Black Widow

by

Colin Demét

Published by Wordcatcher Publications in 2007

Printed in the Isle of Lewis.

A catalogue record for this book
is available from the British Library

ISBN: 978-0-9551318-6-8

Cover: Photograph by Colin Demét

Printed and bound on the Isle of Lewis by
Wordcatcher Publications
Loch á Tuath Cottage
Flesherin, Point,
Isle of Lewis, HS2 0HE

www.wordcatcherpublications.com

CONTENTS

Synopsis

SYNOPSIS

A psychological story of love, abuse and pain as told by the Black Widow, Emerald whose beauty is recognised by all men and most women. People are lost within the enchantment of her deep green eyes. As well as her beauty, Emerald is a kind, innocent girl whose only wish is to find one true love. However, she feels she is to blame for her father's abuse against her. From the depths of her confused emotions Emerald begins to develop a defensive split personality, introducing us to Lotus who is described as her friend and protector. Lotus has no understanding of love, she is cold and calculating and exists through pain and revenge, and **she is the Black Widow incarnate**.

As Lotus grows she begins to take control while justifying her actions to Emerald. The Black Widow leaves a trail of love and abuse as she makes her journey through life, whilst attempting to cover her web of death and trying desperately to hide from her own feelings of guilt. This story is at times light-hearted and humorous, whilst at other times deadly serious, as emotions move between love and hate and commitment while exploring many different sexual perspectives.

I awoke to find I was sleeping.
It was dark yet the room was light.
I knew where I was, yet I was somewhere else.
The Wordcatcher sleeps tonight.

BLACK WIDOW

Sleepless nights spent tales to tell, restless....dark dawn's yawn....nothing?.....A silence to kindle fear....waiting for.....

EMERALD

I sank into the darkness of sleeps void to wander through
ageless times torment, past cries, lost souls, to roam some
endless last lament...seeking...waiting...for such a fool as I
whom..............

I awoke to find myself sitting in a room on a leather
chair and ... and everything was green! The room was
small and barren; there were no pictures on the walls and
no other furniture to be seen. The walls seemed to move ...
vibrate as if ... alive in some macabre way. I reached out
and touched the wall ... it was soft and sticky and I found
my hand was stuck. I stood up and pulled as hard as I
could but to no avail. After a time I accepted that I could
not pull my hand free, and resigned myself to my fate,
whatever that may be. My chair was by my side so I sat to
wait for whatever comes from dreams wells wished or
nightmares needs, some victim trapped in heaven or hell.
The room was cold and I could feel my hand, which was
stuck to the wall, beginning to freeze. There was one door
... a green door which was facing me and I cared not to
wonder where it may lead. I noticed a thick notepad of
parchment paper which was resting on the floor by my
chair. Next to the paper stood an ink-well from which a
long dark green feather quill stood tall.

Am I to write some tale to tell from words caught in
a web to weave? Or! Be, I meant to undo some past time
trapped spells cast last to lost romance ...... Am I to be

some victim, waiting, caught within some tangled dreams repeating pain to what ....?

The door facing me began to open slowly. The room was silent and the door made no sound as it moved in an arching swing. The cold had moved along my arm which felt like it was frozen, and I was aware the ice was creeping towards my heart. The door was now open - yet all that was to be seen beyond was deep, dark, nothing. I stared into the blackness as my heart thumped against my ribs, be some panicking bird trapped in a cage trying to escape..........

Slowly within the darkness was a vague ... something. I sat frozen with fear ... fear of the unknown and a sense of trepidation. I began to see a faint outline which slowly became clearer. What soon came to face me could have been from heaven or hell, for the interpretation of misunderstandings led many the fly to the beauty of Venus. She was small and petite, dark and deep, and radiated a beauty; like the darkness of the blood black rose. She wore a dress of black which seemed to be like a skin of fine hair. Her skin was lily white and reflected the green hue from the surrounding walls, while her short hair was as black as the darkest night. As she stared into my eyes, wells of emotion twirled to swirl and swallow my soul, forever lost in a pain of bliss. Her eyes were of a deep green; ice cold as if frozen from hate, while hot and moist with the warmth of love. As she stared into my soul, I felt powerless ... like an insect trapped in a web. She walked slowly towards me as she pushed the door which closed silently behind her. Her eyes were searching my soul and I knew she could read my thoughts. I glanced down as she stood in front of me and my eyes fell onto her long slender legs. Her dress was short and the silky white texture of her skin flowed over her legs like a mountain stream leading my eyes forever up until they rested on her soft white thighs which seemed to tempt the devil within me.

My glance moved up and up until our eyes once more met to search for ....

Our faces were but separated by inches as I stared into her eyes. I began to feel dizzy and lost, as if falling into two deep wells of green beauty. She smiled and my glance moved to her red lips. As she smiled it was as if I could taste the sweetness from a bursting peach, cool to lick be the taste of forbidden fruit. She leaned forward and took hold of my arm which was stuck to the wall. As she stretched over me her breasts almost touched to taunt my aching lips as they shivered to my delight; gentle waves caressing soft white foreboding sands hiss to kiss. She spoke and her voice was gentle and sweet with a definite strength from the wisdom of life and time, "You should be more careful what you touch my friend ... for some things started must be finished."

My arm was free and as I pulled away, my face touched her breast. Her skin was cool, soft and smooth; it was as if I had placed my cheek against a soft moonlit pool of water. She knelt down to sit on the floor in front of me and her dress rose high to catch my glance for such beauty I had never before seen or known. I began to tremble from a desire which was so strong it was painful. She laid her hand on top of mine and now it was warm ... she put her lips close to mine and spoke softly, "Do you wish to love me Wordcatcher? Do you wish to share my broken heart and to kiss deeply my lips and to taste the nectar of heaven's bliss, for I can bring to you pleasures which you would not believe existed in your wildest dreams, pleasures to turn your soul inside out .... Then my lover you must stay, for once the apple has been tasted it must be eaten for if you leave, you will know of pains beyond your darkest nightmares ... a suffering from which you will beg for the release through deaths oblivion? .... *AH!* You are silent my friend ... then make haste for we have work to do."

She placed some paper into my left hand and pushed the quill between the fingers of my right. She began to speak and I dipped the quill to taste the ink, as the black night's shadows moved uneasily across parched parchment.

~~~

Her voice sounded almost childlike ... playful, happy and full of life. Her eyes became large and round like a child's. Her face lit up with joy and excitement and for the first time of my being in the room of green I began to feel relaxed. "My name is Emerald, and I was named so because of my green eyes ... they are beautiful ... do you think I have beautiful eyes Wordcatcher?"

"Yes ... a beauty I have never known."

She smiled softly and then she pouted her lips and said sadly, "I have asked a thousand times, 'Why am I stuck in this place? Why can't I be free?' I feel as if I am in a prison ... trapped." Emerald became excited and began to shout, "And then ... and then this chair and the paper and pen appeared in the room."

There was a long silence and I did not know what to reply. She pouted her lips at me and took hold of my hand in hers. With a sad expression, she asked, "Can you help me to leave this place?"

"I ... I will if I can ... but I am a writer as is my plight, no more and no less; I catch words from the night and write them at the dawn ... I am the *Wordcatcher*."

"Then catch words for me that I may be set free."

There was another long silence. Emerald stared at me in expectation ... as if I was about to open some magic door which would grant her wishes.

After a while she shook my knee as if to wake me from sleep, "Well! Go on then!"

10

"I am but the same as you ... trapped here ... I have no answer for you."

After another long silence I decided to try and find some answer to the predicament we both seemed to be sharing, "Why do you think you are trapped here Emerald?"

She looked at the floor like a naughty girl and once more pouted her lips, "I don't know ... I have never done anything wrong."

"We have all done something wrong."

"And what have you done wrong Wordcatcher?"

"'Tis not about me."

"Oh! So I tell you but you don't tell me? ... How may I feel at ease with you if you will not confess to me?"

"I am not a priest and neither are you."

"Tell me a truth Wordcatcher. .... Go on! .... I already know! .... You know I know? ...."

"I...I...I want to make love to you."

"Then take me, I'm yours."

"NO!"

"Why? ... Am I not real?"

Emerald pulled my hand onto her heaving breast and moved forward to kiss me, saying, "Take me for I am yours."

I could feel her moist lips against mine as her mouth began to open. I pushed her away and she shouted angrily at me, "Am I not good enough for you? .... Who do you think you are?"

"I .... I am sorry! .... I am married and I love my wife."

"Well done Wordcatcher ... you are honest and you tell the truth. Now I will tell you the truth .... I have never hurt anyone who has not hurt me .... Do you think it is wrong if someone hurts you and you hurt them back? You have hurt people haven't you Wordcatcher?"

"Yes … But now I try to be at peace … to find peace."

"That was all I ever wanted Wordcatcher … peace and love."

"And did you find love?"

"Oh Yes! Many times ….. Yet love and hate walk hand in hand … Do you agree Wordcatcher?"

"I … I have found love through hate … it was a long and painful search for happiness."

"And I … I have found hate through love, it was a long and happy search through pain."

I placed the paper on my lap and dipped the quill to ink for I knew Emerald was about to begin her tale. She sat at my feet and began to speak. Prepared to write, I was full of expectation, and yet could not understand why my heart was filled with dread.

FATHER...

Into thy hands I commend my spirit.

"I was born in a city."

"What city?"

"Does it really matter ... they are all the same ... people rushing everywhere in circles - chasing dreams and buying things they could live without. My mother's name was Mary and my father's name was Peter. My father was a minister and I was brought up to believe that his devotion to God was the correct and only way to be protected from the evil which exists within all people. Everything was godly and had to be right. We prayed before every meal ... we prayed when each day began, to thank the Lord for another day of life and the chance to follow God's ways and to worship him. We prayed at the eve of each day to thank God for our existence and the chance of another day to have praised the Lord. We prayed to God ... we prayed to God to give thanks for giving us the chance to pray to God."

"You sound pessimistic, as if you were not happy."

"Oh! Was I happy? .... Happy! .... What is happy Wordcatcher?

"Ah! A riddle ... possibly with no answer and a riddle which too many people claim to know."

"I think I was happy ... in the beginning ... but then time changes everything .... do you think time changes everything Wordcatcher?"

"Another riddle of life ... I tell my wife that time changes everything but not my love for her."

"Your wife is lucky, but would your love end with your death?"

"Ah! The final enigma."

"I found happiness through perfection. Everything had to be perfect because; as my father would tell me, 'We can never be perfect in the eyes of God'."

"A hard act to follow."

"I was a child, and what I was told was all that I knew. I lived under my father's control ... my father's laws and rules. I found solace through the companionship and love which I received from my mother. It was as if we suffered together ... some unspoken torment. I remember all the countless times when my mother would break down in tears. I was perplexed and wondered what was wrong. I would hug my mother with a heart full of love, and she would cry ... that was the very first time I was confused regarding the emotions of love and pain."

"Did your father love you?"

"My father loved only God."

"Did your father never tell you he loved you?"

"Yes."

There was a long silence. Emerald sat staring with a blank expression on her face. Her eyes, which were full of power and energy, now seemed weak and void ... empty. I reached for her hand to comfort her and recoiled in horror. She snatched her hand away and her expression instantly changed to one of ferocious hate ... a hate which instantly made me fear for my life; her face had transformed and was now twisted and contorted with rage, *"Don't touch me ... don't you ever touch me."*

Emerald burst into tears and held her head in her hands as she sobbed uncontrollably. I sat in silence recovering from shock, as I did not know what to do or say. My heart was beating hard from the fright of Emerald's sudden change. It was as if she had become another person.

I waited a time, and as time past she lifted her head and took hold of my hand, "I am sorry my friend."

Emerald kissed my hand; she had a look of sadness as she said softly, "Do you forgive me? Please? I will not let her near you again."

I was about to ask the question, 'Who is she?' but was left with my question unanswered as Emerald continued to speak, "I don't understand what love means. I once asked my father if he loved me and he told me that he 'loved me through God'. I was twelve years of age at the time and I have often tried to understand what he meant, 'He loved me through God'. Everything was black or white for my father. Good or Evil. There was no in-between for him. I was a good girl or I was a bad girl, and if I was bad he would beat the badness out of me. My father was a strong advocate for punishment and repentance. He had a cane which stood in the corner of his room; he used the lounge as his room and office. We had no T.V. but were allowed a radio, and we were only allowed to listen to the programmes that he had decided were suitable by placing red 'ticks' alongside the programme in a magazine. He would reach for his stick if I had been naughty and I soon learned that if I cried and said 'I have the fear of God in me' I would usually be appointed with some ... lesser punishment such as writing 100 lines -

I must not forget my homework
I must not forget my homework
I must not forget my homework

I could understand my punishments, and even had respect for the hand of discipline ... until ... until ...."

There was an uncomfortable silence and I cannot understand why but I was filled with fear, a fear I could sense more than understand. I repeated Emerald's last word, "Until?"

She was startled and jumped, "Until ... Until my thirteenth birthday. I will never forget the day. My mother allowed me to have some friends visit the house for a party. It was close to Christmas and I was excited. My father was not expected to arrive home until after 7 p.m. so four of my girlfriends arrived about six o'clock and one of the girls brought a record player and some 45s (small records with one song on each side). My mother had prepared some food; sausage rolls, sandwiches, and a big birthday cake.

The cake had thirteen candles and was covered in pink icing. We drank lemonade and danced to pop-music. The girls were dressed in mini-skirts or skin tight hipster trousers, and I was wearing a red mini-skirt that mother had bought me for my birthday. The room had balloons and Christmas decorations pinned to the walls. It was the best time of my life ... I felt free and happy and even my mother was dancing. Time must have passed quickly and I remember that my dream became a nightmare. We were all doing the twist to the song, 'Lets Twist Again' .... It's funny how you remember certain little things isn't it Wordcatcher?"

"Y...Yes."

"I had the fright of my life ... I was spinning around to the music when I saw my father's face staring at us through the kitchen window. I still remember his face ... his expression was like a mask. He was staring down at one of the girls, who was jumping in the air. I suppose she was showing her knickers, but the room was full of girls so we didn't care. It was dark outside as it was December ... December 17th that makes me a Sagittarian .... My father walked into the kitchen and 'all of hell was let loose'. He chased the girls out of the house and shouted at my mother, 'How could you let such evil and debauchery enter our home? Go into the study and pray for forgiveness and I will speak with you when I have driven the devil from this child.' My father took his cane from his office and told me to go upstairs to my room. He followed me as I pleaded with him for forgiveness, 'Please father NO! I was only having some fun ... it was just a birthday party.' My father threw me into my room and pulled me across his knee ... I begged for forgiveness, 'Please NO! It was the devil and he has gone now you have returned father ... Now I am filled with the spirit of Christ our Lord.' All to no avail, my father was wearing his black smock and white collar. He lifted my skirt and pulled down my knickers. He began to whip me with the cane across my bare bottom while, with every stroke of the cane he raged at me, 'You are an abomination to the Lord, you are possessed with the evil of seduction, you tempt salvation with your lust, be gone from here temptation, be gone back to hell from whence you came you harlot, harlot from the sins of the flesh.'

As he whipped me with the stick over and over again something stirred deep from within me. I was confused I could not understand what I had done wrong ... and ... and I felt in some way that my father was punishing himself for his own evil thoughts. For the first time in my life I became angry ... not just angry ... totally overcome with anger ... it was like I was somebody else ... maybe I was possessed and he was right. I spoke to him as I never had before, 'Let me go you bastard ... you filthy swine ... I saw you looking at that girl's body ... it is you who is evil not me ... and leave my mother alone ... you bastard.'

All the time I raged he beat me and I said the Lord's Prayer repeatedly. I think he believed he was doing an exorcism ... I often wondered if he was?

Eventually he stopped and I lay crying on my bed. He walked from my room and to my surprise he returned within moments. I was lying on my front and my skirt was still raised above my waist. He sat next to me on the bed and began to smear ointment onto my bottom. He cried ... I had never known him to cry before and ... I ... I felt sorry for him. My mind and my emotions were spinning around in my head. So many questions ... confusion ... was I Right or Wrong? ... Was I Good or Evil? Was I ... Had I been possessed?

Father smeared the ointment onto my skin and whispered of love through sobs of pain, 'I love you my child, but lust must be overcome ... How can we stand together before God with such thoughts of evil in our minds?'

As I lay on my bed I felt bewildered; as if I was in a dream, or nightmare ... but what disturbed me, was that from somewhere deep inside, I found the touch from my father exciting. This was the second experience which made me feel confused between the emotions of love and pain.

When I awoke the next day I could hardly move my legs to stand as my bottom was stinging from the whipping. I looked in the mirror and my behind was black and blue and there were deep red lines where the cane had struck. I struggled to put on my clothes for school ... I don't understand why, but I felt guilty ... as if I had to keep my injuries a secret ... I felt embarrassed and ashamed. Had I done something wrong Wordcatcher?"

"No! But your father had."

"I travelled to school on the bus and I remember having to stand as I was too sore to sit down. I walked into school and then realised that my first lesson of the day was P.E. I told the teacher I was feeling sick, but she would not excuse me from the lesson as I didn't have a note from my parents. We were to play basketball in the gym and had to wear shorts that look like knickers. I felt so guilty and frightened ... it was as if I had some horrible secret. The girls in my class were divided into teams and we played for several minutes before changing teams. I stood waiting and praying that no one would notice the marks from my beating. Soon it was my team's turn to play and we walked onto the gym floor whilst the remaining girls climbed onto the wall bars to watch. I had to play and jump about as the game was fast and the girls in my team passed the ball to me. My knickers must have moved because suddenly the teacher blew her whistle and told me to wait in her office. As I waited in the teacher's office I began to cry. I felt as if I had been caught doing something horribly wrong. The teacher met me in the office and gave me a hug. Her voice was soft and gentle as she asked me what was wrong. I told her nothing was wrong. She asked me what had happened to my bottom. I tried to lie ... I told her a car had run into me and knocked me over and then driven away. She told me that was a criminal offence a 'hit and run' ... she asked me if I had told the police and if I had been to hospital. It was as if I was digging a hole for myself and making things worse. She told me to turn around ... I was crying and frightened. She pulled my knickers down over my bum, and I winced with pain. I will never forget her words and the shock which was in her voice, 'Oh! My God!' She knew I had been beaten; she could tell by the red lines from the cane. 'Who has done this to you? ... You have been whipped haven't you? ... You poor child!' I begged her not to tell anyone. She tricked me. She asked me to tell her who had beaten me, and then she said she would forget the whole incident. I told her the truth; she made me tell her the whole story, and then she told me to go and get dressed. By the time I arrived at the changing rooms all the other girls had gone. I quickly dressed, and as I was about to leave, a nurse met me at the door. She spoke softly to me, 'Hello Emerald, I want you to come with me so we can have a look at you.'

I was taken to hospital and examined. My mother was at the hospital and she was crying. I was told to lie face down on a bed and I was examined. A lady put swabs into me, and I did not understand what was happening ... I just felt a terrific feeling of guilt ... guilt and fear ... fear as I believed my father would hit me again for 'letting out our secret'.

I was questioned by a lady, and I told her the story of what had happened. I told her I did not want to go home as I was frightened of what my father would say. The nurse told me I would be staying in the hospital overnight to make sure my cuts were not infected. The next day I could hardly move from the bed. I stayed in the hospital for several days and my mother visited me. Mother brought me fruit and chocolate and sat crying. We never spoke a word, she simply kissed me on the head as she was leaving and whispered, 'God Bless'.

Mother met me when I was due to leave, and when we walked outside the hospital, several men with cameras began taking pictures of me and shouting questions. I was frightened and covered my ears. When we arrived home, father was nowhere to be seen ... I was glad, as I was dreading facing him; I felt as if I had done something really bad ... Had I Wordcatcher?"

"No, But your father had."

"The next day I went to school and the girls were whispering about me. I opened my desk and someone had put a newspaper inside ... I ... I."

Emerald began to cry ... I reached forward to console her but stopped quickly as I remembered her reaction the last time I had touched her. I watched as tears dripped to trickle over her breasts; I wanted to help her but knew not what to do. She stopped crying and lifted a deep red handkerchief to her face and wiped her eyes and then continued, "The paper had a picture of me, next to a picture of my father. There was a headline which read,

'DAUGHTER WHIPPED BY THE HAND OF GOD'

I did not read anymore from the newspaper ... I broke down crying and was taken home. I will never forget the day; it was the day we broke-up from school for the Christmas holiday. I stayed in my bedroom for the rest of the day and mother brought me my meals. She told me that my father would be returning home in the evening as he was being held at the police station for questioning but was to be released later. Mother talked to me and explained how she wanted this whole mistake to be over with. She asked me if I was telling lies about father, so I asked her how she thought I could have caused such injuries to myself. She told me my father had denied hitting me and had said I was a troubled youngster. Do you think I was a troubled youngster Wordcatcher?"

"I think we all have troubles."

"It was late evening when I heard my father's voice. I was shaking with fear. I expected him to come charging into my room and beat me for telling what had happened between us ... that's it, isn't it Wordcatcher? ... I felt it was us, not him.

I lay awake for hours too frightened to sleep. It was way past midnight and the house was still and silent. I remember thinking *'it is Christmas time and I am so unhappy and frightened.'* I wanted a drink of cold milk so I crept downstairs as quietly as I could. I was trembling and had the thought of my father suddenly opening a door and jumping out at me screaming. I poured a glass of milk and began tip-toeing silently back to my room. As I was passing father's office I noticed his door was slightly open. I peeped in and the room was lit by a small table light. Father was writing on a piece of paper and on his desk stood several bottles of tablets and a glass of water. He finished writing and then began tipping the bottles of tablets onto his palm and throwing them into his mouth. Soon all the bottles were empty and he sat crying. I knew what he was doing ... I knew he was taking his own life."

Tears ran down Emerald's face as she spoke, "I ... I ... I felt many different kinds of emotions twirling around in my mind ... fear ... hate ... forgiveness ... love ... anger ... freedom ... it was as if all my emotions were separate ...

and yet they all made one feeling within me ... and all my different emotions were trapped inside one big bubble ... I had a terrific feeling of excitement. I was so excited I was wet, and I had an enormous feeling of control ... power ... the power over life and death ... my father's life or death. I was no longer weak I was strong; I had changed; I was someone else, or something else. I walked into his room and closed the door. I walked over and stood beside him. He was weak ... dying, and yet I knew there was still time to call for help and possibly save his life. We stared at each other and he spoke to me softly and slowly, *'My Latrodectus ... my beautiful white Lotus flower which has grown from the deep darkness of the mud.'* He placed his hand on my hand and said, *'Forgive me my white flower.'*

I moved my face to meet with his and I kissed his lips. I could feel that his breathing was becoming weaker and weaker until his last gasp of life left his lungs and entered mine.

I ... I had my first orgasm ... it was as if a new life was born within me from his death. I took the note he had written from the table and I left the room. I gently closed the door and collected my glass of milk from the hall. I returned to my room and drank my milk while reading his last written words from a crumpled piece of paper. At the bottom of the paper was some scribble.

He had written -

Father
Into thy hands I commend my spirit

Latrodectus

LatrOdecTUS

LOTUS

Such a sad story Wordcatcher ... do you think my story sad?"

"Y ... Yes."

"You know Wordcatcher ... I often wonder if my father was trying to beat Lotus from me ... or ... or if he brought her to me. When Lotus comes I have no control. Do you think its frightening Wordcatcher? ...... Do you think it is my fault Wordcatcher? .... Don't be frightened ... I will keep her from you ... after all you are here for me .... You are, aren't you Wordcatcher?"

*****

I awoke at my crofter's cottage, by the sea on the Isle of Lewis in Scotland. The wind was howling as it pushed and pulled at the tiny roof which creaked like old times bones. My room was dark and I could hear my wife breathing deeply as she lay asleep peacefully next to me.   My eyes moved through the darkness as if looking for ... for what? I do not know. I quietly left my bed and crept downstairs. I made some tea and retired to my desk which faced the sea. Rain was beating against the large window which was facing me.   Dawn was creeping over the restless Minch which continued to wrestle with itself as sea moods, green, deep depths, sway waves, searching to find contentment, whilst never realising each conflicting battling wave is but a part of itself. I sipped my tea while staring out to sea.   A small boat was hiding in Broad Bay, taking shelter from the fury of the Hebrides.   As the morning light kissed the waves, white horses stormed like an army towards the shore, framed by the surrounding hills barren beauty dappled from heathers purple and yellow hue. A buzzard rode the storm, searching for food as an angel of death. A spider's web glistened as if covered by tiny sparkling diamonds from the lights reflection through the morning dew; the beauty of nature hiding death's black cloaked shroud beneath a thousand tiny rainbows. A spider sat in the centre of its web with the patience only death respects as time and fate bring restless life into its open arms.

I tried to escape into the natural raw beauty of nature which surrounded me ... to no avail ... for every time I blinked my eyes all I could see within the darkness were two beautiful green eyes staring ... staring and waiting and I knew I would have to sleep and return to Emerald.

I had finished my tea ... I was frightened ... I looked at my computer screen and typed a word into the search engine. The word was a name which had stuck in my mind like a thorn.

LATRODECTUS

My heart was beating hard against my chest ... I felt a fear ... a fear of the unknown ... an unknown you deny yet know will come and must be faced for you cannot escape.

I pressed the search key and waited —

Spiders from the genus *Latrodectus* are referred to as

THE BLACK WIDOW

The Black Widow has a kiss of death. Mating is usually the last activity for a male *Latrodectus* and *he* generally never escapes to tell the tale. The female rewards the male by killing and eating him after mating. That is why she is always known as a...

Black Widow

The thing that makes the female's bite so dangerous is the large size of the poison glands which are not just confined to the chelicerae but extend back into the top of the head.

The Black Widow is renown, for her kiss of death, and literally sucking the life from her victims.

The female Black Widow spiders are commonly known for the red hourglass pattern displayed on their abdoman.

I keyed my next word from nightmares shadows into cyber-space -

LOTUS

I pressed the search key and waited —

Then seated on a lotus
Beauty's bright goddess, peerless Sri, arose
Out of the waves

The lotus is an Asian water lily known for the delicate beauty of its water flowers. It possesses an amazing ability to flourish in a variety of environments ranging from clear ponds to muddy marshes. Legend says that those who eat of it forget of their father and those who are dear to them. The lotus is the two-fold type of the Divine and human hermaphrodite, being of dual sex.

The lotus is called 'the child of the Universe' and relates to creation, regeneration, and the state of the initiate and higher beings, all of whom travel through life's vicissitudes and trials to become at one with the creative source of life in order to return and spread its light to other receptive souls.

The leaves break from the bandage of the green stem, stretch themselves and form a green pool with untidy edges. Now the flower comes from out of the vast surface of the water, just like a very beautiful woman coming gracefully from her bath.

They grow out of the dirty mud under the water, and yet they still keep their pureness, freshness and beauty. Chinese poets often use them to inspire the people to keep on doing what they must do, and to show their best part to the outside world, just like the lotus flower, no matter how bad the situation or circumstance may be.

Another characteristic of the Lotus refers to the plant's stalk. It is easy to bend in two, but it is very hard to break, or separate the two parts completely, showing the powerful bond between the flower and the root.

*****

While I wrote what had been from the previous night, I reflected upon the mystery of my new acquaintance.

It seemed as if Emerald had some kind of split personality. Was the beauty of the Lotus flower, joined by its stem to the dark repression of the Black Widow? Was this the woman who, once kissed, would forever keep your soul ... stolen from your last breath. She was a woman who seemed innocent; almost child-like, and yet she spoke so calmly about death and dying. I remembered her calmness as she told me of her father's death, and how she took her glass of milk to her room after, as if nothing of importance had occurred. I wondered why I had been placed with Emerald, and I remembered the threat from the hangman in Hades.*

When I had finished writing words caught to tell I watched as the blanket of the dusk crept over the land and sea. I felt uneasy as I knew soon, sleep would take me ... take me to this woman of beauty and ... and ....

*(Scotland's Executions 1800-1899)

I fell into a deep sleep and opened my eyes. I screamed in fear. Emerald's face was but inches from mine and her green eyes stared into my soul. She kissed my lips as a mother a child and whispered softly, "Are you awake my darling for I have been alone and waiting ... waiting it seems, forever."

She stroked my brow and softly began to sing. The sweetness of her voice sent shivers down my back and I felt as if I was in another world ... a world of bliss.

So sweet your lips one kiss of honey
To swoon my heart to never part
True love will always once found be
Two hearts as one
For all eternity.

She pressed her lips against mine and the taste was cool and sweet. I felt as if I was sinking ... sinking into bliss ... and yet I was falling downwards and I also felt as if I was drowning. I jumped, and Emerald was startled, "What is the matter my love?"

"Nothing!"

She spoke to me sadly, "Oh! I am sorry ... would you like me to leave?"

"No!"

I found Emerald enchanting. Her beauty enthralled me while the shadows of danger and power which surrounded her excited me. I felt bewildered ... trapped in a web.

I sat back into my green leather chair and waited for Emerald to speak. She was once more sitting at my feet. She was leaning against my legs and as I was looking down at her; I could not help but notice the beauty of her breasts.

Her skin was as white as snow ... freshly fallen snow; pure and unblemished. She stared deep into my eyes and her smile drew my whole being towards her like a magnet. She began to laugh softly and her breasts quivered. She spoke to me seductively ... teasing, "Stop making me laugh ... you're staring at my breasts ... why are you staring at my breasts?"

"I ... I'm not."

"Oh yes you are."

"Well! They are in front of me."

"You like me don't you?"

"Y ... Yes."

"Do you love me Wordcatcher?"

"How can you be so blasé about love?"

"I take love very seriously, but have never found it."

"Well I have found it Emerald, and I am happy."

"Then why do you stare at me so?"

"I ... I ..."

"You have gone all red Wordcatcher."

"Y ...You are beautiful to look at."

"And would you like to touch me?"

"Y ... Yes."

"See! ... You do love me."

"It is not love."

"You want me ... and yet you do not love me ... why?"

I felt confused and tried to explain myself, "Well ... its like if you see a flower and you pluck it, and then you see another flower which is beautiful ... but you do not take the flower you have seen ... you stare at its beauty."

"But why not have a vase of flowers?"

"What we have is more complicated than flowers."

Emerald sighed and snuggled closer to me, "Oh! I realise that daring."

"No! I mean ... I mean you cannot give your heart to one person and then simply say 'Oh! I don't love you now, I am in love with someone else."

"Why not?"

"Because true love never dies."

"But you were married twice before and you ....."

"That is none of your business."

"Ooooow! .... I love you when you are angry Wordcatcher."

"I am not angry ... you twist my words."

"Possibly you do not understand what you are saying ... for two times you have given your heart and then broken a heart ... maybe you did not give your heart but took and did not give."

"You do not know what happened so don't judge me."

"Love is blind! Is it blind Wordcatcher?"

"I do not know if anyone really knows what love is ... that is why it is so easy to make mistakes."

"I think I know what love is Wordcatcher ... I think love is Life and Death ... flying with the clouds in heaven or slowly dying in hell ... do you think I have found the answer my love?"

"Possibly ... for I have been in the two places you speak of."

"Will you take me to heaven Wordcatcher?"

"Sometimes one person's heaven is another's hell"

Emerald stood up and slid out of her dress, it was like a shell which fell from her body, "Be with me Wordcatcher for heaven may lead to hell, but love always has a price."

I was facing Emerald's naked body which looked irresistible. My hands began to move towards her curvaceous hips. Suddenly I stopped ... I was shocked by what was facing me. Upon Emerald's stomach was a birth mark. The birth mark was red and it was shaped like an hourglass.

I awoke to think of Emerald. I could not remove her from my thoughts. I did not love her and yet I craved to be with her ... to have her ... I felt lust, and she enchanted me ... Like some siren luring with an illusion of beauty, the sailor onto the rocks of destruction, and yet one has to taste the forbidden fruit even though it may be poison.

I returned through the sun-set of sleep to awaken through ... the green mists of dawn.

JASON

Emerald sat a distance from me. She stared at the wall and hummed a soft tune. She stopped humming and pouted her lips like a child who could not get what she wanted, "Oh Emerald ... stop sulking."

She did not speak and began to hum a tune. I felt an overwhelming feeling of love for her ... I did not understand the love I felt ... I think it was more as one loves a friend than a true love for a woman. I shouted to Emerald jokingly, "Emerald ... Emerald stop sulking and come here, you know I love you."

She sprang to her feet and dived towards me shouting excitedly, "Do you ... Do you ... Do you really Wordcatcher?"

She knelt by my legs and put her head on my knee. She began to speak through sulking lips like a child wants what cannot be given, "I knew you loved me and yet you hurt me ... see it is true love hurts ... but I will never hurt you my love ... and I will keep her away from you ... have no fear for I know all her tricks."

Emerald jerked about as she made herself comfortable and her beautiful breasts bounced up and down. "Now my lover I will continue with my story ... and take your eyes from my breasts for you will need to listen and to write ... cheeky!"

She laughed and began to speak and as she did so my heart felt heavy for I loved her deeply ... I was trapped within her web ... nothing seemed to matter anymore ... only Emerald.

"Soon after my father's death, mother and I moved away to another city. We never spoke about father ... it was as if he had never existed ... like some guilty secret. If I was asked where my father was I told people, *'Oh! I don't like to talk about him; he died when I was a child.'*

I lived with mother in a small apartment and attended a local school. Mother worked hard; during the day time she worked in a supermarket, and most evenings she served drinks behind a bar. I left school and worked in an office, on a switchboard. The work was boring but I was in a small room alone so I was happy.

Several years passed quickly and when I was twenty years of age mother met a man who she said she loved and had decided to marry. Harry owned a large house with a driveway and a double garage. He was a kind man and I liked him a lot ... I even called him dad. The new family experience was so different from when we lived with my real father. I had my own room and I could buy any clothes I wanted ... and anything I wanted, as long as I 'didn't make him bankrupt' as Harry would say. Harry called me his green eyed princess, and he was the father I had always dreamed of. He had a son called Jason who was five years older than me. Myself and Jason got on fine ... we were always teasing each other and laughing. Jason worked with his father who owned one of the biggest motorcycle shops in the city. Jason had a massive sports motorbike and he would take me to my friends, or meet me if I needed a lift home. I would cling onto him; terrified and yet excited, as the bike screamed from a stand-still to what was like a hundred miles an hour in seconds. I would scream yet I knew nobody could hear me ... I felt so free ... so wild... Have you been on a motorbike Wordcatcher?"

"Yes ... I once owned a 1200cc Harley Davidson."

"Oh! Good ... so you know what it's like on a bike?"

"You sound as if you had found happiness!"

Emerald became still and silent ... and she starred at the floor.

"Why is it Wordcatcher that every time things seem right ... things have to turn bad?"

"I suppose the rain follows the sunshine."

"Oh! ... You do talk silly sometimes ... what sort of answer is that ... *'the rain follows the sun'* I'm not talking about the bloody weather I'm talking about my bloody life ... *Ohhh!* Now you've made me swear."

"Sorry."

There was a long silence before Emerald continued to speak.

"Mother and father were going away for a weekend holiday, and that's when things went wrong."

Emerald was silent for what seemed like half an hour so I decided to try and comfort her.

"You don't have to say anything but..................."

Emerald interrupted me shouting, "Oh! Shut up ... you sound like a policeman."

There was another short period of silence before Emerald continued with her story. She took hold of my hand tightly and smiled. She asked me, "Will you always love me as I am now? Please don't judge me will you? Please don't leave me alone."

Her grip was tight and her eyes were deep and full of love ... I felt weak ... I seemed to fall into her eyes ... our lips met softly and briefly ... there was no lust, only the purest elixir of love. I told Emerald, "All I could ever feel for you is love without question, and a love which must be without lust."

"And yet you crave for a circle of love between us, your whole being needs to be at one with me."

"No! ... I love you as a sister."

"Do you stare at your sister's breasts?"

"No!"

"And I am not your sister."

"And you are not my wife,"

"Ah! Be patient my darling for time changes everything."

I was confused and my feelings were like a broken jigsaw puzzle. I loved my wife and yet Emerald seemed to have a power over me. I found her irresistible … I was too weak to turn away from her … it was as if I had all I wished from the love I shared with my wife, and yet a love had come which I could not resist. I had never before experienced the feelings of weakness which overcame me when Emerald was close. I felt like falling into her arms and simply then … nothing … I wished to be there with my head upon her lap and experience ecstasy in its purest form, as she stroked my head and stared into my eyes, it was as if I wanted to succumb to her power … it was as ……………

"*Wordcatcher … Wordcatcher* … Have you fallen asleep? Am I so boring?"

"No … and I was not asleep … I was ………….."

"I know what you were doing … and sometimes dreams may come true … and sometimes a dream may turn into a nightmare."

Emerald squeezed my hand and began to speak. Her hand was soaking wet with sweat and I could feel her slightly trembling. The feeling I now had was of fear … not a fear of losing my life or even my mortality … No! My fear was; that what Emerald was about to tell me may interfere with my illusion of shattered perfection. I suddenly realised my last thoughts, *'illusion of shattered perfection'* I felt more confusion … I decided to listen and to write … at least for the moment.

"Mother and father were away for the weekend. I suppose I was somewhat reclusive … a loner … I think I became a lot more reserved after my father's death. I kept myself to myself. I was happy to stay at home and watch T.V… I had friends whom I would see and we would go to the cinema, or 'Ten-Pin Bowling', or shopping. I had never been to a disco or nightclub even though some of my friends often asked me to go with them. I think I was worried about boys and sex. I felt confused about sex ... I did not know anything about sex and I was still a virgin. I avoided the subject as much as possible ... I felt as if something was to be feared ... I was frightened of boys. I knew I was attractive because boys were always asking me to go out with them, and girls would tell me they wished they had a figure like mine ... Oh! And some girls were nasty ... jealous ... they would try to belittle me, but I knew really they thought I was beautiful ... do you think I am beautiful Wordcatcher?"

"You know I do."

"Oh! Do you think I am vain?

"I don't think, with you I only feel."

"I thought you said you didn't want t............."

"Emerald ... Tell the story."

"It was Friday evening and I was all set to enjoy a quiet night in and watch a film on T.V. Our parents were away and every Friday evening Jason would leave the house at about 8 p.m. and go to a nightclub in the city. At around 7 p.m. Jason had showered and changed ready for his night out. We ate some sandwiches together and he offered me a glass of lager. I was not used to drinking but I suppose I thought, with our parents being away, one glass would be alright. Jason sat next to me on the settee, and his cologne smelt divine. He was a good looking guy who was always at the gym, and he looked amazing when he was dressed to go out on the town. I had one more glass of lager and began to ask Jason what it was like at the nightclub. He asked me if I would like to go with him, and I said I couldn't. He asked me why I could not go, and told me I would be safe with him. He told me all the clichés ... 'You only live once' ... 'When the cat's away', etc. I was excited and I thought 'why not?' ... Why should I sit in watching a film when I could be out at a club having fun dancing?

I rushed upstairs and got ready. I had lots of clothes as daddy would let me buy what I wanted. I chose a scarlet velvet mini-skirt and black high-heeled shoes. My hair was long and deep black, and flowed down over my shoulders. My dress was low cut at the front ... I knew I was beautiful and I was not ashamed or frightened to show off my beauty. When I walked into the lounge, Jason gasped, 'WOW', he didn't say much more, we rushed to a waiting taxi and headed for the city.

I had a white fur coat which I handed in at the cloakroom when we entered the club. Jason seemed to know everyone. We sat at a table and I waited while Jason went to the bar for some drinks. He returned with a glass of wine for me and shouted, 'Try that and see if you like it, it's a sweet white wine'.

The club was dark and the music was loud ... so loud that we had to shout with our mouths against each others ears to hear what was said. I was not used to drinking and seemed to have had several glasses of wine within an hour. There were lights flashing and the music was playing and I felt better than I had ever felt in my life before. It was a bit like being on the back of Jason's bike as we raced down the open road. Jason pulled me up to dance and I remember there were bubbles floating in the air, and as people danced they popped the bubbles with their fingers. I was having the time of my life ... I had never felt so good ... a slow song began to play and couples danced slowly together on the dance floor. Jason held me in his arms and pulled my body against his. He kissed my cheek and whispered how he loved me and always had since he had first seen me ... he whispered how he had dreamed of this moment and wished it could last forever. The next thing ... we were kissing. I had never kissed before and he thrust his tongue into my mouth. He pulled me against his body and I could feel him hard ... pressing between my legs. I felt so wet ... I felt embarrassed but I remember everyone was soaking in sweat so that made me feel easy.

My head was spinning and I remember Jason saying 'I had better take you home'. We sat in the back of the taxi and kissed. I felt Jason's hand on my breasts and then I felt his hand between my legs, and I remember him saying 'You're soaking wet.' He was very experienced and soon had me crying out with pleasure. He had to stop because the taxi driver hit the curb several times as he must have been watching us instead of the road ... the driver watching me seemed to excite me even more ... is that bad Wordcatcher?"

"It might have been bad for the taxi driver."

"When we arrived home my head was spinning and Jason carried me into our parent's bedroom. We got undressed and I climbed on top of the bed ... it was hot and, as I lay there naked, the room seemed to be spinning around. I felt sick and pushed Jason aside as he was climbing onto the bed; I had to dash to the toilet to be sick. After some time I came back to the bed but felt differently than I had before. I was confused ... I felt as if we were doing something wrong. I lay on the bed next to Jason and we talked for a while. He was feeling me and touching me and I ... I ... I felt like two people ... one part of me wanted to have lustful sex while the other part of me was asking questions ... and questions, and more questions. I asked Jason my questions while the two separate parts of my mind argued between themselves.

Do you love me Jason?	I always have
Will we be together now?	Yes!
What about our parents?	We're not brother and sister
I'm a virgin, will it hurt?	No I won't hurt you
Do you love me?	Yes!

And so we were ... debating for more than one hour until I gave in. There was no love or romance left. It was like the end of a discussion which had ruled that the action should now commence.

I felt like I was at the dentist ... frightened in case it hurt. I was dry so he ran out of the room and returned with some sort of cream. He smeared the cream onto himself and I remember him trembling. I began to rub him and said *'Here let me do it this way,'* he seemed to become angry ... as if his patience was at an end. I felt guilty and frightened.

He dived on top of me and I could not move. I lay still and trembled with fear. He pushed hard into me and I screamed ... he kept thrusting and thrusting ... and that was when everything became a nightmare. I was telling myself over and over ... he loves me and we will be together forever ... and all the while this little voice was crying from the abyss, *'No! He doesn't love you and you know that don't you, and what does this make you????????'* and as he was thrusting away at me I cried ... *Stop!* ... He answered my darkest fears. He began aggressively thrusting at me as if he was stabbing me and shouting, 'You dirty bitch ... You slag ... Take that you dirty bitch.'

My world collapsed and I just lay there crying in pain. He finished and climbed off me; he spoke to me like a piece of dirt, 'Stop crying ... anyone would think you were being murdered.'

He stumbled out of the bedroom and into his own room. I will never forget him yawning and calmly saying *'Good Night'* as he closed the bedroom door, as if nothing had happened.

I lay in the dark crying and feeling just like what he had called me *'A Slut.'* I felt like calling the police and telling them I had been raped ... but then I remembered I had decided to let him do it. I cried myself to sleep ... and as I fell into sleep I can remember, there were now two separate parts of my mind still arguing ... arguing about love and pain."

Emerald squeezed my hand and cried. Soon she spoke once more and what she told me filled me with dread.

"In the morning Jason walked into the bedroom as if nothing had happened the night before. He had brought me some tea and toast. 'Hello! ... Good morning! ... Time to rise and shine.'

I pulled the covers over my chest as I was still naked. He said, 'It's a bit late for covering up babe ... by God you're hard work ... I have never seen a girl going from hot to cold so quickly and so many times.'

I was raging with anger ... I felt like he had stolen my ... my self, 'You bastard ... you raped me!' I said.

'Oh! No!' He said, 'You asked me a thousand questions and then said 'Yes.' I don't know what your moaning about it was a great night and we both had fun ... we can do it again sometime ... now give me a kiss and don't be silly'.

Jason lifted the covers and moved towards me ... I spit in his face and he jumped backwards shouting, *'Bitch!'*

Jason's mouth dropped open from shock as he stared at the bed ... I looked down at the sheets and they were covered in blood from my losing my virginity. I began to cry and held my hands to my eyes. Jason walked out of the bedroom and shouted at me, 'You dirty bitch, clean that lot up, you're a waste of fucking time'."

Once more Emerald sat crying and I remained silent. Soon she looked up into my eyes and asked, "Do you think me a slag?"

Tears filled my eyes and I was angry. I was trembling from my feelings of rage towards Jason. "I love you and if I was there I would have torn him into pieces."

"I know you love me Wordcatcher and I know you would do what you said, but there is no need because I have already done it."

I sat as if in shock ... we all say 'I will kill him for that' but only the few fulfil the act. She placed her lips against mine and they were stone cold ... like ice. She began to open her mouth and I looked into her eyes

NOOOOOOOOOOOOO! her eyes had become all black ... there was nothing ... an emptiness like a black hole in space which, once entered, one could only pass through and hope to live. I could feel her breathing ... sucking my breath from my lungs while all the time her eyes simply stared ... like an angel of death's last commandment. I pushed at her body but it was useless ... as she sucked at my breath. I cried from my deepest inner self, "Emerald ... I love you ... it's me."

It worked and Emerald had returned ... her lips once more became warm and her eyes shone like glistening emeralds, "What is wrong my darling?" She asked as if nothing had happened.

"You ... you changed and my life was being ...."

Emerald interrupted me and began to stroke my head, "Don't worry my darling I will always be here for you ... it was only Lotus ... I think she is jealous of the love we share."

Emerald snuggled against my legs and stared up at me. She smiled and my heart melted. I knew I was lost within the wheel of fate, and that, whatever was going to be, would be. I knew I shared some ... some kind of deep love with the beautiful woman I was with, and yet I knew that danger was ever near. I felt as if I could not leave Emerald, trapped as she was ... I loved her too much.

"Stop day-dreaming Wordcatcher ... Now! Listen to the rest of my story, I think this part is good, and I want to know what you think.

It was Saturday morning after Jason had used me and he had left the house to go to the local shop for a newspaper. Every Saturday morning he followed the same routine ... he called for a paper and then he would return home to leave for work on his motorbike. When he had left the house I took the bloodstained sheet outside to the rubbish bin. We had cleaners who came to the house and I planned to turn the mattress over and remake the bed. It was a terrible feeling ... a feeling like I had experienced with my father ... Yes! I felt guilty ... as if I was dirty ... I had a terrible feeling of guilt ... It was as if I had done something really bad, and then I felt guilty because I had a feeling I was going to do something terribly wrong. I didn't do anything wrong ... it was Lotus ... she had taken some garden cutters and snipped a pipe on Jason's bike. Red liquid squirted out from the bike like blood ... but don't worry Wordcatcher she wiped it clean. When Lotus took over it was as if I was outside of myself ... it was like I was there watching but I knew it was someone else. I was glad she was doing whatever she was doing because I hated him and I knew she was looking after me ... sometimes I think she is my guardian angel. I was in the house when he returned; I had my dressing gown on and was making some coffee. He came into the house as if nothing was wrong ... he walked past me and slapped my bottom, 'Ah! Glad to see you've pulled yourself together. It's only fun you know ... we only live once so take life by the throat and choke what you can from it. You should chill-out more and ....'

I shouted at him angrily, 'You think it's a bit of fun to tell me you love me ... steel my virginity ... and then simply continue as if nothing has happened?'

Then he said, 'I didn't steel anything ... you took your clothes off and jumped onto the bed first ... what did you think we were going to do ... read *'Rag-Tag and Bobtail'* and fall asleep dreaming of butterflies ... get over it and get a life ... if you got out more you wouldn't be so fucking soft'.

'You Bastard!' I said, 'You told me you loved me and then when you had got what you wanted you called me a dirty slag ... how dare you ....'

Jason spoke softly and tried to hold my hand which I pulled away. I screamed at him, 'Don't touch me you animal ... No! Calling you an animal is an insult to animals.'

41

'Listen babe ... I do love you ... that doesn't mean we are getting married this morning ... and when I called you names ... that's just sex talk ... I know your not a slag ... you've never had sex before so how can you be a slag ... a slag is a girl who sleeps with anyone ... it's just sex talk ... it turns me on ... I have to go to work now so chill-out and remember life's just a game.'

He leaned forward to kiss me on the forehead and I moved away. It was so confusing ... the part of my mind that was broken into pieces was trying to make some sense out of what he had said. Questions that may have led me back to normality flicked into my mind. It was like someone drowning and clawing at ice with the hope of escaping and moving back through time. Did he love me? Were his derogatory remarks meaningless words that simply turned him on? ... I remembered when I was in the taxi and he was making me come ... over and over again ... I had called him a bastard ... I had shouted at him, 'You bastard', and yes! It was just sex talking. Maybe it was just fun and I was taking everything too serious ... maybe it was my religious upbringing that was stopping me from chilling-out ... I did not know then .... I heard the roar from the bike as its engine yawned like a dragon and spit fire. I moved over to the window and watched to see what Lotus had done. The driveway led steeply down to a duel carriageway and was busy with fast moving traffic. This was no problem to a sports bike which could reach fast speeds within seconds. Jason revved his bike down the drive and at the bottom, the red brake light on the back glared as if with anger. Instead of stopping, the bike shot like a bullet across the carriageway. There was a terrific explosion as an artic-truck hit the bike. The truck must have been travelling at about fifty miles per hour and the bike seemed to vanish in an explosion of sparks and fire beneath the vehicle. Wheels locked and tyres screamed.

The whole thing was like a holocaust from hell. That was when it happened for the first time."

"W....What?"

"I found myself to be completely out of my body ... I was watching myself ... or ... not myself but Lotus. I could see her face and her eyes were black ... empty like holes ... and her hand was inside her dressing gown and she was touching herself. She was trembling and breathing deeply and I could see a frosty white mist coming from her lips. She seemed to double over as if in pain ... but I knew it was not pain ... she was having an orgasm. Within seconds Lotus ran from the house and down the driveway ... I remember her dressing gown was not fastened and she was showing her naked body as she ran. As she ran onto the road she screamed as if from shock and horror, yet I knew it was a cry of victory. The road looked as if a bomb had exploded. There was chaos everywhere. People were injured in their cars and a car's horn was sounding like a siren of war. No emergency services had arrived and people were standing staring; frozen within death's shroud of shock. Lotus ran towards the rear of the lorry and ... and what I saw I would not wish on my worst enemy. There were body parts which had been torn from Jason strewn across the carriageway. I watched as Lotus ran looking for Jason ... or should I say ... what was left of him. She saw his torso under the wagon and crawled underneath to be with him. I was frightened now for I knew if Lotus was to be caught and blamed for this killing I would be put in prison for years. I could see under the truck, and I watched as Lotus leaned over Jason ... he was semi-conscious and groaning. I was horrified as there did not seem to be much of a human-being left. His legs and arms were missing and his body was a mangled mess ... I remember his intestines were strewn along the road. I don't want to say what I saw next Wordcatcher."

"You don't have to say or do anything you don't want to."

"Well ... the story is over ... it wasn't me was it?"

"No it was me!"

I jumped in my chair as Emerald's voice had just changed to a deep sunken groan. "What ... What did you say Emerald?"

She spoke again as she always had, "I was just finishing my story. Lotus climbed on top of Jason and opened her dressing gown ... she was naked ... I watched in horror as she lay on top of him ... he was groaning in pain and Lotus lowered her head towards his blood splattered face. She whispered two words to him, *'Game Over'* and then gently placed her lips against his. I could see her breathing in and swallowing his last breath of life ... and as she sucked the life from him she trembled within an orgasm of ecstasy.

Is that what you would have done Wordcatcher ...Wordcatcher ...Wordcatcher are you dreaming again?"

"N ... No!"

"Well! I want to know what you think ... is that what you would have done to Jason ... the dirty beast ... remember you said you would tear him into pieces. What do you think Wordcatcher? ... Well ... answer me?"

"I ... I don't know if I would have done it ... after all you didn't do it ... Lotus did."

"Yes ... She's good isn't she? I mean ... even you said you would tear him to bits didn't you?"

"Yes ... I did."

"And don't worry Wordcatcher because everything worked out fine. I was found lying unconscious on top of my dead brother which was accepted as normal under the circumstances of shock. I was taken to hospital where I stayed for several days ... I can still remember the warm feeling of comfort and contentment as I lay snuggled in the cocoon of my hospital bed. No one would ever know what

44

had happened that night ... I came to the conclusion that love is a peculiar thing ... it's like life ... it can be there one second and gone the next.   Do you still love me Wordcatcher?"

   "Yes."

HARRY

I fell into sleep as rain bashed angrily upon the ceiling window of my bedroom. I drifted through the darkness as I tried to avoid a void of nothing where only something must remain. I did not stop for I was driven by ... whatever hand waves tests of judgements trials. Be I some humble floating leaf to drift on a breeze of ....*AHHHHHHHHHHHH!*
I was startled by a face zooming towards me shouting......

"*OOOOOOOOOOO! Har Har!* It's me Wordcatcher *Har Har!* Did I scare you ... it's a joke ... where have you been? ... I will sit against the wall and you can lye on the floor with your head on my lap ... Come on then! ... That's good ... is that nice Wordcatcher?"

"Yesss."

I was lying on the floor with my head resting upon Emerald's lap ... she was lightly stroking my head and face ... it felt like feathers brushing against my skin ... I felt myself sinking into bliss ... I was staring into her eyes which filled with kindness and loving.

"I know what you like Wordcatcher ... don't I?"

"Yesss."

As I bathed within bliss, Emerald began to sing ... her voice was like an angel's ... I began to feel I was in heaven.

"When all life's troubles surround us my love
My hand will reach out for you
For together forever we will always be
Be one circle of love floating free
And if ever a dream, in a dream be true love

Our hearts will always be bound
In our secret room the Lotus will bloom
By the beam from the silvery moon."

"Do you like me singing to you Wordcatcher?"
"Yesss."
"We are happy together ... we're happy and in love ... I mean at this moment ... now ... are we in love Wordcatcher?"
"Yes."
"Will you write me a poem ... a poem for me ... a poem about our love?"
"Yes."
"Ooooo! ... Go on then!"
"I have to be in the mood."
"Well what comes first the Mood or Love?"
"They're only words Emerald."
"Then why waste your time writing?"
"Because the words are the only way I know to find the answers to the riddles."
"Why look for answers when you have everything?"
"We never will have everything."
"Then stop looking ... *SHHHH!* ... Relax and be with me in the moment for now everything has become nothing."
I lay with my head resting on Emerald's lap and stared into her loving eyes. She would lean forwards and kiss my lips softly ... she would lean forwards and move her wet warm tongue around my lips and the taste was of honey ... she would smile and I was happy ... I was content ...was I in heaven? Had I found the answers to all my questions? Emerald began to hum a tune and words came into my mind ... so softly,
So soft your touch, green eyes so kind
The heart beat deep
You hum a lullaby's caress

47

> *One sweet-lipped stolen kiss*
> *To taste loves nectar from the Gods*
> *For when I look into your eyes*
> *Time and all become one moment*
> *One moment for ever with you ...true love.*

"Oh! That was beautiful darling ... nobody has ever given me a poem before ... quickly ... write it on the paper."

Emerald passed me the parchment and quill and she held the ink-well while I wrote her poem.

"I will keep this next to my heart forever ... *Wordcatcher ...Wordcatcher ... where are you going? ...NO! Please! .... Don't fall asleep and leave me ..... Don't leaaavveeee..............*"

*****

I awoke at home and my wife kissed me on the lips, "Are you alright ... you were mumbling in your sleep ... Oh! Your lips taste sweet ... what have you been eating?"

"I had a taste of honey."

"We have no honey ... you're always dreaming, but at least you're having sweet dreams ... now kiss me again I like it ... and again ... *Mmmmmmmmmmmmmmmmmmmmmmmmmm.*"

I sat to write and felt confused ... I loved my wife and we were happy together. I loved Emerald ... I know I should not love Emerald but what could I do if I did? My first answer was *'not to see her again'* and yet I had no choice for I knew that sleep would take me to her and that once I looked into her eyes I would be weak and lost; lost in love. I decided I had no choice ... I had to return and face whatever was to be. I could only steal moments with Emerald as my heart was given to my wife.

I sat watching T.V. It was 2 a.m. and the next film was about to begin. Everything became black … I had fallen into sleep and unfortunately, I knew I had.

Floating through black shrouds, cascades of swirling mists, where the place exists where all must travel a time in a space … empty! Is that why we move to search … is to be still, to be swallowed? … Why must we always move?

*****

"My Darling … My Darling … you have returned to me." Emerald grabbed hold of me, as if I were her long lost husband returning from a war. "I was alone … why did you leave me … I want you with me forever?"

"I have a wife I love."

"You love me."

"I do love you."

"You just said you loved your wife."

"I do."

"But you said you loved me … see you wrote me a poem …a poem of love … you do love me don't you?"

"Yes … but……"

"No buts love is love."

Emerald began to laugh and threw me to the floor like a child playing, "*Har … Har … now I have got you …*
now I have got you …
now I have got you …"

I was laughing as Emerald sat on top of me. Her face was full of love and beauty and she wrestled with me joyfully. I found it amazing how her mood could change so quickly … in one moment she could transform from a mature woman into a young girl, "*Har … Har Ha …Har Har*
now I have got you …
now I have got you …

> *now I have got you ...*
> *Har ... Har Ha ...Har Har"*

She was sat on top of me with her legs open and her short black skirt was almost around her waist. She was wearing brief black knickers and I could feel her pressing hard onto me and wriggling from side to side. She leaned forwards and pushed her breasts into my face as she held my arms down flat against the floor, she was laughing and chanting,

> *"now I have got you ...*
> *now I have got you ...*
> *now I have got you ..."*

I could feel her hips thrusting against me. I could feel her drawing my excitement into the wet heat of her thighs. I found something very disturbing about what was happening, as I was pinned to the floor. It was as if there was some kind of control from Emerald taking place. I didn't want sex with her ... and yes I longed for sex with her, and yet through my confusion my choice was being stolen. As she began to take me I felt a terrific panic. She was sinking onto me whilst laughing and joking ... I knew if she sank onto me and took me, some kind of unspoken agreement would be imposed by Emerald. I had to summon every bit of strength I could from where ever such strength awaits ... I pushed her from me and rolled towards my chair. I stood up laughing as I took cover from her blanket of humour.

I sat in my chair and calmly said, "Oh Well! That's enough fun let's carry on with our work."

Emerald stared at me angrily, "Oh! You bastard."

She seemed confused ... it was as if she did not know what to say. She stood to her feet and she was half laughing while her mouth was twitching from anger. She whispered at me while tilting her head coquettishly as if teasing me, "*Ha Har* ... what are you doing? ... What do you think you are doing?"

"What's wrong?"

She became angry and shouted in my face, "How could you?"

"What?"

"What! What! You flirt with me and then stand up as if nothing has happened."

"I didn't ... I didn't ."

"Oh! Oh! I just imagined you rubbing against me ... Oh! Well that makes everything fine."

"It was an accident."

"Oh! You decide to make love to me and then call it an accident."

"It just happened."

Emerald was shouting in my face and I could see the darkness rising behind her eyes, "Oh! It just happened. We almost made love, I could feel you sinking into me."

I was becoming annoyed with Emerald ... frightened, but also annoyed, I shouted back in her face, "It was you who was trying to fuck me ... you tried to rape me."

"I was making love to you, and you rejected me."

"But I didn't want to make love with you."

"Then why were you so hard?"

"It just happened ... you're beautiful."

"Don't you want to sink into me ... body and soul?"

"You want all of me but only a part of me is here."

"You're like all the others Wordcatcher ... all you want is to use me."

"No! You want to use me!"

"Which of the two is the worst kind of abuse Wordcatcher ... to be used or to be rejected?"

"Which of the two pains is the worst, being with you or having to push you away?"

Emerald fell at my feet and began to cry. She held her face in her hands and her body shook as she sobbed. I began to stroke her hair and to hum a tune softly. I felt as if I was going crazy ... I was so confused my head was spinning. It seemed like hours had passed by before Emerald raised her head and looked into my eyes with a love which stole my heart. She was sniffling and crying as she spoke to me. I felt for a handkerchief to wipe away her tears, then realised I had none. She mumbled, "Tell me you are sorry."

I did not know what I should be sorry for so I asked, "Sorry? ...."

I was about to ask Emerald 'Sorry for what' but I did not have a chance as she interrupted me, "I accept your apology ... but don't make me angry ... you won't like me if I am angry ... now you have wasted enough time ... your trouble is you take things too seriously ... remember Wordcatcher ... life is just a game. Now where were we? Ah! I remember ....

Mother and Harry returned from there holiday and I had to tell them the bad news. I had not taken a note of where they had gone for the weekend so could not call them ... anyway I thought ... why spoil there weekend because of a beast like Jason. Of course ... they walked into the house shouting happily, 'Hello-o we're back ... put the kettle on for tea ... where are *yoooou? Are yoooou* in?'

I walked into the lounge where they were taking off their coats and I began to cry ... I mean how do you tell someone their son is dead?"

Emerald suddenly began to jest, *"Oh! Hi! Did you have a good time and Oh! I almost forgot ... Jason your son is dead."*

I was beginning to think that Emerald would find it quite easy to have spoken in the way she had described ... Emerald suddenly shouted angrily spitting into my face, "Don't you dare think of me like that."

I was shocked ... even my thoughts were now Emerald's.

"As I was saying ... before you had nasty thoughts about me. I began to cry and they both hugged me and asked me what was wrong. I did not answer and they asked where Jason was. I looked at them and mumbled through tears, 'Jason ... Jason is ... Jason is dead.'

It was as if I had hit them with a sledge hammer. They both fell back onto the settee and sat still like a pair of ghosts with their mouths open. They could not accept what I had told them ... they thought it was some kind of sick joke. I explained how Jason had left for work and I suddenly heard a terrific crashing sound, and how he was killed by a truck. Eventually they both broke down crying. After a while mother made some tea ... but ... but daddy was hysterical. I have never seen anyone so upset before. He walked into his bedroom and stayed in there for days. I was very upset and disturbed by daddy's reaction ... after all, I loved daddy more than anyone ... I had never loved anyone the way I had loved him ... no one had ever cared for me or loved me like daddy ... Oh! Except you Wordcatcher, you are the love of my life. Anyway ... love and pain once more became confusing and Lotus had to kill daddy. What's wrong now Wordcatcher ... you look all white, come closer darling ... that's right ... snuggle close to me and don't worry.

Daddy eventually emerged from his room and he began to ask questions. Not just questions ... hundreds of questions ... I mean, you can't bring someone back from the dead by asking hundreds of questions can you ... and you never know ... if you ask too many questions you might end up dead yourself. Harry said he knew every nut and bolt on Jason's bike and could not understand why he had shot out into the road. I told him that people make mistakes and his foot may have slipped from the brake peddle. Daddy said that was impossible because there were two brakes ... one for the hand and one for the foot. He said one may slip but not the two, and he said Jason was one of the best bikers he had ever known having been riding motorcycles since he was able to walk. He would not stop asking questions and looking ... searching. He spent hours outside on the drive. He saw some fluid marks on the drive which he said had been wiped up and looked like brake fluid. Ah! I said maybe his brakes were leaking. He looked over every inch of the drive leading down to the road with a magnifying glass and eventually, he came to the conclusion that the brakes could not have been leaking because there would have been some drops on the drive, especially at the bottom where the brakes were applied. Daddy would look into the sky and shake his head as if looking to heaven for an answer to a riddle. He would shake his head while whispering, *'Something is not right ... this doesn't way up.'*

I was worried Wordcatcher ... very worried. Why could he not have let things be and we could have been such a happy family. No! He had to dig ... deeper and deeper and deeper. He arranged to see the wrecked bike. I told him it was a mangled mess and there was nothing to see, but he insisted. When he returned he stood for hours staring out of the window. I asked him what was the matter, and he said, 'I think the brake pipe on the bike had been cut.' He explained how the pipes had woven metal wire inside and would survive even the worst of fires. He told me he had seen a brake pipe which had been cut through cleanly and that there was no way this could have happened by accident. He said he thought someone had murdered his son and that he would not rest until he found out who it was or he was in his grave. I think Lotus may have heard him and I was becoming more and more concerned for daddy. He was obsessed with Jason's death ... he wasn't going to work and he talked of nothing else. Problems really began when the cleaner found the blood stains on the mattress. She said she was lifting it to tuck the sheets under while making the bed and wondered if someone had hurt themselves. Daddy looked at the mattress and asked me if I knew anything about it. Stories filled my mind. Should I say that Jason had taken a girl to bed while they were away? Should I tell them I had slept with a boy before Jason's accident? I decided to plead ignorance and said, 'Oh! I wonder how that happened!'

Daddy said he was going to have a sample taken from the blood and have it analysed to see if it was Jason's. I think what really upset Lotus was when daddy collected all the cutters from the garage. He said he was going to have them tested to see if there were any traces of brake fluid on them because, if a pair of cutters had been used, brake fluid would have squirted over them.

Daddy was a frail man and he had a weak heart. He retired to bed at about 10 p.m. as he usually did. Mother was out at her friend's and would not return home until after 11 p.m. I lay on my bed trembling. I knew something was going to happen ... I loved daddy and yet ... I suppose this is simply another part of love. I was playing music in my bedroom ... I remember the song was 'Nights in White Satin' by the Moody Blues. My curtains were open and the bedroom light was turned off. Moonlight flooded into the room ... and then it happened ... Lotus took over ... I shouted at her, 'Please don't harm Daddy ... Please'. She stood up and began to dance to the music. She began to undress until she was naked. As she moved with the music she seemed to wreathe like a snake. Her body was white in the moonlight ... it was as if all colour had gone ... everything was black and white. The music stopped and she walked to the bedroom door and opened it silently. She walked to my daddy's room and opened his door. She walked into his room and I followed trembling and crying. His curtains were drawn and Lotus walked over to open them. Daddy was shocked and began to clutch at his chest saying, 'What are you doing? ... Emerald ... What are you doing?'

Lotus stepped over to the side of his bed and pulled the covers from him. He was naked and he began to panic, 'What ... What are you doing ... What are you ....' Lotus lay on top of him. She wrapped herself around him like a spider and daddy seemed to be choking. He was gasping as if he was drowning. Lotus threw her head back and groaned with pleasure … I knew she was having an orgasm. Daddy was becoming weaker and she began to place her lips against his … it was like a spider with a trapped fly … she kept teasing him … licking his lips while her mouth dribbled saliva into his. Eventually he became so weak that his breathing was hardly noticeable. Lotus placed her lips tightly onto his and sucked the last breath of life from his body. She then calmly stood up and covered him with the bed sheets. She walked back to her room and climbed into bed.

I awoke to the screams from mother. An ambulance arrived and took daddy away. I was sad to have lost daddy because I loved him … but I must admit, I felt as if a weight had been lifted from my shoulders. I was sorry Lotus had killed daddy but … Well! I suppose that's what friends are for. It's funny how one thing leads to another isn't it Wordcatcher. I think it's another riddle from life … one minute you are with the person you love more than anyone else in the whole wide world … and then … then, in the next minute they are dead. Do you still love me Wordcatcher? I love you more than ever … more than I have ever loved anyone."

DEXTER and MOTHER

"Emerald?"

"Yes Darling?"

"I think we need to have a talk."

"I love to talk … You go first."

"Everything is like a game to you."

"Oh! Let me snuggle up close … are you going to shout at me?"

I shouted, "No!"

She looked into my eyes and it was as if a magic spell had been cast … I was lost once more … sinking into the beauty of her smile.

"You don't really know what to say do you my love?"

"No."

"I know you are worried but I will never harm you."

"It's not you I am frightened of … it's Lotus."

She pushed her face close to mine and began to rub our noses together. Even her nose felt soft and smooth. I could smell the sweetness from her breath … suddenly her lips pressed tightly against mine and we kissed … I opened my eyes and stared into hers … I could see nothing but love … our lips separated. She smiled softly and asked, "Was that nice?"

I answered, "Yes."

"Then stop worrying and trying to find answers because sometimes there are no answers and sometimes what will be will be … Now tell me where you live?"

"No! ……… What for?"

"There you go again trying to find answers."

"Well! I will ask you a question, what is through that door?" I pointed to the door leading from the green room.

Emerald seemed startled, "Nothing."

"See! You have your secrets and I have mine."

"But I am telling you all my secrets."

"And I have none from you because you see into my mine."

Emerald stared at me and sighed, "I will carry on with my story darling, and I hope you do not judge me, for I have never hurt anyone, and Lotus has only hurt those who would hurt me.

When daddy died from a heart attack everything he owned was left to mother. Unfortunately he also had a lot of debts as I suppose businesses do. Mother could not run the motorbike shop so sold it and paid off any remaining debts. She had enough money to live and maintain the house but had to 'cut back' with her spending. The cleaners had to go and she had to sell her car. She was contemplating selling the house to buy somewhere smaller when Dexter appeared on the scene. Dexter must have been around sixty five years of age which put a twenty five year age gap between him and mother who was forty. When I asked Dexter where he worked he told me that he was an 'Entrepreneur.' I had no idea what he meant but thought it to be some sort of circus act as he reminded me of a clown. He seemed to have money and he definitely had the 'gift o' the gab'. He was a flash sort of guy; you know … fast talking … lots of gold jewellery … and he had an answer for everything. He was the sort of guy who, if he had been on the Titanic when it sank, would have some way made a fortune from the ships contents. Mother seemed to like him and he made her laugh a lot … she told me he made her feel like a young girl again and she was happy with him. She said she had no intention of marrying him, and she was simply going to take one day at a time. He was a friendly guy and would often give me money. He would push fifty pounds into my hand and tell me, 'There you are gorgeous … now go and have some fun … life is too short to be sat in the house all the time.'

I had a feeling he wanted me out of the house and he was paying me off … I didn't care to think or imagine why, but mother seemed happy so I left them to it. Dexter had been living with us for several weeks when I began to become suspicious of him. He was a very tactile sort of guy … you know … always touching and hugging. He was always patting my bottom but I didn't mind as no harm was being done and I just presumed that was the sort of guy he was. The first time I was offended and frightened was one Saturday morning. I had left my bedroom and gone into the kitchen to make some tea. I would often make tea and take it back to my room. I was standing in my silk pyjamas making tea when Dexter came into the kitchen. He began making tea at the same time I was, and I noticed he kept placing his hand on my bottom as he moved about behind me. My heart was beating hard and I was frightened. I did not know what to say … I was embarrassed. I returned to my room and passed it of as, 'Well that's what Dexter is like.' The next morning the same thing happened again only this time I could feel his fingers pushing in between my bottom so I said, 'Dexter! Stop it! What are you doing?'

'I'm making tea!' he said, 'Why! What's wrong?'

And I replied, 'Just behave yourself Dexter.'

I hoped my warning would be sufficient but alas it was not. I used to visit the gym often because I enjoyed keeping fit. I returned home from the gym and it was a hot summer's evening and I was still wearing my tiny basketball skirt. Mother was out and as I walked past Dexter he pulled me onto his knee and said, 'How's my girl then?'

At first it seemed quite normal for him to do this as he was very extravert; and then while he was talking to me he put his hand on my bare leg and I noticed it was working its way towards my knickers. I tried to pull away saying, I had to have a shower and that was when he went too far. He pushed his hand up my knickers and tried to kiss me saying, 'Come on honey you know you want it!'

He threw me onto the floor and ripped my knickers off ... he was trying to kiss me and I felt like being sick. He was pulling his pants down when the door opened and mother walked in and shouted, 'What in God's name is going on?'

I ran from the room crying and locked myself in my bedroom. Dexter used his 'gift o' the gab'. I don't know exactly what he had told mother but she came to my room and called me a dirty whore. Apparently Dexter had woven a story about me asking him for money and my seducing him so that he would pay up. He had told mother that I had come home in a tiny skirt and been bending down in front of him and had tore my own knickers off and sat on his lap. Of course what man could resist such seduction ... Oh! And Dexter was very upset and I had to apologise to him and promise never to let anything like this ever happen again. Mother called me a whore and said I was jealous of her happiness. She said some terrible things to me which I can never forgive her for ... unforgivable things ... she said that it was my fault father had died and I should not have let him touch me. I shouted back at her, *'You should have stopped him touching me,'* she slapped me across the face and ran from my room crying. I was left feeling guilty again. I felt as if I had done something wrong."

Emerald began to cry. "Isn't that terrible Wordcatcher?"

"Yes ... he was a dirty rat."

"Well don't worry Wordcatcher because I told Lotus."

A FRIEND IN NEED

"Snuggle up close Wordcatcher. Are you ready? Then I will continue.

I began to talk to Lotus. At first she didn't answer me. I often spoke to her at night when I had gone to bed, and she would speak to me in my sleep. I told Lotus how I hated mother for letting me be abused by my father and not stopping him. I told Lotus how mother had once more let some 'creep' touch me … and then had the audacity to blame me for his abuse. I hated the two of them. You see Wordcatcher … it was as if I was sinking deeper and deeper into a well of guilt. And there was a whole lot of guilt … I mean! People were dying and I was stood in the middle of it all … it was as if I was in the eye of a tornado … there was chaos all around me as I calmly watched. I seemed to have no control over what was happening … I explained my feelings to Lotus and she explained how I needed to feel in control … she explained how she was my friend and would be there whenever I needed her. She was really helpful and helped me to understand what was happening. She told me I was like a boat at sea without a rudder and simply sailing anywhere. She said I needed to stop people from hurting me, and that I should find ways to take my revenge. She said we could work together as a team and that she would help me to be strong … she told me she would always be there for me and that she would never let anyone hurt me. I felt better after talking to Lotus … Lotus told me she would make mother and Dexter sorry for hurting me. It's good to have a good friend isn't it Wordcatcher?

When mother and Dexter were in the house with me the two of them would ignore me. Lotus explained how terrible this was as I had done nothing wrong. She explained how people were trying to drown me in feelings of guilt. She told me it was time to fight back and that *'all was fair in love and war'*. I spoke to her for hours in the night, and slowly I regained my pride and respect for myself. I became very angry and wanted revenge. Lotus told me there was nothing wrong with revenge if someone had hurt you. She would have lots of little sayings like, *'It is better to die on your feet than to live on your knees'*. I was very excited and felt like a new person. I was really looking forward to my revenge on Dexter and mother.

Dexter had a weakness so I should use it Lotus said. It was a weekend and Dexter and mother were having breakfast in the kitchen. Dexter would always return to their bedroom to wash and dress after having breakfast. I made sure I was taking a shower. I left the door to the bathroom slightly open and there was a tiled mirror where I could watch the doorway. As I stood naked with my back to the door I saw the reflection of Dexter's face appear in the crack of the door. It was a peculiar feeling. I was frightened and yet excited … I had a terrific feeling of control. I rubbed soap over my bottom and bent over washing my feet with my bum in the air. When I stood up again and looked in the mirror, his head was shaking and I knew he was playing with himself. I turned the water off and took the towel to dry myself. I was finding the whole experience extremely stimulating, and I groaned with pleasure. I took my mobile phone which was hidden in a towel, so that Dexter could not see it. I bent forwards and put the towel over my head drying my hair. I sent a text to mother who was downstairs as I knew she always had her phone close by. I sent her a simple message, *'Mother come upstairs.'* It worked and there was one hell of a commotion coming from the stairway landing. I quickly stepped from the shower and locked the bathroom door. I could hear mother shouting, 'What are you doing you dirty man ... you disgusting excuse for a human being.'

I had never felt so excited in my life. I stood in the bathroom, facing the door and as they argued I pleasured myself ... it was amazing ... orgasm after orgasm ... such an exhilarating experience.

My mother was shouting at the door, 'You dirty girl ... why didn't you lock the door?'

I didn't care anymore ... the more she shouted the more excited I became. I was even looking forward to facing her and acting innocent ... I laughed inwardly, 'Oh! Mother ... what has happened ... I was sure I had locked the door ... *sorrryy.*'

I wrapped a large bath towel around myself and opened the door. The two of them were still shouting on the landing. I was finding the whole scenario extremely amusing. Lotus was right ... I was in control. Mother flew at me, 'Why didn't you close the door properly?'

'I thought I had ... why? What has happened?'

'Why did you text me, and tell me to come upstairs?'

'Because I thought I saw the bathroom door open and someone peeping at me. I was frightened.'

Mother pushed me shouting, 'You knew exactly what you were doing ... you whore.'

As mother pushed at me the towel fell to the floor. As I stood naked, I calmly said, 'Oh! Now look what you've done.'

Mother proceeded to hit and chase Dexter along the landing as he attempted to turn his head and have one more peep.

After my first taste of blood I could not stop. It was like a drug addiction. I would walk into the kitchen wearing a short shirt and tiny knickers. Of course Dexter was making his morning tea and mother was upstairs. I knew he was looking and I would deliberately drop something and bend down to pick it up while I pushed my bottom into the air. Dexter would call me a *'Bitch'* and I would shake my breasts at him. Whenever he attempted to touch me I would begin to shout *'Mother'*. It was real fun and it excited me. Lotus and I would laugh together in the night. And then the inevitable happened and the fun had to end.

It was a late summer night. It must have been about two o'clock in the morning. I was lay on top of my bed naked as it was so warm. I was in a deep sleep when suddenly ... I felt a hand over my mouth and a naked body lying on top of me. I thought I was going to die of fright. My heart seemed to be pounding out of my chest. There was a faint light in the room and I could see that the person on top of me was Dexter. His face reminded me of a wild animal. All his teeth were showing as he snarled, and he was dribbling saliva onto my face. He growled at me, 'You bitch ... you think you're clever ... well I am leaving now and I have all of your mother's money. Before I leave I have something for you ... you slut.' Dexter began to force his hand into me and that is when it happened. I instantly found myself standing outside my body watching what was happening. I even hit Dexter with my fists, but my hands passed through his body. I watched as he began to rape ... to rape ... Lotus. I could see the white from my eyes turning to black. I jumped up and down frantically screaming, 'Lotus ... Lotus ... Stop him ... Stop him.' Dexter forced her legs open and slung his head back as he thrust his hips forward. I remember a terrific feeling of sadness ... as if Lotus had let me down. I believed that Lotus was powerful and could protect me and ... it was as if she was just accepting being raped by our worst enemy. I was beginning to crumble to the floor. Dexter had flung his head back groaning in pleasure as he thrust into my body.

As Dexter brought his head forward again he was laughing and said, 'Now I have you my dark beauty … how does it feel?'

There was an unnerving silence as Dexter groaned in pleasure. I was crying and watching from the side of the bed… my heart was broken as not only had the man I hated more than anyone else in the world taken me, my only friend, whom I trusted with my life, was not even fighting him.

Dexter groaned and spoke once more, 'See! I told you! You wanted it.'

Dexter began to move as if to climb off Lotus and … and that is when it happened. Lotus spoke calmly and in a deep voice, *'Now you must stay.'*

Dexter's mouth dropped open … I will never forget the expression on his face. I could almost see the thoughts flashing through his mind … all leading to that one simple question which even I was anxious to know. Dexter began to ask, 'What ….' He never finished the word for instantly the long finger on Lotus's hand was thrust deeply through his eye. I … I felt as if my whole being … my whole life was returning to me. It was as if I had been saved from the gallows. I shouted, 'Yes! Yes! Yes!' Dexter wriggled like a fish on a hook. Lotus took hold of my hand and smiled at me. As Dexter wriggled she pumped her finger in and out of his skull; blood and grey stuff squirted across the room as Dexter groaned; only this time it was from pain not ecstasy.

Lotus spoke to him, *'Now my lover … you must not leave for we will remain together forever as love and pain lie hand in hand.'*

She took hold of Dexter's hands with the tender care of a lover. She placed her lips over his and breathed in. Dexter became limp as his last breath escaped from his body, and he fell like a rag doll onto the bed. I began to heave as I felt physically sick. Lotus took hold of my hand saying, '*Oh! Don't worry darling ... I know he was an evil man but at least there was a happy ending.*'

*****

I awoke at home to bathe in silence. I could hear the faint whisper from the waves of the sea like the turning pages of an everlasting story. The bedroom was dark and I lay awake with my thoughts. I knew I would not sleep ... nor desired to for the rest of the day. I decided to go downstairs and write. Possibly through writing, some answer may be revealed to the situation I was facing.

I went into the kitchen to make a drink of tea. There was no milk left in the fridge so I took the few steps from the back door into the barn where we had a freezer in which we kept a store of bread and milk. I switched on the light and collected the milk from the freezer. As I was walking from the barn I looked up and saw a large spider's web. In the centre of the wed sat a massive black spider. I watched the creature in awe. I always liked spiders because they kill the insects which I hated. I noticed several empty husks or shells of insects resting in the web. It reminded me of a graveyard. Suddenly a large beetle fell from a beam above into the web. The spider did not move as the beetle began to struggle frantically. The more the beetle struggled the more trapped it became. I was watching for a long time. Eventually the spider slowly walked over to the insect and began to pull it apart. The spider seemed to have had all the time in the world; patiently waiting, knowing that eventually some victim would arrive to fulfil its needs. The spider would then wait and wait while the victim struggled as if toying with its forthcoming meal.

I walked across to the house and I was worried.

*****

"I don't know why you keep leaving darling because you will always have to return," Emerald shouted as I awoke to sit in the chair in her room.

"Now! Take your quill and I will continue with my story ... You are naughty going off near the end ... I think you should stay here with me ... would you like that? Oh! I do hate it when you sulk ... Now! Where was I ....

I was still standing by the bed watching Lotus. She stood up on the bed and stretched, flinging out her arms and throwing her head backwards. She stood naked in the moonlight and I was amazed at the beauty of her body (the body we shared). Her skin looked like pearl as the moon flowed downwards and over her like a spotlight. Sweat trickled down her body to leave lines, like streams to veins of marble, through the dark valleys and chasms clefts. For the first time ever I realised how beautiful I really was, and I began to understand why men would risk losing there lives for one taste of my love ... Yes! I had a love to die for ... they may love me but then they must remain forever, for how wrong it is to steal a woman's love and then to just walk away ... isn't that a 'cold' thing to do Wordcatcher?"

"Yes."

"Well I can be cold if I want to ... I mean! It's only fair to treat people the way they treat you, and what could be worse than to break a woman's heart?"

"Dying?"

"No Wordcatcher! ... I would prefer to die rather than to live each day with the pain of a broken heart ... but each love will remain with me forever for each one is important and will always be as it was, for my moments of love will last for eternity; and each love was my love and I will always know I was their last love ... forever. *Oooo!* It's so romantic isn't it Wordcatcher? ... I feel all dreamy. Let us not diverse my darling as I have a lot more to tell you. Now! Are you comfortable my love?"

"Yes."

"Then I will continue. I felt frightened now as I had a dead body on my bed, and I realised it would be hard to hide the evidence as blood had squirted all over my room. Lotus could tell what I was thinking and placed her finger against her lips, '*Shhhh.*' Lotus laid Dexter's body on the bed; he looked so peaceful. I wondered what she was doing but I trusted her and believed in her ... I knew she would not let us down. Lotus calmly walked into the shower, washed herself quickly, then put on a towelling robe and slippers. She went downstairs, opened the basement door and walked down the steps. She stared at me with those dark eyes of hers and giggled while shrugging her shoulders. I felt like we were two naughty girls stealing cream cakes ... *Oooo!* It was fun, it was really exciting. I never know what Lotus will do next. She walked over to the central heating boiler and kicked the oil feed pipe. Red fuel began to spread over the cellar floor. Lotus took some matches and an old rag from a shelf and dipped the rag into the fuel. She set the rag on fire and dropped it into the oil. Soon the basement was a raging fire of fury. We ran upstairs and Lotus pulled the batteries out from the smoke alarms. Mother's bedroom door began to open. Oh! I was frightened and ran to hide behind Lotus. Mother shouted angrily, 'What are you doing? Where is Dexter?'

Lotus pushed mother hard and she flew backwards into her bedroom and landed on the floor. She shouted, 'Who are you? Who are you?'

I will never forget ... Lotus turned to her and said to her slowly ... in her deep sunken voice, '*I am your last mistake.*'

Lotus lifted her knee and kicked forwards with her heel at the door handle in mother's bedroom. The handle flew off the door and Lotus calmly picked it up. As she stepped from the bedroom she looked at mother and said, '*Go to sleep my love.*'

The door slammed shut and I could hear mother screaming from the other side. Flames and smoke were roaring through the house and we ran into one of the spare bedrooms which were at the opposite end of the house from where the fire was spreading. Lotus undressed and got into bed, she looked at me and picked up the telephone which was by the bed. She dialled the emergency services and handed me the phone. I was back in my body and smoke was seeping into the bedroom. I was coughing as I screamed for help down the phone, '*Help! Help!* The house is on fire and I can't get out of my room.'

It must have been about ten minutes before I could hear the fire-engine's siren. My room was full of smoke and flames were licking around the door. The windows had top openings and were not large enough for me to climb through. I tied a pillow case around my head in an attempt to stop the smoke which was now choking me. I began to hit the window with a chair, but it must have been special glass because I could not break it ... the last thing I remember was seeing someone on the other side of the window who was dressed in yellow. I must have passed out, for the next thing I remember was waking up in the hospital. A nurse leaned over me and spoke softly, 'You have been in a fire Emerald, and you are going to be alright ... you have no burns but breathed in too much smoke.'

I immediately shouted, 'What about mummy and daddy?'

The nurse replied slowly, 'I ... I am sorry my dear but you were the only one to survive.'

I burst into tears from relief ... I mean to say ... imagine if mother had survived to tell the tale. Eventually a policewoman visited me, 'Hello Emerald I hope you are feeling better?'

'Thank you ... but what ... what happened?' I asked shocked, but continued, 'One minute I was going to sleep and then I woke up choking.'

'It seems to have been a leak from the boiler in the cellar which caught alight, and with there being a lot of fuel for the fire it spread quickly. Your mother and father had no chance of escaping and you were very lucky to have woken up. If you had not woken at that moment you would not have survived.'

'Oh! Oh! Poor mummy and daddy ... what will I do now?'

'Don't worry! We will send someone who will talk with you and help you decide what you are going to do when you leave the hospital. Have you anyone to stay with when you leave hospital?'

'No.'

'Well! Don't worry you will not be left on your own when you leave the hospital Emerald.'

'Yes! Thank you ... I know I am not alone.'

KEN

I was surprised later that day when I saw a handsome man walking towards my hospital room. He had some flowers and ... and he walked through the door as if he knew me. I shouted to him, 'Hi! But I think you have the wrong room ... I don't know you.'

The handsome man passed me the flowers and replied, 'Yes! You're the one ... I never forget a beautiful face ... I'm the fireman who saved you.'

I must have turned bright red ... I felt embarrassed. The handsome young man pointed to a chair and asked, 'Do you mind if I sit with you awhile ... or would you like me to leave? ... I understand if you would like me to go.'

'No! No! I am glad to have someone to talk to ... and ... and how can I ever thank you for saving my life?'

'Seeing you alive is thanks enough.'

'You must have the best job on earth ... I mean saving peoples lives ... what could be more rewarding?'

The young man reached out his hand to me, 'My name's Ken.'

I reached for his hand, 'My name ......'

I was interrupted, 'Emerald! I know ... and what a beautiful name, I wondered why you had been called Emerald ... but now I can tell by your eyes ... you have the most beautiful eyes I have ever seen.'

I suddenly realised that my eyes would have been closed when he saw me last as I was unconscious. My face must have become bright red again because Ken said, 'Oh! I'm sorry … I am embarrassing you and being too forward?'

'Oh! No … you can flatter me all day … as long as you mean it … I mean it isn't nice to lead a girl on is it?'

'I mean what I say … your eyes and your smile … you're beautiful and ………..'

'Oh stop! Now … tell me about yourself.'

Ken stayed with me for several hours … until dinner was being served. I could tell he did not want to leave and he promised to call back the next day as he was working nights.

Ken arrived about two o'clock in the afternoon and sat in the chair next to my bed. I told him to bring his chair closer and I held his hand. He had brought me some chocolates and some more flowers. I told him if he continued buying me flowers I would be able to open a flower shop. We talked and talked and Ken told me all about himself. He said he lived with his mother who was sixty-four years of age. Ken was twenty-five and told me how his girlfriend, whom he had loved since being at school, had died in a car crash along with his father who was driving the car. He said he had never loved anyone since and could not think of a girl in that way until … until he saw me. He explained that he could not understand why but he had been drawn to me in some mysterious way. He asked me if I believed in love at first sight. I told him, 'Yes!' And I believed love could last forever … even if someone died. Ken said he could understand what I meant and he … he said the weirdest thing.

He said, 'I love you!'

'Ken! You have only known me for a few days.'

He was so romantic. He spoke to me in a way I had never known, 'How long does it take to find an emerald in a field of mud?'

'Oh! Ken ... I think I love you too ... but promise me you will not hurt me? ... Promise because I have been hurt through love so many times.'

'I would prefer to die rather than hurt you my love.'

'Oh Ken promise?'

'Yes my love ... I promise.'

As Ken sat in the chair by my bed he fell asleep while I stroked his head. I hummed a lullaby as we bathed in our feelings of love ... I knew whatever happened, that moment would last forever ... I knew a part of Ken would remain with me forever.'

*****

"That's an amazing story of love Emerald."

"Yes! Thank you darling ... do you ever live in the moment Wordcatcher?"

"I never have the time to."

"What sort of answer is that ... you are silly sometimes ... Wordcatcher! Did you hear me? ... You are silly sometimes!"

"Yes I suppose I am silly, most of the time."

"Oh! Don't go all sulky ... I still love you! Are you jealous?"

"Your story ... It sounds like when I met you."

"And it was ... but love is like seeds ... there can be many."

"And yet only a few may grow?"

"Ah! But the husk from the seed will live on for ever."

"But Emerald ... the husk is a dead shell."

"Yes. A trophy! ... Sometimes I think that all the collected moments of love are like trees which make a forest."

"And what became of Ken?"

"How dare you speak to me like that? You are not so high and mighty are you? ... You broke two women's hearts and some others along the way."

"We all make mistakes Emerald ... I have never hurt anyone for no reason."

"And neither have I ... see, we are alike ... are we alike Wordcatcher?"

"I have never killed anyone."

"But there were times you wished you had?"

"Maybe."

"See! Lotus has only done what we all wish for at times ... I think everyone would love a friend like Lotus ... Do you think so?"

"Maybe."

"You nearly killed a man once Wordcatcher ... you forget I can see through you."

"Nearly never killed anyone, and neither have I"

Emerald became angry and stood up shouting, "Don't sit there judging me you bastard ... all you are is a 'pen-pusher' ... your not my judge."

"I am not judging you ... I don't really want to be here."

She instantly changed her mood as if a switch had been turned ... "Stand up and hold me darling it is silly for us to be arguing ... we are victims of circumstance; both trapped by fate ... Hold me! ... Kiss me!"

She pressed her lips tightly against mine ... I was shocked ... shocked by how sudden her mood could change ... I was shocked at the power she seemed to have over me. I opened my eyes, to find our eyes staring into each others with less than an inch of distance between us. Her eyes were beautiful like deep swirling magical pools of green ... I felt her tongue push into my mouth and I felt myself becoming weak ... weak and excited. She pulled me harder against her as she thrust her tongue around the inside of my mouth. I was beginning to succumb to her every whim ...

as I stared into her eyes I noticed her tiny black pupils. Instantly I was horrified as I could see death as if incarnate ... the black in her eyes were like tunnels ... I felt as if I was falling; falling into death. My whole being shivered and I felt frozen. I pushed Emerald away from me and screamed, "*Ahhh!* I have seen inside you."

"Oh! Wordcatcher, you do over react ... sometimes you can be really boring. Let us carry on with the story ... and don't worry for I love you and always will."

"Do you believe in love at first sight Wordcatcher?"

"Yes ... but y........."

"Oh! Shut up and listen ...

*****

It was like a whirlwind of love between Ken and me. He met me when I left the hospital and insisted on my staying at his home. He was tall, strong and handsome ... I called him my knight in shining armour and he joked, 'You mean yellow plastic armour.' Ken carried me upstairs and laid me on a bed in the room I was to use. I had a double bed and my own bathroom which had a shower. *Oooo!* I was so excited ... a new home and a new love. I was greeted by Ken's mother Amy and she seemed to be a nice, kind lady. Amy told me I had to relax and take things easy. She told me that if I wanted anything, then all I needed to do was to ask her. The house was big. It had five bedrooms and two lounges and the kitchen was as big as a garage. Amy was a small elderly lady who walked with a stick. She wore glasses on the end of her nose and she always seemed to be dressed in black. There were a lot of religious pictures in the house ... and crosses with Jesus on. There was a bible by my bed and psalms in frames on one wall. From my past religious experiences with my father I came to the conclusion that Amy was Catholic. I told Amy that my father had been a minister. She was surprised and asked in a whisper, as if it was some dark secret, 'Oh! .... You are not Catholic then?'

'No, I am of the 'Church of England' but I don't go to church much. I believe in God and I often pray ... but it's usually when I want something ... Oh! I am naughty ... that must sound awful.'

'Well at least you tell the truth my dear.'

Amy asked me hundreds of questions. After several hours my head was spinning and I was fed up of all the tea and biscuits she had been giving me. I went to my room and lay down for a rest. Ken was at work and would be home around dinner time.

I was awoken by a kiss on my head from Ken. He sat on the side of my bed and asked me if I had a nice day. I told him I had spent most of the day talking to his mother. He said, 'Oh No! She hasn't been giving you the third degree ... has she?'

I told Ken she was cute and I had enjoyed talking to her. Ken told me we would be having dinner soon and that he was going to take a shower. I said to him, 'You can use mine if you want ... I don't mind.'

I sat up on the bed in front of Ken. I was naked and I pushed my belly into his face jokingly. Ken's mouth dropped open, 'You are beautiful!'

'Do you like me naked darling ... am I a sight for sore eyes?'

Ken ran his fingertips softly over my body saying, 'I have seen you naked before but you won't remember will you?'

'When! ... Oh! I remember ... when you rescued me. Well I hope you covered me up?'

'It seemed a shame to cover such beauty but ... what is that red mark on you stomach? ... I noticed it when I rescued you.'

'It's a birthmark!'

Ken began to kiss the red mark, '*Ummm! Yummy Yummy* it tastes good! ... It looks like an hour glass?'

I pushed Ken's head between my legs and thrust my hips into his face, 'You do as I say you naughty boy, *Oooo!* Harder! ... Harder! ... *Oooooooo!*'

Suddenly there was a knock on the door and the handle moved. The door opened slightly and Amy's head popped into the room. 'Dinner is ....Oh! Oh! Mary Mother of Jesus, Oh! Oh!'

Ken hastily emerged from between my legs and began to panic, 'Oh shit!' He was as white as a sheet.

'Well Ken!' I said, 'She should knock before she walks into peoples rooms.'

'Yes ... I know.'

I had to have a shower before going down the stairs. I was soaking wet and as frustrated as a woman could be. I put on some slacks and a t-shirt and went downstairs to join Amy and Ken for dinner. I sat down facing Ken and felt embarrassed about what had happened. Amy placed three plates of food onto the table and I began to eat. I tried to begin a normal conversation, 'Oh! That looks lovely ... I am starving.'

I was interrupted by Amy, 'We will say grace and thank the Lord for our food.'

I placed my knife and fork onto my plate, 'I am sorry; I was so hungry I forgot my manners.'

Amy was abrupt, 'I would imagine that to be a sentence often used by yourself.'

After prayers Ken said the most stupid thing to his mother, 'Oh! The burn on Emerald's leg seems to have gone now ... that's what I was looking at when ... when you walked in the room mother.'

Amy was quick to reply to Ken, 'Well I think you should stay out of her room. Remember ... the best way to prevent temptation from the devil is to avoid it.'

I was really annoyed at Amy ... I felt that she was calling me the devil and ...."

~~~

I could not resist interrupting Emerald, "Oh! Your cover was blown?"

"That is not funny Wordcatcher." Emerald leaned towards me to give me a playful slap.

She smiled with a twinkle in her eye and continued, "You are a real cad sometimes ... I was upset and felt Amy had invaded my privacy. I almost wished she had barged into my room a bit later when our loving had reached a climax. Yes! I thought that would have given her something to think about. I decided to stand up for myself.

~~~

'I am not the devil and you should knock before going into a room where someone is staying.'

Amy's reply was instant, 'Oh! Now I understand you ... you have been in my house for a few hours and you are making up the rules. Well! Young madam ... this is my house and I say what is right or wrong. And you! Ken!' *Amy poked Ken with her fork,* 'you will not go into her room again ... I will pray tonight for forgiveness for the two of you, and you will do the same if there is one ounce of decency left between you.'

Later that evening Amy was praying, 'Please Lord keep all fornication from my home and deliver us from evil Amen.'

The door to Amy's sitting room was ajar, and as she prayed, two deep black eyes stared at her. I prayed in my room ... I was worried in case something may spoil my love with Ken, 'Thank you God for bringing Ken to me and thank you for Lotus, my guardian angel who is always here to protect me.'

AMY

The next day I stayed in bed until 10 a.m. I was hoping that Ken may have called in before he left for work, but he didn't. I could not believe I was separated from the man I loved because of his mother and her beliefs. I felt uncomfortable as I sneaked downstairs to make some tea. I had some magazines in my room and my intention was to make tea, then return to my room to read. I was wearing a short nightdress but nothing on my feet. I crept into the kitchen and switched on the kettle. There was an instant blast like a fog-horn, 'What are you doing child? ... Go and put some clothes on and I will make the tea ... NOW! ... Go on ... Snap! Snap!'

I was absolutely fuming with anger. I was also feeling sick from a kind of fear because I felt trapped. It was like a panic. I did not know how to handle the situation. I knew what I wanted to do, and say, but I was also aware what Amy's answer to me would be, '*This is my house and I make the rule.*' I returned to my room mumbling obscenities.

'What are you mumbling child? ... Now hurry up.'

I could not believe I was in the twentieth century. Had I stepped into some horror film? ... Was I asleep and having a nightmare? After dressing I sat on my bed waiting for the inevitable Amy.

'I have made you some breakfast ... come on now! Snap ... Snap.'

At least she did not stick her head around the door. I walked into the kitchen where a place was set for me at the table. Amy was cooking and shouted across the kitchen to me, 'How are you this morning young lady?'

'I was alright till I fucking saw you.'

'What! What did you say?'

My heart was pounding in my chest ... I had not spoken ... I immediately realised it was Lotus who had replied to Amy.

'I ... I was just saying there is a lovely morning dew.'

'Oh! Well I didn't see any morning dew.'

I must admit, Amy made me a wonderful breakfast; eggs, bacon, sausage and mushrooms. When I picked up my knife and fork I hesitated and began to say grace, 'For what we are ....'

Amy interrupted me, 'It is alright my child ... you eat your breakfast and the Lord will wait until you are ready ... He's very patient you know?'

I was starving and could not eat fast enough. Amy sat facing me but I was not concerned about her. I thought I would eat breakfast and then go out shopping, and I had to see a solicitor regarding my mother's will. I was finishing breakfast when Amy began to ask questions. While I was eating she stared at me from across the table, which was nothing unusual for me as people often stared. 'You really have the most unusual colour of eyes my darling.'

'Well ... Thank you Amy and thank you ......'

I was hoping to make my escape but was beginning to realise it was not going to be as easy as I thought, as Amy interrupted me, 'I think Ken is hooked on you and I can understand why. You really are a beautiful sight to behold.'

'Thank you I ......'

'I have not finished speaking yet ... Emerald! I can see why you have the name Emerald! ... Your eyes are ... are hypnotic.'

'Oh! Well ... thank you for ....'

'Be patient my dear ... you will get indigestion rushing your food. I would find it hard to believe that any

81

man would not be attracted to your beauty. And you do
know how to tempt the devil don't you my dear. Those
skin tight pants you are wearing and the low-cut top you
have on ... you certainly leave little for the imagination ...
Don't you darling?'

'Well ... I am not responsible for your imagination. I
have been given a beautiful body by God so why should I
walk about in baggy black clothes hiding it?'

'There is something unusual about you ... Emerald.
A mother's instinct is to protect her son.'

'Your perceptions overwhelm me Amy ... but
remember the word you create if you place the letter 'S' in
front of mother ... now I would love to sit and talk all day
but I have an appointment ... Bye for now.'

'Goodbye for now ... Emerald.'

I was relieved to leave the house, while in my mind,
a disturbed debate was questioning the complicated issues
surrounding my love for Ken, and the interference from his
mother. How lovely it would be if I were to live alone with
Ken in such a lovely house. I sighed and felt sad because it
always seemed as if the perfect dream was always side by
side with a nightmare. I met with the solicitor and he told
me my mother had not made a will, but explained that
everything she owned was now mine. The latter was
another dream with a parallel nightmare. I now owned
everything mother had, while everything mother had was
changed into cash by thieving Dexter, and which was now,
most likely, turned into ashes along with Dexter. The
solicitor explained that the house was insured, but there
was a dispute in relation to the fire as the boiler had not
been serviced for several years, and the insurance company
were claiming that the fire was caused through negligence.
It was explained to me that all the money from mother's
accounts seemed to have been withdrawn on the same day
as the fire. I was left with about £2000 if I was lucky, and
from which the solicitor would need to deduct his fees. The

bottom line was that I could end up actually owing money. I thought of where the rat, Dexter would have hid all the cash he had withdrawn. I remembered he was leaving the house when the fire started. I realised he would have hidden the cash in a case ... a case which would have been burnt to ashes. I left the solicitor's office feeling despondent. I felt lost as I had no home to go to and like a beggar as I had no money. What was I to do? I could apply for benefits ... that made me feel even worse. I returned to Ken's and began to cry ... I began to cry because I had to knock on the door and 'the old bag' must have gone out. It was raining so I walked into the garage and sat on an old tea chest. I cried and cried ... why was there always someone in the way of my love? I stopped crying and became angry ... that's when Lotus came and I knew she would help me.

Amy came home at about 3.30 p.m. She seemed to know I was in the garage as she stuck her head around the door to greet me, 'Oh! What are you doing sitting in there you silly girl ... you should have asked me if I was going out ... I can't sit in waiting for you all day you know! Now come on and stop being silly and it's no good puffing up your lips and sulking with me girly .... Oh no! I'm too old and wise for your tricks.'

'Bastard.'

'What ... What did you say?'

'I said I am tired.'

I entered the house and told Amy I was going to my room to lie down. It was not long before Ken was home ... I lay on my bed feeling sad because I could hear him talking to his mother, and her saying, 'Emerald is having a sleep ... she asked me to tell you not to disturb her and that I was to shout her when dinner is ready.'

I lay on the bed thinking, *'You lying bitch'* for all your religion your nothing but a liar. I could hear Ken go into his room. I was determined to break her rules. It was as if she was spoiling my dream and I had to stop her. I sneaked into Ken's bedroom where I could see he was having a shower. I tiptoed to the shower door and waited. He turned off the shower and stepped into the bedroom from a cloud of steam. I took him in my arms and kissed him. I slid down his body and took him deep into my mouth ... I rolled my tongue around and I remember wishing that his mother would walk into the room now, and how I would look into her eyes as I continued with what I was doing. Something was wrong as I noticed that Ken was still soft. He pulled me to my feet and kissed me, 'I'm sorry darling ... it's mother, I ... I just think she will come to the door.'

I was shocked by his reaction and rejection, 'So when do we make love? ... I have needs ... I need you!'

'We will work something out ... I know! We can go away at the weekend to a Bed and Breakfast.'

I ran from the room crying. I felt like a prisoner ... I felt second best to Ken's mother. I felt like some thing kept in a room to fulfil some need, which neither Ken nor his mother understood. I returned to my room and lay on the bed crying. I heard a knock on the door and it was Ken, 'Darling I'm sorry ... please come out and let's talk this over?'

I heard Amy's voice shouting, 'Don't worry son it is probably her time of the month ... women have these funny moods. Come down and have your dinner and I will take her a sandwich later.'

I was beginning to realise that I may have made a mistake in thinking that I could build up a relationship between Ken and myself. Two is company while, in this instance, three is a crowd. I did not hate Ken ... I simply realised that our meeting was a mistake and that it was best to end it now. Lotus whispered to me, *'You fucking hate her though ... don't you?'*

I held my hands over my ears, 'Please go away Lotus ... I will leave here tomorrow and start a new life.'

Later that evening Amy knocked on the door and walked in with a tray, 'Here's some milk and a sandwich. You are a sulky girl! ... Oh! Look at those puffed up sulky lips ... I think you need a good spanking.'

'I will fucking kill you bitch'

'What ... What did you say?'

'I said nothing.'

'Ha! That is where we differ, Emerald ... if I have something to do, or say, it will be said or done. You sit in your room and cuss and mumble ... if you were my daughter you would have had a good whipping when you were younger ... you cheeky girl ... you wont pull the wool over my eyes ... I know what you need.'

'And I know what you need.'

'Ah! And what do I need?'

'Help.'

'You cheeky girl ... I just pray Ken sees how evil you are.'

The door slammed shut and I was frightened ... frightened for the first time, of Lotus, *'How dare she say that to me ... Whip me! ... Whip me! It happened once and it will never happen again. .... Emerald!'*

'Yes Lotus.'

'I am going to kill her ... slowly.'

Lotus! ...Please? ... Let's just leave here.'

'No one speaks to me like that ... You may put up with it Emerald but I demand respect.'

It must have been midnight when Ken sneaked into my room like a frightened mouse, 'Darling ... I thought we might have some time together.'

Ken began to climb into my bed and to slip out of his pyjamas. Within seconds he was in the bed. We were both naked and I pushed him onto his back and sat with my legs open on top of him, 'Now my love, I will take you to heaven ... I will make you feel as you have never felt before.'

I rubbed my wetness over him while keeping him from slipping into my body, 'Oh! You like that don't you?'

Ken was trembling and begging for more. I knew he had lost control ... I knew I could do anything with him now. He begged as he thrust his hips towards me, 'Please! Please! I need it.'

I quickly got off the bed and stood by the door. I put my hands onto the wall and pushed my bottom into the air, 'Take me darling ... Now! Take me.'

I could hear movement in the hallway. Ken ran behind me; he was so big I knew he was about to explode. As he grabbed hold of me like a wild animal, I screamed, and the door suddenly burst open. It was Amy ... her mouth dropped open as Ken stood tall trying to cover his wet erection. I looked at Amy and shouted, 'Can't you keep your filthy son out of my room? ... He almost raped me! ... He's like a wild animal! ... He's possessed by the devil.'

Amy hit at Ken with her stick as he ran down the hall groaning ... she chased after him while beating him, 'You dirty fornicating evil boy ... I will beat the devil from you.'

Ken ran into his room squealing like a pig. I quickly put on my nightdress and gown. I picked up Ken's pyjamas and waited for the inevitable visit. The door burst open and Amy was spitting fire. I handed her Ken's pyjamas while shouting, 'I have never been so humiliated! ... I have a good mind to report this to the police ... Do you know it is called rape when a woman is jumped on by a man when she is asleep in her bed? ... Oh! But I suppose it is your bed so it doesn't matter. I come from a good family and I am not used to this sort of behaviour.'

Amy was frothing at the mouth and I was praying she would have a heart attack. She growled at me like a mad dog, 'I want you out of my house in the morning.'

'Oh! You don't have to worry about that. You keep that wild animal away from me! He should be locked up.'

I returned to my bed where I giggled with Lotus ... I was so excited I let Lotus play with me, as I was still wet from my fun with Ken. I felt happier than I had for a long time, 'Lets go to sleep now Lotus ... We have a busy day tomorrow.'

'Yes my love ... I have to kill the bitch.'

I awoke the following morning ... it was a beautiful day and the sun was shining. I opened the window and stood naked letting the hot sunshine flow over my body. I breathed in the fresh air. I looked outside and several elderly women were staring up at me. They were wearing the sort of hats I had seen religious people wear in the past. I hoped they would be friends of Amy's. I began to stretch and rub my breasts. The women stared, shocked by my behaviour. They irritated me because all they had to do was look away and carry on with their boring lives. I slid my hand between my legs ... that did the trick ... the women disappeared in a bustle of dust. I smiled as I thought to myself, 'What will the neighbours say to Amy?' I was interrupted by a familiar voice in my head, *'Amy will never know ... Now stop showing off we have work to do.'*

I tried to reason with Lotus but she told me she could never forgive Amy for threatening to whip her, and said she had to be punished as she reminded her of our father and the whippings he gave us. I showered and dressed before packing what little belongings I owned into a holdall. I went downstairs and sat at the kitchen table; I knew Ken would be at work. Amy walked in, spitting fire,

'Get out of my house you whore.'

'Oh! Mummy! Are you to send me out with no breakfast?'

'Get out or I will phone the police.'

'Yes! Phone the police and I can make a statement as to how your son tried to rape an innocent girl.'

'You are as innocent as the devil ... I can see the beast within you!'

'Oh! Is she here now?'

Amy screamed at the top of her voice while raising her stick to hit ... Lotus ... *'That's a big mistake you wicked woman.'*

Amy screamed as Lotus grabbed the end of her stick, 'What are you? Your eyes are black! ... Your voice is deep!'

Lotus sat on top of Amy as she struggled, and struggled. She spat and screamed and swore and fought like a wild cat. I had left my body and was frightened as I watched. I wasn't worried about Amy ... I was frightened of being caught. Lotus must have held Amy down for over an hour. The weaker Amy became the more pleasure Lotus seemed to derive. Eventually Amy became still as she lay on her back exhausted while staring at Lotus who was wriggling her hips about and I knew she was aroused. I wanted to leave this hell-hole and carry on with my life. I shouted to Lotus, 'Hurry ... let's go!'

As Lotus moved her hip's she lowered her face towards Amy's. She began to kiss her lips and speak to her slowly, *'Now my lover ... you are going to heaven with the taste of forbidden fruit upon your lips'* ... Lotus kissed Amy and I could see her breathing in deeply as she sucked the last breath from her victim. *'Now be at peace my lover for you may resist me no more.'*

Lotus stood up and left Amy lying on the floor. There were no marks on her body ... she simply looked like she had fallen asleep. Lotus looked at me and smiled as I returned to be with her ... Lotus told me, *'Her body is at rest while her soul will be forever tormented in hell.'*

STARLIGHT

"Are you comfortable Wordcatcher?"

"Yes."

"Give me a kiss ……….. *Oooo!* That was good … See! You can be good if you want to … can't you?

"Yes! … You sound like a teacher who is going to spank me."

"I can be anything you wish darling … and also some things you may not wish. Now! Do you want me to spank you?"

"No thanks."

"Then I will continue with my tale.

~~~

I left Ken's house and began to walk. I didn't know where I was going. I enjoy the feeling of comfort I feel when I walk. Movement seems to bring a satisfying and comforting feeling; a kind of escape through transition which one may only experience when walking towards nowhere in particular. I was walking along by the side of the road when I looked up, and found myself approaching a café. I suppose Ken would return home to find his mother had died from a heart attack … well! She had been very stressed out. I suppose Ken would blame himself for her death. Poor Ken. A tear ran down my cheek as I thought of him … Ah well! Love hurts.

Inside the café I handed over all my remaining money to pay for the meal and drink I had chosen. I was tired, it was dark and I was feeling despondent. I visited the toilet and changed from my tight jeans into a short skirt. I knew I would be given a lift now, for no man could resist me. I stood by the side of the road and placed my hand on my hip. I stood seductively with my thumb in the air and stared down the road. I felt nervous so shouted to Lotus, 'Lotus! I feel frightened,' Lotus replied, *'Don't worry… I won't kill anyone.'*

Soon a massive lorry stopped and the driver shouted to me, 'Jump in babe!'

I climbed into the truck while attempting to keep my legs together.

The driver was about forty years of age … I felt comfortable with him as he seemed like a nice man. He shouted across to me as the lorry began to move, 'Where you headin' babe?'

'I shouted back to him, 'The next city.'

He began to ask me questions such as where had I come from, and what was I doing hitch-hiking in the dark. I told him, 'No questions … No lies.'

He seemed to understand me. We talked about the weather and his work. He was a long-distance lorry driver and his name was 'Starlight' that was his call sign on the radio, as he preferred to drive at night. He told me how he loved to drive at night and time seemed to fly by. I fell asleep in the cab and when I woke up he had covered my legs with a blanket. I began to feel close to Starlight and put my head on his shoulder as I slept. It must have been dawn when I awoke to the hissing of the wagons air-breaks as we pulled into a café. We stopped and the sky looked like it was on fire. *'Oooo!* Look at that sky! … Isn't it lovely?'

Starlight yawned and stretched as he was tired from driving all night, 'Yes … that's a part of my job I love … you see some beautiful sights … like yourself of course.'

I blushed as he stared at me. He seemed surprised, 'Wow! I never noticed your eyes. Probably because you have been asleep most of the night ... Your eyes are the most beautiful things I have ever seen ... Sorry! ... I don't mean 'things' I mean eyes ... they're amazing ... have you some sort of contact lenses on or ... something?'

'Oh! Stop it you are making me blush.'

Starlight opened his door and jumped down from the cab. He came around and lifted me down, 'You know girl ... you should wear some proper clothes ... there are some bad people out there ... I mean people who would not think twice about killing someone.'

'Yes ... I know.'

'Well! ... Follow me then. I suppose you are hungry?'

'But I have no money!'

I began to cry and Starlight held me, 'Don't be getting upset I think I can afford an extra plate of food.'

'Thanks.'

'Here take my hanky ... Oh! Don't worry about that it's only a bit of oil ... *Ha Ha Har!* Come here you have a black nose now.'

Starlight wiped my nose and my eyes and I began to cry even more ... he asked, 'What's wrong now?'

I whispered, 'I love you.'

'What did you say?'

'I said ... I could go a brew.'

'That's right ... food and tea and you will feel like a star ... Did you hear! ... Star! ... *Ha Ha Ha!* Starlight!'

We walked into the café laughing and Star shouted, 'Two big mugs o' hot tea Mandy, and two 'Full-Monty's.'

We sat down while Star explained that a 'Full-Monty' consisted of bacon, eggs, sausages, mushrooms, beans and tomatoes. He explained how much he appreciated his food since driving long-distance. I told him I could tell that by the size of his belly. He grabbed my nose and shouted, 'Cheeky monkey.' He stared at me from across the table and took in a deep breath, 'Well if the good Lord is my witness! You are beautiful … I couldn't see you properly in the dark … I have never seen a woman as ….'

'Oh! Stop it Star you are embarrassing me.'

Mandy brought the food and tea and we ate heartily. I felt like I had known Star for years … I felt comfortable with him. When I had finished breakfast I went to the toilet and changed back into my jeans. I returned to the table and sat facing Star who said, 'Well! Those pants are better, but you still leave little to the imagination.'

'Oh! Stop it Star.'

'It's true … some women you could dress in old sacks and men would still see the beauty beneath.'

Star paid for breakfast and I heard Mandy say to him, 'You have yourself a beauty there Star … an angel from heaven.'

We walked outside and I shook Star's hand. I thanked him and said goodbye. I kissed him on the cheek and began to cry. I walked away from him swinging my thumb in the air in the hope of another lift. I pulled the hanky Star had given me from my pocket and wiped my eyes. I felt a hand on my shoulder … it was Star, 'Now where are you going, crying like that … your tempting the devil and someone might get hurt.'

I sniffled and looked sadly into Star's eyes, 'Yes … I know … that's what worries me.'

'Come on jump into the truck.'

We jumped into the wagon and Star pulled a curtain back which was behind the seats. He looked embarrassed, 'I don't know what we are going to do … I mean … I sleep up here now for six hours before continuing with the journey. I will sleep on the seat below and you climb up top.'

I climbed up top to find a comfortable mattress with blankets and pillows. I removed my tight pants and top then made myself comfortable. I looked down at Star and I could see he was uncomfortable ... He was twisted and squashed in his seat. I said, 'You can sleep with me up here Star! ... Please! There's lots of room ... you look uncomfortable down there.'

'No! ... I'm alright.'

'Come on Star ... I promise not to kill you.'

'Oh! ... I suppose if I sleep down here I will have a twisted neck in the morning.'

'I wouldn't want you to twist your neck Star ... There! ... That's good, let me snuggle close to you ... *Oooo!* You're all cuddly! ... You're my cuddly Star aren't you?'

'Yes!'

I snuggled up to Star ... he was like a ... a real friend ... I just wanted to hug him and be held by him. 'Star!'

'What?'

'Are you asleep?'

'No!'

'I love you!'

'And I love you ... now go to sleep.'

When I awoke I looked at the clock on the dashboard and it was four o'clock in the afternoon. The sun was shining brightly through the cab windows. I looked around and I could not see Star anywhere. I jumped from the cab and tried to grab my clothes from inside. There was a barrage of *'wolf-whistles'* as I tried to reach for my clothes. The latter was not surprising as my knickers were tiny and riding high. Star suddenly appeared with a tray of tea and some food. There was a barrage of comments coming from an audience of lorry drivers,

'*WOW!* No wonder Star works nights!'
'Is that your daughter Star?'
'You dirty old man!'
'Some guys get all the luck!'
'Hey! Have ye' won the lottery?'

'Is this a new type of bed warmer?'

I felt flattered by all the comments … I mean … a girl loves to be worshipped doesn't she? I turned around and bent down to pull on my trousers … of course my breasts were hanging on by a thread in my bra. I wriggled into my jeans like a snake and the men became silent. They all had their mouths wide open so I was flattered.

Star shouted at me, 'Emerald! … What are you doing?'

'I'm getting dressed.' I walked off towards the wash room wiggling my bottom.

There was another barrage of remarks and whistles … I loved being a lorry driver … I was happy … I mean … I had never been loved by so many men so quickly … I felt like a queen. I washed and returned to Star. I was disappointed as the other drivers had gone. Star shouted to me, 'Your tea will be cold darling.'

My heart swooned … it was the way he called me darling … it made me feel all week. Star tried to tell me off, 'You shouldn't flaunt yourself like that in front of the men … they will get the wrong idea.'

I pouted my lips and looked at the floor. He grabbed me and threw me jokingly over his shoulder. He began to laugh and spank my bum, 'I will spank your bottom for you girl.'

'Oh! I wouldn't do that if I were you.'

Soon it was dark. I loved the coloured lights in the cab and how we were sat up so high. It was as if we ruled the world. As we travelled I would ask Star questions,

'Do you think we rule the world?
Do you think we have found true happiness?
Do you think we will always be together?
Do you believe in fate?
Have you ever loved a woman as much as me?
Would you die for me?'

94

Star would answer my questions and we would discuss the universe. He would turn the radio off while telling me, 'O.K. Let's put the world to rights.'

We talked and talked and the hours seemed like minutes."

~~~

"Have you ever found that the hours pass like minutes Wordcatcher?"

I was feeling tired and moody, "Or minutes seem like hours?"

"Wordcatcher! Why do you always have to be so sarcastic? ... Sometimes I think you are being nasty to me and want to hurt me."

"Sometimes I feel the same about you Emerald."

"I have never been nasty to you Wordcatcher, not yet."

"That sounds like a threat."

"It's not a threat if you make a promise."

"So! If people don't give you what you wish ... you become a threat?"

"No! Wordcatcher! ... People are a threat if they use me ... and then they wish they hadn't."

"I haven't used you."

"Then why are you here?"

"I don't know ... Why are you here?"

"I don't know either, but it is my web and you are in it.

~~~

The sun was rising again as we pulled into another café. We ate as we talked and we were both tired. We climbed into the bed at the back of the cab and I undressed. Star took his pants and shirt off. I snuggled up to him in bed and rubbed my naked leg along his. He whispered, 'You behave yourself.' I jumped on top of him and laughed. I was lying with my legs open and I was soaking wet. I had never known a man like Star. He whispered softly words of love as he stroked my hair, 'Go to sleep now darling ... you are the flower of my heart and I will always love you and be here for you ... *Shhh!* Just go to sleep my baby.'

'Do you love me Star?'

'*Shhh!* Go to sleep ... I love you more than any one in the world.'

'Will you always stay with me Star?'

'Yes! Forever.'

~~~

Star was twice my age, but love may bridge the gaps of time. Do you believe that age doesn't matter Wordcatcher."

"Not if you love someone ... but ... but ...."

"Don't but ... but ... ask your question."

"But you know my question."

"Yes! And the answer is NO! He did not make love to me. I lay on top of him soaking wet and he would touch me with his fingers while talking to me and stroking my hair. I knew he loved me but I could not understand what was wrong. I would ask him if he had a problem, but he always avoided the answer. He would ask me if love was not enough ... he used to tell me, 'You have all my love and that is the most precious thing in the world' ... I would go all weak at the knees and kiss him. I thought he must have had an accident or something which he found embarrassing to talk about. Anyway, we managed because love conquers all ... Doesn't it Wordcatcher?"

"Yes."

~~~

"Star had the most marvellous hands ... he would touch me, and take me to heaven.

I suppose I knew deep down that something was wrong .... *'I told you that.'* Shut up Lotus.

I awoke one day in the cab and it was pouring with rain ... I had a strange feeling that something was wrong. I lay awake listening to rain drops beating on the metal roof of the cab. I looked around and Star was gone, which was not unusual as he would often return from the café with tea and a sandwich for me. I wanted to go to the toilet, so I dressed and ran to the ladies room inside the café. I looked around but could not see Star. I thought he must have returned to the lorry. I rushed through the rain, back to the cab. Star was nowhere to be seen. I sat in the cab and turned on the radio; country music was playing. As I looked into the rear-view mirror I noticed Star, he was stepping down from his friends cab. I had seen him laughing with this man before and thought nothing unusual about their meeting, as Star had lots of friends - being a lorry driver. I was irritable as I was waiting to go for some tea. The two of them were standing, talking in the rain. I was just about to shout to them when ... it ... happened. I could not believe what I was seeing. The two men were holding each other and hugging. They were holding each other like passionate lovers. I had to open the window, put my head out and look back ... as they parted, Star kissed the man ... my mind was screaming NO! My thoughts flitted about like someone drowning, grasping at floating leaves. I thought, NO! It's not Star ... but when he began to run towards me I knew it was.

Suddenly I understood everything. No wonder he did not make love with me ... he was Gay. I could not understand why he had not told me the truth. I felt deceived ... he was making love to another person ... I mean we were an item ... it was me and him in love forever.

When Star returned to the truck, he jumped in as if nothing had happened. I was shivering from the shock of what I had seen. He asked me if I was alright and I told him I did not feel well. He asked me if I wanted him to hug me, and I nodded my head. While he held me tightly in his loving arms Lotus killed him.

It happened in an instant. I remember his last words as the screw driver was stuck through his heart, 'Your ... Your eyes have turned black.' Lotus kissed his lips and it was all over. She wiped the handle of the screw driver and climbed down from the cab. It was as if I was sucked back into my body. I screamed angrily at Lotus, 'How can you leave me like this? What am I supposed to do now?'

Lotus answered me ... she usually did, '*Oh! Stop being a baby and pull yourself together. I do all your dirty work and all you can do is moan. Do you want me to go and never come back?*'

'No!' I said.

'*Exactly! ... You would still be getting your bottom spanked by daddy if I had not grown from your mistakes to help you. We all need friends and friends look after each other, and always remember, 'You find out who your friends are when you are in trouble.' Well! You are in trouble now and I am with you. Just carry on ... it's no good giving-in is it?*'

'No Lotus.'

'*Do you want to lie down in the bushes and die?*'

'No Lotus.'

'*Well start moving ... and stop crying ... you are always crying.*'

I began to walk down the road. It was pouring with rain and the only possessions I owned were the wet clothes I was wearing.

I walked into a phone box and called the emergency services, which was a free call. I asked for the police and explained that I had been given a lift by a lorry driver, and that we had parked outside a café where I had gone to the ladies. I continued to explain that when I returned from the toilet, I had seen him struggling with another man in his cab. I gave a description of the man as I had seen him dismount from the cab and return to his lorry which was parked behind. I said to the policeman on the other end of the telephone that the incident worried me so I thought I had better report what I had seen. I also added that I had noted the registration number of the vehicle which the man returned to after the struggle. I was asked if I could supply my name, to which I replied, 'Yes! My name is Lotus … Goodbye.'

RUBY

I had not been walking for long before a car pulled in alongside me. The driver wound down the car window and said, 'Hello ... Are you alright? ... Do you need a lift?' She was an attractive lady with short red hair. The car was a white Mercedes.

I shouted, 'Thank you,' and jumped into the front passenger seat. I was dripping wet and shivering from the cold.

The lady looked at me with concern and said, 'Are you alright? Have you been in an accident? Why are you walking in the pouring rain?' I began to cry and the woman put her arms around me, 'Oh! You poor thing ... I will take you to the police station.'

'No! Please,' I said, 'I am fine ... I have just had an argument with my boyfriend.'

'Well! The cad! ... If you ask me, you are better off without him. I hope he rots in hell!'

'Yes ... I am sure he will!'

'Now! Where are you going?'

'Oh! Look at the car seat its soaking wet.'

'Don't worry about that ... people are more important than cars. I only live a few miles away ... do you want to come with me and change your clothes?'

'Oh! I don't like to bother people.'

'Well we can't leave you here can we?'

'No.'

'The lady who was very kindly helping me was about 28 years of age. She wore deep red lipstick, and her full red lips complimented the colour of her hair. She turned towards me and I apologised, 'I'm sorry … I was admiring your hair … you have lovely hair.'

'Thank you,' she said, 'My name is Ruby, what's your name?'

'Lotus … I mean Emerald.'

'Ha! You have two names?'

'Well! ….. It depends what mood I am in.'

The car stopped outside a lovely, big house which a drive the size of a car-park. Ruby jumped out of the car and shouted to me, 'Come on Emerald, let's find you some dry clothes.'

When we entered the house a butler opened the door and greeted Ruby who seemed excited. She ran upstairs and shouted for me to follow her. Once upstairs, we walked into a massive bedroom. Ruby threw her coat onto her bed and pointed to the shower room, 'You have a hot shower through there, and then we will find you some clothes … you look about my size.'

The shower was bigger than any I had ever seen; it was like a room in itself. I threw my clothes onto the tiled floor and turned on the hot water. It was wonderful; hot water gushed over me from power jets. I laughed as jets of water tickled me. Ruby shouted, 'Are you alright in there?'

'Yes thank you … It's brilliant.'

~~~

Shelves were filled with different soaps and perfumes. I shampooed my hair and … and guess what Wordcatcher?"

"What?"

"Go on guess."

"You thought you had found eternal happiness."

"You are a real bastard sometimes Wordcatcher."

"I'm sorry … I don't know what to guess."

"Well! I found a bottle of perfume that was called *'Emerald'* isn't that amazing Wordcatcher?"

"Yes ... It really is."

"Are you being condescending?"

"No darling."

"Oh! I love you when you call me darling."

~~~

I stepped from the shower room wearing a towel-robe. Ruby seemed all excited, 'Come and sit in the chair Emerald and I will dry your hair.' Ruby brushed my hair whilst holding a hair-dryer in her other hand, 'Oh! You have beautiful hair ... it is so dark, deep, black ... and Oh! ... Look at your eye's.' Ruby lifted my chin up with her hand. She leaned forward staring at my eyes. 'Are those eyes real? ... Darling, you have eyes to die for.'

'Yes ... I know.'

~~~

I was enjoying the attention from Ruby, and I felt like I had fallen into the lap of the gods. Ruby opened another door and ... and guess what was in there Wordcatcher?"

"Not again ... can't you just tell the story?"

"You are a misery at times ... aren't you?"

"I'm sorry."

~~~

Well the other room was a walk-in wardrobe ... well it was a room that was a wardrobe. It had one whole wall that was one whole mirror. There was a table in the middle of the room and I asked Ruby what it was. She shouted while she was opening sliding wardrobe doors, 'It's a massage table ... have you never had a massage?'

'No!'

'Jump on then ... you will like it.'

I climbed onto the table and lay on my back.

'No! *Ha Har* ... Take your gown off.'

I jumped down from the table and removed my gown, 'You have a remarkable body Emerald. Your skin is so pale and you figure is amazing ... you have a body to kill for ... you must have been told that before?'

'Yes ... many times.'

'Jump onto the table then! Let's see *Mmmm!* I think this will do ... a blend of the essential oils of Jasmin and Bergamot.'

Ruby turned on some soft music, then tipped some of the oil (which she had blended with some almond oil) onto her palm. She massaged my feet first and it was amazing. I would never have believed so much time could be taken to massage someone's feet. It sent shivers down my spine and all through my body. When she eventually finished my feet it felt like my whole body had been massaged. And then Ruby massaged my whole body. Her fingers and hands were so strong. I felt like I was sinking and sinking into bliss. I turned over and she massaged my back. In the end I felt like ... I had no feeling in my body ... I just felt like a feather floating. Ruby's hand slid onto my bottom and that's when it happened ...."

~~~

"What ... What happened?"

"I'm not telling you Wordcatcher ... see how you like it?"

"Stop being silly and tell me."

"Well say you are sorry for upsetting me before."

103

"Sorry."

"NO! Give me a kiss on the cheek and say, 'Sorry Darling.'"

I kissed Emerald on the cheek and said, "Sorry Darling."

"Oh good I forgive you ... now kiss me ...."

"You said you would tell me."

"Tell you what? ..... Oh! ... Ruby!

~~~

Ruby began to massage my bottom and I had my eyes closed as I listened to the music; I was enjoying the most heavenly experience I could ever have dreamed of. As she pushed and squeezed my bottom my eyes opened and I found myself staring into my reflection in the mirror. That was when I saw my eyes had turned black. I jumped with fright as the whole of my body became tense. Ruby asked me, 'What is wrong honey ... have I hurt you?' I did not reply and Ruby continued, 'It's something to do with your bottom isn't it? I can see very faint lines. You don't have to talk about it if you don't want to honey.'

I felt comfortable with Ruby and I trusted her, so I told her the truth. 'It's where my father beat me when I was a child ... and he would rub cream on after ... I suppose it brought back memories.'

'Well I am here for you if you need me honey.'

'And I will always be there for you Ruby.'

'I have finished now honey, so jump down and let's find you some clothes ... Oh! You are crying ... come here and let me hug you ... there now ... that's good ... you don't have to worry, I love you and will not let anyone hurt you anymore.'

'Do you really Ruby?'

'What?'

'Do you really love me?'

'Yes of course I do.'

I must have been trying on clothes for hours. Ruby had endless amounts of clothes, and shoes, and ... and everything. It would have been easier to tell you what she didn't have ... but that would not be easy because she had everything. It reminded me of the time when I was young and had the party at home with my friends ...

~~~

Remember Wordcatcher?' ... just before my father died.

~~~

I was wearing a skin tight black P.V.C. mini dress while Ruby wore a deep red one. The dresses were so tight Ruby said it was best not to wear underwear. Ruby had shaken sweet smelling powder over our bodies before we put the skirts on. She told me we would not slide into them without the powder as the dresses would stick to our skins. It felt like a plastic skin. I felt naked and sexy. Ruby played pop music and we danced ... or tried to ... as our dresses seemed to have a life of there own. We stood sweating while we looked at ourselves in the mirror. We looked a pair ... a pair of what? I will never know. I had this black dress on and my skin was white while my hair was black. Ruby's body was tanned and brown and her red lips matched her dress and hair. We laughed uncontrollably and promised each other we would go to a nightclub together in the same dresses. Ruby said, 'we will leave a trail of dead men behind us', and I asked her how she knew. She hesitated a moment and we both burst into laughter. Eventually we attempted to remove the dresses. They were stuck to our bodies like a second skin. We had to help each other peel them off. Ruby suggested we take a quick shower as we were sticky with sweat. When we were in the shower, Ruby showed me some exciting tricks to play with the water jets. We fell to the floor laughing; I have never laughed so much in my life.

At about 6 p.m. a gong sounded and Ruby told me it was dinner time. We slipped into some jeans and t-shirts. I asked Ruby if she had some bras. She laughed and shouted, 'What for ... we're liberated.'

We walked into a large dining room with a long table. A butler was standing by the door and as we walked in he accompanied us to our seats. I was nervous because I had never had 'much to do' with etiquette. I felt as if I was attending some banquet and was improperly dressed ... I mean; as I walked across the room my breasts were bouncing so much I had to hold the bottom of my t-shirt which only made matters worse because then I felt my nipples were going to burst out. The butler moved the chair from the table for me and I sat down. There were four other people sitting at the table. A big man, who was sitting in a wheelchair at the head of the table, spoke to Ruby, 'I wish you would dress more appropriately for dinner Ruby ... you think your whole life is a fashion show ... now introduce your guest.'

'I wish you would not be such a worrier daddy ... This is my friend Emerald, and you have to guess why she is called Emerald. Emerald! ... This is daddy, and sitting next to him is mummy, next to mummy is Melissa my sister, and sitting next to you is Thomas my brother.'

Everyone shook my hand and I was particularly flattered by Thomas who could not take his eyes off my breasts. Thomas was about 17 years of age and covered in acne; I presumed his hormones would be 'playing him up'. Melissa was about 13 years of age and had blonde hair. She was pretty and sat smiling at me while swinging her legs under the table. Ruby's mother was tall and slender, she looked tired and had a lot of 'wear and tear' which was evident by the lines on her face. She had long dark hair and looked as if she was about to break down crying at any moment. Maids appeared and placed large dishes of food onto the table. I decided to sit and watch everyone else and to copy them. Soup was served and I waited and watched as Melissa chose one particular spoon from the collection of cutlery which surrounded each of our dishes. Ruby's daddy shouted to me across the table, 'And where do you live Emerald? Are you local?'

Ruby interrupted, 'Emerald is between addresses at the moment ... she has had a traumatic experience happen in her life and she is staying with me while she recovers.'

Ruby's father shouted again while peeping out of the corner of his eye at his wife, 'Ah! Bet it's to do with love! ... Take it from me ... if every man counted the ups and downs of love, then every man would be down in hell ... *Ha Ha Har!* ... Do you agree Emerald?'

'Yes sir! ... Most of the men I have known are in hell.'

Peels of laughter echoed across the room from Ruby's father, '*Ha Har Ha Har Ha Har* ... I am going to like you *Har Har Ha Har* ...Did you hear that mother? ... A woman who finally admits she enjoys torturing men.'

Ruby's mother glared at her husband and replied, 'Well at least she seems to know how to treat them.'

Once more father burst into laughter, '*Har Ha Har Ha Har*. I will have to be quiet or I will never eat my soup *Ha Har*.'

Melissa shouted out, 'I know why you are called Emerald!'

There was an immediate silence from the table before Melissa continued, 'It is because you have green eyes ... Am I right?'

Ruby answered Melissa, 'Yes sugar ... you are right.'

We finished our soup and the maids exchanged our dishes for plates. The family began helping themselves to food from several large dishes. I took some food and paused. I had several sets of knives and forks and was waiting for guidance from my peers. Melissa picked up a large knife and a peculiar shaped fork ... 'Ah!' I thought, and followed suit. Melissa instantly dropped her cutlery back onto the table and shouted out, 'LOOK! Emerald has the fish knife to eat beef.'

Everyone looked at me and there was silence. Suddenly everyone in the room burst into laughter. Even the butler was laughing. Ruby's father shouted out, '*Ha Har Ha Har Ha Har*, I don't know who you are or where you are from but *Ha Har Ha Har Ha* you're a killer.'

~~~

Wordcatcher! Wordcatcher! Are you asleep ... wake up ... have you been listening to me?"

"Yes..s."

"Then what have I just said?"

"You said, 'Have I been list......"

"NO! .... Before that?"

"You were telling the story of how you were sat at the table with Ruby's family and how Thomas was touching your knee with his leg."

"How did you know that? I never told you that!"

"That's what I do."

"So can you see into my mind ... as I can yours?"

"Only one page at a time."

"I felt like I had lived with Ruby forever ... I felt part of their family ... isn't that good Wordcatcher?"

"I hope so."

"Why are you always so pessimistic ... it's as if you want me to be sad. Is that it? ... Do you want me to suffer?"

"No! I love you."

"Ha! I don't think you know what love means."

"I know it can hurt so you have to be careful with it."

"I give love Wordcatcher, and people take it and then hurt me with it."

"Maybe you should be more careful who you love."

"Oh! So now you're the expert ... are you?"

"No! I am simply one who wonders at the riddles of life."

"There is no riddle to love ... it is as simple as black or white. Love is there, or it is not ... nothing more and nothing less."

"What about all the shades in between?"

"What do you mean Wordcatcher?"

"There are different kinds of love and different depths of love ... I loved my motorbike but when it had to be sold I wasn't heartbroken."

"I understand what you mean. I loved Starlight and the lorry. When Starlight died I still loved the lorry and that's what hurt, but I wasn't heartbroken ... I suppose I can always find another lorry."

"And I suppose there is always another love, like a flower waiting ... somewhere."

"Yes Wordcatcher and if someone hurts me with it they will pay for it."

"Emerald ... Starlight may have loved you as a friend ... you may have been the best friend he ever had."

"Then why did he hurt me?"

"He was gay ... he couldn't help being gay and maybe he loved you, and cared for you."

"He did ... but he betrayed me."

~~~

After dinner Ruby and I returned to her bedroom. Ruby told me to choose a coat from her collection as we were going out to visit one of her friends.

While I was waiting for Ruby to come out of the bathroom I sat watching the T.V. that was in her bedroom. The news was on and I had the shock of my life; a picture of Starlight filled the screen. I began to look for the remote control so I could turn off the T.V. ... I expected the newsreader to shout out my name. I scuffled about in a panic searching for the remote as the bathroom door opened and Ruby walked towards me, 'What are you looking for honey?'

As I replied, 'The T.V. remote', I could hear the newsreader speaking, *'The body of a man was found dead at the steering wheel of an articulated vehicle earlier today. A man is being questioned by police in relation to the man's death, and is to be charged with murder. Police are asking for the woman to come forward who ....'*

Ruby found the remote and turned off the T.V. 'Come on let's go honey.'

As we travelled in the car, Ruby told me her friend's name was Eugene and that he was her best friend. I asked, 'Oh! Is he your boyfriend?'

Ruby laughed, 'I don't think so honey ... Eugene is Gay.'

We drove towards another big house and stopped the car outside where several expensive looking cars were parked. As we jumped from the car I shouted, 'It looks as if Eugene has a lot of visitors.'

Ruby shouted back to me, 'I doubt it honey ... all the cars are his.'

Ruby rang the door bell, and a butler opened the door, 'Good evening madam.'

We walked into the house and Ruby threw her coat onto a settee. A tall thin young man walked into the room. He had blonde hair which was short and wild. He was wearing a pink cardigan and white trousers; he was about 27 years of age. He said, 'Hello darling …*Mmmm* hugs and kisses and … *Ooooo!* Who is this angel? … *Ooooo!* Look at your eyes … they are the most beautiful enchanting eyes I have ever seen … come here darling *Oooo!* Hugs and kisses … I love you darling! … I absolutely adore you! … Look at that bottom … so round and firm … I bet you have broken a few men's hearts my dear.'

Ruby shouted jokingly at Eugene, 'Her name is Emerald and she is mine so leave her alone.'

I felt flattered that I was receiving so much attention, and confused by the way they were talking about me; as if I was not in the room; like an item you would own. Eugene asked a maid to open a bottle of wine, 'You will love this wine my darlings and ….'

We were interrupted as a tall woman walked into the room to join us. She was slim and had long blonde hair. She wore a mini-skirt which was golden coloured and had a matching top. Her midriff was bare and she had a diamond stud in her navel. She was about 30 years of age. The attractive lady walked over to Ruby and kissed her on the lips, 'Hello darling, how are you and who is your beautiful friend?'

Eugene interrupted excitedly, 'Look at her eyes … she has the most amazing eyes.'

Ruby shouted out, 'Will you stop … Emerald, this is Clair.'

Clair walked over and kissed me on the lips, 'Hello darling *Mmmm!* … come and sit next to me and tell me all about how you two met.'

I was led to a settee by Clair and we both sat together. She linked her arm through mine and snuggled close, bringing her feet up onto the cushion next to her. Ruby kicked off her shoes and sat with Eugene. They snuggled close and both lifted their feet onto the settee. I thought I might as well join in and kicked off my shoes and lifted my feet and legs onto the cushion next to me. We were served wine and I sat nervously waiting as if I was about to be interrogated. Ruby was there to save me, 'Now! I don't want you two asking Emerald too many questions. She has just been through a bad relationship and is recovering.'

Clair asked, 'What was her name darling? Do I know her?'

Ruby interrupted, '*HIM!* ... Darling it was a 'him' not a her.'

Clair lifted her hand to her mouth, 'Oh! I am sorry ... I assumed you two were ....'

Eugene interrupted, 'Yes Clair? ... Put a sock in it ... there's no need to give her a shovel she will dig a hole anywhere.'

I was beginning to realise that my present company was gay. I did not mind ... I was pleased to be among friends. The three of them talked about people they knew, and while they talked I snuggled close to Clair and drank wine. I was confused ... I was thinking about how Eugene had told me he loved me. Questions floated through my mind. How could he love me so quickly? He reminded me of Starlight; the way he loved me as a friend. Is this the way gay men talked of love to women who were close friends? And the worst question of all ... I tried to avoid but could not ... Had I killed a man who loved me and had cared for me by mistake?

I began to cry and Clair hugged me in her arms, 'Oh! Now don't cry darling you are safe with us ... just forget that brute now, he's gone.'

Clair wiped my eyes with her handkerchief ... I remembered Star when he wiped my nose and smeared it with oil. I began to cry more. I mumbled through tears, 'It's alright ... it's just the wine and everything ... I'm sorry.'

Of course I was lying; some voice in my mind was screaming out, 'You have killed someone who loved you.'

Several hours flew by as did several glasses of wine. My head was resting on Clair's shoulder and I was almost asleep. I heard Ruby saying it was time to go home, and Clair replying that her butler would drive us home as we had been drinking. As we were hugging and saying our farewells Clair asked us, 'Did you hear about the killing of Star?' - That resulted in my almost fainting.

Ruby replied, '*Star ... Star ...*' She stared at the ceiling and frowned as if searching her memory for an answer to a riddle, 'Ah! *Starlight* ... one of daddy's drivers! Yes! I remember now ... a nice guy ... he had an accident that damaged his spine and it took him several years to return to walking ... but ... his wife left him because he ....'

Clair interrupted Ruby, 'Yes! ...Yes! ... There is no need to cover every detail darling. Well! He was murdered this morning ... stabbed by his own brother through the heart.'

Beach Boys

I was dreaming of swimming and twirling in a tropical blue sea. Everything was perfect. I glanced towards the shore where my handsome lover was sitting at a table. A waiter was serving a large jug of red wine. He waved to me and pointed at the jug which was now standing on the table with two glasses. I waved and began to swim towards him. I was swimming and yet I was moving backwards. I thought to myself, 'The tide is going out and taking me with it.' I began to panic. I stopped and waved to my lover and began screaming, '*HELP! HELP!*' But my lover calmly waved back to me as he drank the red wine from his glass. I looked to my left and there was something black in the water moving towards me. I began swimming with all my

113

strength. I glanced over my shoulder and the black object was closing in on me. I swam and screamed and cried ... the black thing was a shark and it was almost upon me. I looked at my lover and he was calmly waving as he drank from his glass and pointed to mine ... it was as if he was saying, 'your wine is here getting warm ... stop playing games and come back.' Suddenly ... I knew I would never be with him as the shark was about to bite me and drag me forever down and ....

I awoke to be smothered in silky blue sheets. The room was light and the curtains were open. '*Emerald!* ... *Emerald!* Wake up honey ... you are alright ... it's only a dream.' Ruby was holding me in her arms as I cried. She comforted me and stroked my back as she hugged me, 'Don't worry honey I am here and you are safe.'

'Thank you Ruby ... I ... I am alright now it was just a nasty dream.'

'Do you want to talk about it honey.'

'Oh it was silly ... there was ... there was a big black shark chasing me through the water and I couldn't get away from it.'

'Ah! That will be your nasty ex-boyfriend. Well have no fear of him now ... he will never bother you again.'

'Yes ... I know!'

'You have a rest honey and I will bring some tea.'

'Ruby put her gown on and left the room. While I was waiting for Ruby to return I recalled the previous evening's events. Starlight had hugged and kissed his brother, and of course that was a normal thing to do. My stomach ached from sunken remorse, too deep to ever heal, deep sadness as can only be buried to hide, while the foul aroma of death's last mistake will forever ferment. I composed myself ... I had to ... I had no choice. I looked through Ruby's CDs and put some lively music onto the player. I danced and sang loudly as I laughed, whilst at the same time, swallowing sin. Ruby came into the bedroom carrying a tray and shouted over the loud music, 'Somebody has made a quick recovery.'

> *Some boys take a beautiful girl*
> *And hide her away from the rest of the world*
> *I want to be the one to walk in the sun*
> *Oh girls they want to have fun*
> *Oh girls just want to have*
> *Fun.*

By Cyni Lauper

~~~

I danced and swung my hips for it was a new day ... the first day of the rest of my life ... I mean! You never know when you wake in the morning, if the day you are beginning will be your last ... do you Wordcatcher?"

"No ... that is true."

"Oh! Don't look so sad Wordcatcher ... mistakes are made and people die ... I suppose it's a part of life."

"And death."

"Oh! Now you are sad and sulky my love."

"You didn't have to kill him!"

Emerald put her face close to mine and her eyes began to turn dark ... she spoke in a deep growling voice, ***"She didn't, so leave her alone."***

~~~

"Ruby opened the curtains and began to dance with me."

> *Oh girls they want to have fun*
> *Oh girls just want to have*
> *Fun*

"I was wearing pink pyjamas which Ruby must have dressed me in the previous evening and she was wearing red pyjamas. Soon we were sweating and our tops and pants dropped off as if to submit to our youthful frenzy. We danced in our knickers while our breasts bounced freely; liberated as if with minds of their own. Something suddenly caught our attention. At the window, a man was staring in, wide-eyed and open-mouthed, as if he had seen a ghost and been instantly frozen ... or maybe the window cleaner was wishing what he saw would last forever.

~~~

We were naughty Wordcatcher. We taunted him ... I wiggled my bottom at him while Ruby bounced her breasts in his face. We had to close the curtains in the end as we were worried the poor man may fall and have an accident.

~~~

We showered and slipped into silk gowns before going downstairs for some tea. We were both naked beneath our gowns, but I didn't care; every moment I shared with Ruby was unpredictable and exciting. We sat down in a large conservatory and, upon summoning a maid, Ruby asked for some tea and toast. Morning papers were resting on a glass table and my heart jumped into my mouth as I caught site of a picture of Star on the front page. Ruby had her back to me and was talking to two love birds that were in a cage. I picked the papers up and placed them under the table. I felt as if I was trying to hide; a bitter ocean of guilt by tipping a glass of salt water down a grid.

~~~

It is a terrible thing to experience Wordcatcher!"

"What ... What is?"

"Having to try and hide a murder that your friend has committed. I mean! If you are a true friend you have to stand by them whatever ... Don't you?"

"Yes ..."

~~~

"The maid soon arrived with tea and toast which we ate with marmalade; we were hungry so we ate quickly while looking into each others eyes. It was an unusual experience; surreal ... I don't know what one would call it ... but as we stared into each others eyes, there was a kind of understanding between us ... like when you're a child and you are waiting for something really important to happen and you look into a friend's eyes and there is this complete 'oneness' you both bond as if one.

We finished eating, and another first experience literally hit me in the face. I could feel some marmalade on my chin so I was about to wipe it away with a tissue when Ruby took hold of my arm. She leaned over and licked the marmalade from my face. I was shocked and yet it seemed so natural; like dusting some fluff of your friends shoulder. As I sipped my tea I felt confused. I sat looking into Ruby's eyes and I had a marvellous feeling of 'living in the moment'. I had no predictions. I did not know where I was going; where I would be tomorrow; what was happening. I didn't even know what clothes I would be wearing that day. I could not predict anything anymore ... it felt like my dream, when I was floating and playing in the sea happily. I simply stared into Ruby's eyes and waited for whatever would be.

We walked back to Ruby's bedroom and she slipped her silk robe from her body. The robe floated from her like a second skin. I did the same, then we both lay on the bed naked while Ruby held my hand. She asked, 'What would you like to do honey?'

I replied, 'Nothing ... which would seem like everything at the moment.'

Ruby jumped to her feet and opened the curtains again. I covered my eyes as sunshine filled the room searching for hidden shadows, 'Your wish is my command ... Come on then! We will go down to the beach and laze in the sun.'

Ruby threw me a tiny bikini and asked me if I liked the colour. It was black; I replied, 'The colour doesn't matter does it? ... There is not enough material here to see it.'

Ruby shouted back laughing, 'Slip them on and wear this towel gown over the top.'

Ruby shouted to the maid downstairs, 'Janice ... would you pack a cool bag for us we are going to the beach.'

We left the house and Ruby placed the cool-box into the boot of the car, and I threw a cloth beach bag in full of towels. I was surprised to see the Mercedes had been returned to the house. Ruby told me, 'Daddy has lots of drivers and cars.'

Within minutes we were at the beach. I felt nervous as I had a feeling of what was going to happen next. We stepped from the car and Ruby handed me some sun-glasses. It was a burning hot day and people of different ages, shapes and sizes were walking about slowly, enjoying the sunshine. We walked around to the boot of the car and Ruby removed the cool-box. She then dropped the bag of beach towels at my feet and took off the towel gown she was wearing and threw it over her arm. She then took the cool-box in one hand and looked at me while shouting as if to wake me up, 'Come on then honey let's go!'

I began to follow her but the inevitable happened, 'Emerald ... don't be silly ... take off the robe honey.'

I think my white face must have turned bright red. I looked at Ruby and she was beautiful. People were turning their heads to look at her. Women frowned at their partners lustful glances, as they tried to steal a dream, trapped within one moment, shadowed from the equation of reality. Ruby placed her hand on her hip and looked over her sunglasses at me. We both burst into laughter and I threw my robe into the car boot and slammed it shut. Ruby shouted to me, 'That's my girl!'

We linked arms and walked across the beach while wiggling our bottoms which were thonged by a thread of hope which we no longer cared about. We spread towels onto the beach and I told Ruby that I was worried about getting sun-burnt. Ruby shouted, '*Ha! Har!*' as she produced a bottle of sun-oil. She rubbed the oil over my skin and as she covered my breasts her fingers slipped over my nipples. I was shocked and surprised, 'Oh! Don't Ruby.'

She smiled and looked into my eyes, 'Sorry honey! Well I'm not really.'

Ruby handed me the oil and I began at her heels before working my way up her legs. Her bottom was firm yet smooth like a peach. I could hear her groaning and she was making slight movements as if trying to push my fingers deeper. The feelings I had were confusing. I felt aroused and yet ... I was touching a woman. It was as if there was some written law declaring, '**NO!** You do not become sexually aroused with another woman.' I felt we had a special closeness, a bond which was in some way growing ... in some way which I could not understand. Ruby turned onto her back and I smeared oil over her legs and body. My heart began to beat hard in my chest ... I didn't know why ... I was shaking as I began to rub oil between the top of Ruby's legs. My fingers were slippery ... I remember hoping that the oil bottle would be empty ...

but of course it was not. I reached the 'final spot' which I had avoided and left until the end. I had a little oil left which I spread onto my hands. I frowned ... I knew I could have been in this position with an empty bottle. I could imagine myself saying, 'Oh! Dear ... sorry darling the bottle is empty.' The bottle was not empty and my fingers automatically slid between Ruby's legs. She jumped and groaned as her legs opened slightly. My fingers slid as if they had a mind of their own ... she seemed shocked and her mouth opened as she breathed in deeply. I remember thinking, 'Why does she seem so surprised'. She groaned as she whispered, 'You bitch.'

I moved my face close to hers and whispered, 'Yes ... But do you love me?'

I pushed my fingers deeper and she twisted as if in pain. She groaned, '*Yess! ... Yess!*'

I asked, 'Will you always be mine?'

She arched her back as her head dropped back ... it was as if electric was shooting through her body, '*Yess! ... Yess!*'

We were suddenly interrupted by two guys; their shadows invaded our space. We looked up startled as the two lads stood over us. They looked fit and had muscles built upon muscles. One of the guys shouted, 'Hi Girls! ... We have some sun-oil here ... we can do that for you if you want?'

I looked into Ruby's eyes and we both smiled. We lay on our stomachs and Ruby shouted, 'Well I hope you have two bottles because ours is empty ... and we are so hot boys ... you wouldn't believe how hot we are.'

The two boys started to panic as they had only one bottle of sun-oil. Ruby threw them our empty bottle and shouted, 'Here! Stop arguing ... you have two bottles now.'

The two boys began rubbing the oil onto our backs as we groaned with pleasure ... but our pleasure was from the torment we were putting the boys through. I was experiencing feelings and emotions I never knew existed, and there was this kind of … telepathic communication between Ruby and me. It is difficult to explain but … as we stared into each others eyes, as the boys hands slid over our bottoms with fingers trembling from excitement, we were both sexually aroused through the boys, and yet it was between us. We were using them, and that was even more erotic. We had control and power; we had an understanding of lust which made the two fumbling boys attempts to arouse us seem nothing more than a joke. I giggled and said to Ruby, 'I think the boys are about to burst.'

Ruby replied, 'But all good things must come to an end.' .

One of the hulks asked, 'Where do you girls hang out … I mean … what clubs do you go to?'

Ruby's face was inches from mine. She answered the boys' question, 'Mermaids.' Then she kissed me on the lips.

Their hands moved away as if they had been stung. The two boys walked away and when at a safe distance, one shouted back, 'Pair o' lesbians.'

We both laughed … we had no cares … we were in love."

~~~

"Do you like my story Wordcatcher? Wordcatcher! Where are you?"

I awoke to write. Right or wrong, I know no judge, some simple scribe to scribble secrets lest be lost to all, tell tales. Loves lust be cussed to cost as souls are weighed while the sea-saw pivot sways, be left, now right, as we all go *UP* or *DOWN* for the pendulum ever sways with hearts from dreams to swoon … 'tis but the fool's own wheel.

The Wheel of Fortune.

Falling down and down through a tunnel of green and then to come face to face with

Emerald

"Wordcatcher! Where have you been? Hold me close … look into my eyes. Kiss me my love … your lips are wet … do you love me?"

"Yes for I am mortal and no man could resist you."

"Nor woman Wordcatcher … Nor woman."

Emerald pushed her tongue into my mouth and kissed me as I had never been kissed before. She breathed deeply and I could feel myself being sucked into her. I became unconscious. There was nothing! This was a place I had never been before as there was always something, even if it was darkness.

"Wake up! Wake up! Wordcatcher!"

My eyes opened as I sank into pools of sunken green. And a sweet voice whispered sighs from angelic harps, "What are you mumbling about my darling?"

"Emerald!"

"Yes … my love."

"I think I … I love you."

"But of course you do! You are so complicated at times … aren't you darling?

~~~

We returned to Ruby's home and showered. We washed each others bodies and shared love … yes there was lust … sexual excitement … but there was a deep understanding between us. In the shower I thought I was going to die from pleasure. My head was pounding as if it was going to explode. Ruby covered me in oils and introduced me to ways of loving I never would have believed existed. I was lost in ecstasy … it was like the whole universe had stopped, or was continuing without us. When Ruby had finished with me I felt exhausted. Then she turned to me and said, 'Now my love you know the secrets only a woman can know.'

I stared dreamily into her eyes and whispered '*Yess.*'

She whispered, 'Now you must share them with me.'

I began to kiss Ruby while searching every inch of her body with my tongue, I then continued with all I had been shown. Ruby wriggled and cried and screamed … we were interrupted by someone banging on the bedroom door which fortunately had been locked. We ran like naughty girls from the bathroom giggling and laughing. Ruby's mother shouted, 'Are you alright Ruby?'

Ruby always had an answer, 'Yes mummy! I am just coming.'

We both burst into laughter whilst holding our hands over each others mouths to keep her mother from hearing. Her mother shouted, 'Well come quickly … dinner is ready … and is your friend coming?'

Ruby could not reply as we were both on our knees choking with laughter. Tears were running down our faces.

'Ruby can you hear me … come immediately and if your friend is there she must come as well.'

Fortunately her mother disappeared and we were able to come together.

When we eventually arrived at the dinner table the mood was dire as we were late. Ruby's mother glared at us both and we dug our nails into each others legs in an attempt to stop any desire of bursting into laughter. 'You two must learn to come on time and at the same time … I will not be kept waiting at the table.'

We both coughed and suppressed our emotions. Ruby replied to her mother, 'We are sorry mummy and we will come together next time.'

Ruby's father boomed a question across the table at me, 'And what have you been doing today 'Green Eyes?'"

His wife interrupted, 'Do not be so familiar. I apologize for my husband's manners Emerald.'

'I don't mind ... I have been called a lot worse.'

Her husband burst into laughter, 'See I know her better than you mother.'

His wife looked at me, 'I will thank you not to encourage him Emerald.'

'I am sorry ... We went down to the beach today.'

Ruby's father replied, 'Bah! It's fine for some ... I've been stuck in a hot office all day.'

As we ate our dinner I asked Ruby's father, 'Where do you work sir.'

'Bah! Don't call me sir ... I have enough of that at work all day. Call me dad. I run a haulage company ... probably the biggest in the country. Where do you work my dear ... Ah! But you're too beautiful to work. I always believe a beautiful woman should be kept in luxury. How old are you?'

'I am 21 ... dad.'

Ruby's mother interrupted, 'It is bad manners to ask a lady her age.'

Dad glared at his wife, 'Oh! Stop moaning, we're only talking.'

Desert was served. I shouted out, 'Oh! I love strawberries.'

Everyone laughed. It was then I felt something on my leg. At first I thought it was the edge of the table cloth. I was wearing a short skirt and I realised to my shock that a hand was on my left leg. I glanced towards Thomas and my assumption was confirmed. Thomas was eating his strawberries while holding his spoon in his left hand; his right hand was beneath the table fumbling and trembling. Thomas was only 17 years of age and covered in pimples. I was not concerned about his promiscuous youthful feelings of lust, but I was worried about my bubble being popped. I was so happy it was painful, and I did not want anything to interfere with that happiness. I could feel his hand moving up my leg and I did not know what to do for the best. If I caused an embarrassing situation I might be asked to leave. His hand was moving slowly towards my groin and his fingers felt sticky and sweaty. I felt like shouting to Ruby 'Thomas has his hands up my skirt' and then things got worse. I heard a voice in my head ... a deep growling voice *'What the fuck is he doing?'* I immediately told Lotus in my mind, 'He is only a young lad touching my leg so don't make a fuss.' I squeezed my legs tightly at the top so as to keep his hand from moving any further. Lotus growled, *'If he doesn't stop I will tear his throat out.'* I thought things could not get worse when I was proved wrong. Melissa was staring at me with a puzzled expression on her face. She shouted, 'Look at Emerald's eyes! ... They keep going black!'

I coughed and stood up knocking the dish of cold cream onto Thomas' lap. Thomas jumped to his feet shouting 'Shit.' He was standing in flimsy shorts which looked like a tent with one pole supporting the middle.

I shouted out, 'Oh! I am sorry ... I felt something crawling on my leg.'

Everyone's eyes fell onto Thomas whose guilt was confirmed by his own embarrassing position. Their mother turned deep red and shouted at Thomas, 'Go to your room you disgusting boy.'

Thomas left the table and shouted, 'Dyke!' in my direction.

His mother shouted, 'What did he say?'

Father who was almost choking from laughter shouted, 'Well! ... At least the lad is normal. I would have done the same myself thirty years ago *Ha Ha Harr Ha Harr*.'

Their mother left the table in a huff and only Melissa was left sitting facing me while staring into my eyes. Ruby, who was still sitting next to me, shouted at Melissa, 'Stop staring like that ... it's rude to stare.'

Melissa shouted excitedly, 'Do it again Emerald! ... Make your eyes go all black.'

I held Melissa's hand and spoke to her softly, 'Don't worry darling, it was only the light and the darkness from the shadows.'

We left the table and returned to Ruby's room. Ruby was furious about her brother touching my leg, 'That dirty little spotty pervert.'

I tried to defuse the situation, 'Don't worry love ... if anything I am flattered. He's only a child really.'

'It's an insult ... him touching you like that ... and at the table in front of mummy and daddy.'

I pushed Ruby backwards onto the bed and we both burst into laughter. I shouted at her, 'You are even more beautiful when you are angry.'

She replied, 'Yes! And I want to see you bursting with anger, because I bet you will be even more beautiful than you are now.'

'Oh no darling ... you won't like me when I am angry.'

I kissed Ruby on the lips as I sat on top of her. We were suddenly interrupted by a voice shouting from the door which I had not closed properly. It was Thomas, 'Pair of dykes.'

Ruby jumped from the bed in a rage throwing me to the floor. She flew out of the bedroom in pursuit of her brother, 'Bastard! You're fucking dead when I get hold of you.'

Thomas ran along the landing shouting, 'Ruby's a dyke ... Ruby's a dyke.'

As he flew into his room and flung the door shut, Ruby just caught it in time to push it open. I was panicking; I thought Ruby was about to kill her brother. I rushed into Thomas' bedroom and Ruby had hold of his collar. She was holding him against the wall, 'You little zit-picking pervert ... you keep looking at your girly books and dreaming. Leave my friends alone ... Where are your magazines anyway? That's the closest you will get to a girl.' Ruby let Thomas fall from the wall where she was holding him, and lifted his mattress, 'Ah! Here they are ...LOOK! ... LOOK!' Ruby threw his girly magazines across the room as she shouted from shock, 'Oh! You dirty little bastard they're all sticky.'

Thomas' face turned bright red and we were interrupted by a voice from the direction of the door, 'Will you two give it a rest,' It was dad; as he sat in his wheel chair he twisted his neck in an attempt to look at a picture of a blonde model with massive breasts. The picture was on the front cover of one of the many magazines left strewn across the floor. Dad spoke to out loud with a puzzled tone, 'Goodness it's a wonder she doesn't topple over.'

We all began laughing and dad shouted, 'Now you two stop arguing and let's have some peace for once ... as if I haven't got enough problems with your mother.

A voice unexpectedly shouted from along the hallway, 'I can hear you! ... Come here!'

We returned to Ruby's room where she washed her hands while exclaiming in disgust, 'LOOK! I have stuff from his zits on my hands ... *oooww!* I feel sick.'

'I don't like to say Ruby but ....'

'WHAT!!!! ... WHAT!!!'

'Well ... how do you know the sticky is from his spots.'

'OH!!! ... NO!!!'

The next day Ruby and I went shopping in the city. We bought lots and lots of clothes. Ruby was choosing clothes for me; I didn't mind, I loved the attention. 'Oh Emerald you look marvellous in black. Your skin is so white … Yes! We will take that!'

'But Ruby it costs too much … that's a weeks wages to most people.'

'*Shut up Emerald* … you're embarrassing me.'

We walked into a jewellery shop and my heart was pounding. I was looking at diamonds … and gold … and endless glittering jewels. Ruby looked at me and whispered, 'Close your mouth and blink your eyes.'

Ruby pinched my arm, '*Ouch!*'

'See! You're not dreaming!'

Ruby was greeted by a small man in a black suit, 'Hello Miss Valair, I am pleased to see you … may I offer you some refreshment … *Pétrur* or possibly a glass of *Romanée Conti* madam?'

'I think a glass of *Romanée* would be most refreshing on such a hot day, thank you.'

We were escorted to a private area of the shop and offered seats at a round glass table. We all sat down and a lady came over to our table. The man with us ordered the wine and Ruby introduced me, 'Emerald this is Maurice, the manager of 'Crystals' … Maurice this is my love … Emerald.'

Maurice bowed his head and took hold of my hand which he kissed, 'Madam I am honoured to meet you but I must apologise.'

'Oh!' I was surprised.

'Yes madam for I have no jewels in my shop which may compete with the ones in your eyes.' I brought my hand to my face; I was speechless.

Ruby was never speechless, 'Now Maurice … you say that to all the girls.'

We all laughed and the wine was served. Maurice asked if there was anything in particular we would be looking for. Ruby held my hand and kissed me softly on the lips. I felt as if I should shout 'NO! We are in public and ... and you don't kiss another person of the same sex in public.' Until this moment it had been as if our love was a secret ... secret because of? ... I didn't know. All I realised was that this woman loved me. She looked into my eyes and I was swallowed within an ocean of love and caring. I felt a momentary flash of anger ... why should I deny my feelings and keep living and hiding behind guilt ... from the purity of our love there was no guilt. I lifted my hand to Ruby's face and kissed her passionately. As our lips parted an unwritten bond was sealed between us ... a bond of love.

Ruby described to Maurice what she would like, 'Maurice! What I want is two special rings. Each one will be an engagement and an eternity ring. Ruby placed her hand on the side of my face and spoke softly ... Eternity because I wish us to be together forever, and engagement because I hope you will accept my proposal of marriage. Tears ran down my face as we softly kissed. I looked into Ruby's eyes and replied, '*Yes! Yes!* I want to be with you forever.'

Our magic spell was interrupted by Maurice sniffling into his handkerchief. We both started laughing as Maurice ran off to compose himself. Ruby wiped my eyes with a tissue. I said to her, 'It feels so funny.'

'What?'

'Oh! You know ... kissing you in front of someone.'

'Well there is no need to worry about Maurice.'

'Why?'

'Because he's gay ... see that guy over there?' Ruby pointed to a handsome man who was also dressed in a smart suit.

'Yes.'

'That is Maurice's partner, and they are married.'

Maurice returned with a tray of rings, 'You should not make me cry so ... the jewellery will become rusty.'

Maurice pushed the tray towards us. There must have been over one hundred rings of all different types. Ruby looked towards me and spoke excitedly, 'What I was thinking of was ... a gold ring with a black onyx band with gold edged bars and a large Ruby and Emerald next to each other. We can have a band of tiny scattered diamonds ... like stars all around the band of black ... What do you think my love???"

'Yes! ... Yes! ... Yes! We will have one ring each, so we are joined by the two rings ... and on each one, a ruby and an emerald to represent us.'

Maurice had a computer brought over to our table and he designed the rings as we requested. We drank more wine and I felt so happy I wanted to cry. I felt tipsy as we stood to leave the shop. On the way out something caught my attention and I had to stop to take a closer look. Ruby walked over to join me, 'What have you seen honey?'

I pointed, 'There see ... Oh! Can I have it?'

'But it's so ugly darling ... but yes if you want it I will buy it for you.' Ruby held my hands and kissed me on the lips as she whispered softly, 'I will do anything for you my love.'

I replied, 'All I ask is that this day will last for eternity.' I ran excitedly towards the shop assistant and pointed with my finger, 'That! That! Yes! That's it!'

The assistant reached for the brooch I was pointing towards. Ruby was laughing at me, 'Don't panic honey ... no one is going to steel it.'

'Oh Ruby I am so happy! ... I have never been so happy!'

We walked across to a table where the brooch was resting on black velvet. I shouted out, 'Oh! It's just what I always wanted ... it's beautiful.'

As I pinned it onto my black dress the shop assistant told us, 'It is a 'Black Widow'. The spider is made from gold and has black onyx eyes. Upon her abdomen is an hourglass motive made from rubies, which also represent the figure of eight for eternity. I believe it is the only one of its kind to have been made by this particular artist ... would madam like the item gift wrapped?'

'No! No! I will take her with us everywhere ... with you and me Ruby ... she will always be with us.'

Two Black Widows

We lay on the bed in Ruby's room and held each others hands while we waited for dinner. I reminded Ruby, 'We had best be early for dinner or your mummy will eat us. Shall we tell everyone about us ... at dinner I mean?'

'I don't think so my love ... they don't know I am gay.'

I was surprised, 'But what about Thomas? Surely he must know ... I heard him call us dykes.'

'No ... he is only guessing, he doesn't know for sure.'

'Why don't you tell them Ruby?'

'Because I don't think mummy could handle it. I know daddy would understand ... Oh! But he wouldn't if it was his son ... No, the time is not right, but if they find out, they'll just have to accept it. I love you and will never leave you my love.'

We began to kiss; there was no lust, only love, 'Ooooo! Ruby I feel all weak in your arms darling.'

We began to kiss more passionately and Ruby stopped, she pushed me away and frowned. I was concerned as she looked as if something was wrong. She said, 'We had best stop now or we won't come for dinner.'

We both laughed and went downstairs. We were early and Melissa was the only other person sitting at the table. I sat in my usual place but Ruby suggested that she should sit in my place, 'Let me sit there honey ... I don't want that zit-faced prick mauling Emerald.'

I looked at Ruby and laughed, 'It's alright my love ... I have had to deal with a lot worse than Thomas.'

Melissa shouted across the table, 'Will your eyes go black? ... Will they? Make them go black.'

I noticed that Melissa had a black eye, so I replied to her, 'It looks as if you have your own black eye!'

She replied sadly, 'It's nothing.'

'Ah! See Melissa ... We all keep our own dark secrets.'

'I fell over at school ... that's all.'

Soon, Ruby's mummy and daddy arrived and joined us for dinner. I had to give Ruby a kick because when her parents arrive she said to her mother, 'Well! At least you two have come together.'

Mother crinkled her brow, 'What do you mean? What does she mean daddy?'

Daddy grumbled, 'Well by the way they are giggling I think it best not to know.'

Mother continued frowning and trying to understand the unknown, 'I simply think that the English language has been reformed ... I mean! ... I have been trying to understand all day why Thomas called you a 'dyke'. I do not understand ... a dyke is an embankment to stop flooding ... why does he call you that Ruby?'

'He's only a child mummy ... take no notice of him.'

I was biting my lip to stop myself from laughing and I knew Ruby would be doing the same as her mother confirmed, 'You two are like a pair of cackling old hens ... I do not know what is going on ... I hope you are not on drugs or something.'

'No mother we are happy, that's all.'

Thomas arrived at the table and Ruby threw him a glance that Medusa would envy. Mother spoke to Thomas with an expression of bewilderment, 'Thomas! I am going to ask you a simple question and I want a simple answer ... do you understand me?'

'Must we mum, it is dinner time and I am tired. Dad has had me writing letters all day at the office and I'm bored out of my skull.'

Mother continued, 'Now there you go again speaking in riddles. I think you should see a specialist ... I will make you an appointment."

'Mother! ... What is it you want to ask me? ... Please!'

'What is a 'dyke?'

Thomas pointed towards Ruby, 'That's easy ... Ask her?'

Mother looked at Ruby, 'What is a dyke?'

Ruby answered, 'I should make his appointment with the hospital mummy ... I have told you for years he is a loony.'

We were saved by the maids as they arrived with dishes of food which they placed on the table. Thomas had placed his hand on my leg again which I presumed was an attempt to annoy his sister. I was not concerned anymore about being careful of upsetting the family; I considered myself part of the family. I relaxed my legs and opened them slightly. I could feel his sticky fingers moving towards my knickers. I think he was so excited he was going to burst his pants. As his fingers began to edge there way under my knickers, I moved my hand slowly under the table. I had a fork with long sharp prongs. I stabbed the fork into his hand. *'ARRRRRR!* You bitch!' He jumped to his feet holding his hand; once more he had his flimsy shorts on; he always changed his clothes after finishing work. And once again his shorts looked like a tent with one large central supporting pole. Mother jumped from the table and chased Thomas from the room, 'You dirty, foul, disgusting boy, go and take a cold shower.'

Melissa jumped up and down shouting, 'She did it! She did it! Her eyes went black again! I saw them! I saw them!'

Daddy sat laughing, 'I have not had so much fun for years, *Ha Ha Harr Ha Ha* I think I will die laughing ... you will be the death of me Emerald ... but at least I will die a happy man ... is that why you wear the Black Widow brooch? I have two Black Widows now! Are you a man killer?'

'Well you know what they will say about you when you are gone daddy?'

'W...What?'

'At least he went with a smile on his face.'

'*Ha Ha Ha Harrr Ha Harr Ha Ha Harr Ha Ha Ha Harrr Ha Harr Ha Ha Harr Ha Ha Ha Harrr Ha Harr Ha Ha Harr.*'

The moon shone brightly through the open curtains as lace danced like a moth upon the cool breeze from the open window. It was 1 a.m. and I lay silently next to Ruby. I watched as my lover slept peacefully while shadows caressed her naked breasts. Ruby's tanned body looked like stone in the moonlight. I stared in amazement at her beauty ... I craved to touch her body, to explore ... to search within the heaven I had finally found. I began to notice the beat of my own heart. At first I thought nothing of it ... then it became harder ... I bit my lip ... soon my heart was pounding against my ribs ... my body began to shake as adrenalin flooded through my veins. I shook my head as tears flowed down my cheeks ... I whispered as I shook my head from side to side ... '*No! No!* Not now ... everything is perfect.'

A pair of black sunken eyes stared at Ruby's face only inches away. Lotus watched and waited as her cold breath floated like mist to be breathed-in slowly by Ruby as she dreamed ... in the distance she could hear the pain of a child crying ... she rose from the bed with the silence of a ghost ... for this was why she had come. Lotus seemed to walk on air ... to float through the darkness of the hallway. When she came to Melissa's door it seemed to open on its own as if 'what had to be would be' and nothing could resist. Lotus moved into the room and the door closed silently behind her. She stood naked like a statue in the middle of the room. Melissa was lying in her bed sobbing. She was facing the wall and had her back towards Lotus. Lotus held her arms out from the sides of her body and tilted her head back as she bathed in the moonlight. She breathed in deeply as moonbeams caressed her body like a stone statue resembling a crucifixion. Moonlight endeavoured to vanquish the darkness, from where all light finally finds a final end. Her body was pure white like marble, with delicate blue veins; a translucent white light reflecting energy through her skin from within her. Lotus looked down at Melissa who was still crying. She did not know why she was with Melissa, only that Melissa had asked to see her ... no one had ever asked to see her before ... it was a strange feeling to be ... wanted ... and there was a pain to be shared, and pain should be shared ... nobody should suffer alone. Lotus lifted the sheets and climbed into the bed beside Melissa. The young girl spun around terrified at the sudden intrusion. Lotus pulled the young girl's naked body against her and held her tightly. Melissa began to scream and Lotus placed her hand over her mouth. Lotus stared into Melissa's frightened eyes and whispered, *'Shhhhh! You asked and I have come.'*

Melissa's body was shaking with fear as Lotus held her tightly. Lotus was used to fear and felt comfortable. After an endless time Melissa stopped shaking and Lotus removed her hand from her mouth and asked, *'Do you wish me to leave? ... If I leave now you will have to come with me.'*

Melissa was frightened yet amazed, 'Who are you? Your voice is deep like a groan and your eyes are black?'

'You asked for me and I am here, is that not enough?'

'What is your name?'

'Lotus.'

'Lotus you are hurting me … you are squeezing me so tightly.'

Lotus relaxed and lay still while staring at Melissa.

Melissa's eyes searched over the naked body of Lotus as if looking for more magic. She touched the skin of Lotus with her fingertips, 'You're cold … you're freezing … let me hug you and make you warm.'

'I don't hug and I don't want to be warm.'

'Are you my friend Lotus?'

'Do you want me as your friend?'

'Yes! Please be my friend.'

'Friends share things … they have no secrets.'

'Then we will share everything Lotus … and tell each other everything.'

'Let me share your pain?'

'What pain?

'You were crying.'

'I don't want to talk about it.'

'Yet we have no secrets.'

Melissa spoke sadly and slowly, 'It's a girl at school … her dad worked in my father's business. He was fired and now she blames me. She is older than I am and really big. She picks on me all the time and takes my money and……..' Melissa began to cry and put her arms around Lotus. Lotus flung her head backwards and hissed as she breathed in deeply while Melissa sobbed and sobbed. Lotus tasted Melissa's tears and licked the salt from her face slowly and softly. The sun began to rise and Lotus told Melissa she had to leave and that their meeting should always be their secret. Melissa hugged Lotus and said, 'I love you! Do you love me?'

Lotus rose from the bed and placed her lips against Melissa's. She breathed in and Melissa's back arched from a pain deep within. Lotus stood away from Melissa and said, *'Whatever bond we have is through pain ... a pain which some may love.'*

Lotus returned to her room and slept deeply next to Ruby. As she rested, Lotus suckled a seed from pain, for she knew that before the next setting of the sun she would take a life. She hissed as she breathed-in deeply and was content. Lotus thought, ... *'that's what friends are for.'*

The next morning Ruby shook me saying, 'Wake up it's breakfast time ... come on!' She had already showered and was dressed.

I said, 'I'm tired leave me alone.'

'If you don't get out of bed I will throw this glass of cold water over you.'

I didn't make a move. Suddenly, Ruby threw the glass of cold water into my face and began to run. Lotus was there in an instant running across the room with deep black eyes and a nail-file she had instinctively clawed from the dresser. Ruby never saw Lotus as she was running from the room like a naughty girl screaming ... well it was just a bit of fun. Luckily the bedroom door slammed shut and what could have been would never now be known.

I cried as I showered and whispered to ...myself ... 'Why did you do that ... you always have to spoil things don't you. I love Ruby and she loves me and we will be married and spend our lives together.'

From somewhere deep inside, I heard a deep voice groaning, *'And what about me? Don't I exist anymore? Don't I matter to you now? Is this how you treat a friend?'*

I arrived for breakfast just as it was being served, 'I'm sorry I'm late.'

Mother spoke to me, 'Good-Morning Emerald ... I AM!"

I was confused, 'What?'

Mother repeated, 'I AM!'

'You are what?'

'You do not say 'I'm … I'm …The correct pronunciation is 'I AM!''

'Sorry mother.'

Thomas sat chuckling as he ate, while daddy came to my rescue, 'Why don't you give the girl a break?'

Mother began again, 'Don't … Don't … Don't.'

Daddy put down his knife and fork and shouted, 'Don't what?'

Mother replied, ''Don't', does not mean anything … the corre…..'

Daddy stood up mumbling and left the table shouting, 'I'm goin' tae wurk I won't 'ave breakfast so don't bloodee wurry.'

I continued eating in silence. I glanced up to meet Melissa's staring, unblinking eyes. A shiver shot down my spine … sometimes she was really creepy. Ruby shouted at Melissa, 'Will you stop that staring … you are doing it all the time.'

Melissa became angry and pouted her lips, 'Well! She's not just your friend … she's my friend as well.'

After breakfast Melissa put on her school blazer. She ran over and hugged me shouting, 'I love you and I am sorry for being a pain.'

'I love you darling and any pain you have is mine.'

Melissa began to cry, 'I don't want to go to school … can I stay with you?'

Mother was close by and shouted, 'Stop being silly and go to school.'

Melissa looked at me with pleading eyes, 'Will you meet me tonight Lotus?'

Ruby interrupted, 'What did you call Emerald?'

Melissa replied, 'I wasn't speaking to Emerald.'

Mother pushed Melissa towards the door, 'Come on now or you will be late for school … your car is waiting.'

As Melissa was pushed through the door she shouted back to me, 'Don't leave me will you?'

I shouted to her, 'No! I promise.'

Ruby told me it was time to 'keep fit.' In our bedroom she threw me some running shorts, shoes and a top. Once dressed, we set off jogging towards the park. We talked as we ran and Ruby showed me the local shops and other places of interest. She pointed to a large building, 'That's Melissa's school.'

We arrived home after sprinting out of the park. Dripping in sweat, we both jumped into the shower. Then we ate some dinner, after which I mentioned to Ruby that I felt tired and sickly. She gave me a kiss, 'You poor darling ... I have pushed you too hard with all the running. You have a lie-down ... I have to go with mother to see some boring curtains ... I wouldn't wish that experience on anybody.'

'Well ... if you are sure you don't mind my love I will stay at home and have a rest.'

I fell asleep on the bed and awoke at around 3 p.m. I knew Lotus was with me but there was nothing I could do. The feeling is like ... when you fall, and you feel you are floating through the air in slow motion and you know you may hurt yourself, and yet you also know there is nothing you can do to stop whatever is going to happen.

I dressed in a green track suit and left the house for a walk. I knew Melissa would be leaving her school at 3.30 p.m. It didn't take me long to walk through the park to where I had been shown the school by Ruby. I stood watching and waiting behind some trees. I could see Melissa standing by the school gates. She was agitated and looked around anxiously. I presumed she was looking for the car which would arrive to take her home. Then I saw her ... I instinctively knew that the girl approaching Melissa was the bully. I felt like shouting, *'Melissa! Melissa! Here I am!'* but I knew I could not shout. I looked to my right; I had left my body ...Lotus had taken over.

A group of girls surrounded Melissa and they all walked across the road and into the park. Once in the park the girls, who were aged between 12 and 15 years, formed a circle around Melissa and the big girl. The big girl was twice the size of Melissa and looked a lot older. The circle of girls began to chant, *'Fight! Fight! Fight!'* I felt sick and I looked towards Lotus. I shouted at her, 'Stop it! Stop it!!'

Lotus turned to face me and replied, *'I will.'*

The big girl moved towards Melissa ... I felt sick and began to cry ... Melissa slapped hopelessly at the big girl who grabbed hold of her hair spinning her through the air to land screaming on the floor. The big girl then sat on top of her and punched her in the face. Melissa was crying and the bully held her arms down while she spit into her mouth and face whilst taunting and teasing her, 'You're not so important now are you bitch ... sacking my dad ... who does your family think they are? Give me your money bitch and bring me more tomorrow or you will get worse.' The big girl stood up and kicked Melissa in the ribs, leaving the poor girl curled up in a ball, crying on the grass. I was on my knees crying; the pain of her suffering was unbearable. I looked towards Lotus ... she was standing with her head thrown back and her arms slightly held out from her body. She breathed-in deeply and I knew something bad was about to happen. The girls dispersed and Lotus followed the big girl to a shop and watched as she asked someone to buy her cigarettes from the money she had stolen from Melissa. The girl began to walk home through the park; still followed by Lotus. We came to a wooded area and Lotus walked closer to the big girl who could hear footsteps and looked behind her ... she spit green phlegm onto the path in front of Lotus ... she could see no threat from a petite young woman who was a lot smaller than herself ... and after all she was the school's 'hard case' and the best fighter in the area.

Lotus did not have to look around she had an animal instinct which told her that nobody was close. She walked close behind the girl and I could see her body shaking ... I knew she was not shaking from fear ... she was shaking from excitement. Lotus hissed like a snake and the girl turned around. She was tall and looked down at Lotus, 'What do you want you little bitch ... I'll pull your fucking head off and use it as a foot ball.'

Lotus stood staring at the girl. I shouted, 'Lotus! Lotus! Run! Run!'

Too late ... the big girl took a grip of Lotus' short black hair and flung her to the ground. The big girl dived on top of Lotus and sat on her like she had done with Melissa, 'Who the fuck do you think you are ... you're pretty ... I like pretty girls.'

The bully began to let saliva drip from her mouth into her victim's. Lotus opened her mouth as if she was enjoying the whole experience. The big girl became uneasy, 'You're a weird bitch you are ... why are your eyes black?'

The bully stood to her feet and kicked Lotus who was still lying on the floor. She turned to walk away whilst shouting, 'Don't come near me again or I'll kick your teeth down yer throat.'

What happened next happened within the blink of an eye. Lotus reached for the girl's foot as she was walking away. The girl seemed to try and spin around, kicking with her other foot towards Lotus. She lost her balance and as she fell to the ground Lotus wedged a pointed stick in the grass so that one end was pointing upwards. The big girl landed on the stick and lay groaning in pain. Lotus stroked her face and brow, as the girl pleaded for help. Lotus spoke to the girl softly, *'What we share will last forever ... this moment is ours, for only within the shadow of death which grows from the seeds of pain, can the true devotion and*

bond of love between warriors be found.' Lotus then placed
her lips upon the girl's and breathed-in deeply ... and all
was over.

I returned home and ran up to my room for a
shower. I felt dirty and, although I washed and washed, the
feeling would not leave me. I threw the track suit into a
wash basket and found a pretty black dress to wear for
dinner. I pinned my brooch onto my dress and spun
around while looking in the mirror. I was beautiful and the
black widow sparkled as it rested on my breast.

We sat to eat dinner and Melissa sat silently without
eating. She looked up at me sulkily while her chin
quivered. She had another black eye and a sore lip. Father
shouted across to her, 'What's wrong with you're face? ...
You been fighting? Well I hope you won! *Ha Ha Harr*, I
remember the story of the lad who came home from school
and had a black eye and his father asked him, 'Did you
win?' The lad replied, 'No' so his dad gave him the kicking
of his life and then told him, 'That's what you get for
losing,' *Ha Ha Harr*, that was a good story ... never forget a
good story. That is the trouble with being a woman
Emerald ... you never see the rough side of life ... never
have a good old scrap.'

Melissa shouted at me, 'I thought you were my
friend ... you're just the same as everyone ... I hate you!'
She ran from the table crying.

Daddy said, 'Women! I will never understand
them, curious creatures ... most peculiar.'

I said, 'She will be alright tomorrow ... everything
will be perfect tomorrow.'

The next evening I arrived for dinner early with
Ruby. I waited for Melissa. She came skipping into the
room happily. She sat staring at me with one eyebrow
raised. She smiled and winked. I winked back and nothing
more was ever said.

I had been living with Ruby and her family for four weeks and the love between Ruby and I had grown stronger and stronger. We decided to start a business together ... maybe a clothes shop or a gymnasium. We had decided to get married as soon as possible, but Ruby was worried about her mother's reaction. We had talked with father about having our own clothes shop, and he thought it was a splendid idea and told us jokingly, 'The money you save from buying clothes at other shops will make it worth while ... even if you never sold anything.'

We knew daddy would finance the shop and we hoped it might be a wedding present when our big day arrived. We planned the wedding together in secret. I had met all of Ruby's friends at 'Mermaids' nightclub but we had only told Eugene and Clair our secret. We were planning a big wedding in the summer-time with marques and hundreds of people, and a top celebrity pop group to play music in the evening; we planned our honeymoon and we wanted to go to so many places that we decided to go on a tour to them all ... Las Vegas ... Hawaii ... Egypt to see the pyramids ... I had always wanted to see the pyramids, and even Lotus said she would like to see inside them.

I could not believe how lucky I had been, meeting Ruby. Her father was rich and loved to have me around as I always made him laugh ... I didn't mean to be funny, I suppose he liked the things that Lotus said to him that nobody else ... including myself would ever dare to say. I remember one day when I was lying on my stomach by the swimming pool and daddy came over on his wheelchair (he often sat by me). He would rub sun oil on my back – spending a lot of time on my bottom but I didn't mind, and he had told me jokingly 'not to worry as everything below waist is dead.' This particular day we were talking and daddy's fingers slid deeply where they shouldn't have. Lotus cried out, *'Oh! You bastard.'*

Actually it was quite nice but it was a bit of a shock. I mean! ... There you are talking to someone about different countries and travelling abroad when all of a sudden 'a hand full of fingers slips between your legs!'

Daddy apologised, 'Oh! I am sorry my hand slipped!'

Lotus had to interfere and groan in her deep voice at him, 'Well! *If your fucking hand slips again it will be so far up your arse you will be picking your nose for the rest of your life.*'

Daddy laughed and laughed until I thought he might die, and I was worried I might be told to leave the house. Eventually he smacked my bottom ... several times lightly ... and said, 'You're some gal ... you really are ... I wish I had met you forty years ago ... I wish you would work for me ... you're a killer.'

Daddy seemed to like all the macho stuff, and Lotus seemed to 'take to him' ... it was as if they had some psychic link through the pain of his disability.

I would lie by the pool, and if daddy was at home and I was alone, he would always come over to me and talk while rubbing sun oil onto my back. I would always lie face down with my head turned away from him as I was frightened of him seeing Lotus' eyes. I was frightened because nothing like this had ever happened before. I mean!! ... There I was lying on the sun-bed and Lotus was talking in her deep, slow, groaning voice to daddy. I did not leave my body as I had when Lotus was angry. It was as if I was in a light trance ... I could hear everything the two of them were saying but I was merely a spectator.

I spoke to Lotus when we were alone, 'What do you think you are playing at?'

'What?'

'You know what! Talking to daddy?'

'I like him … he suffers and he believes in fighting and punishing others … he watches men punching and ripping each others faces apart until they are brain dead.'

'No! That's a sport called boxing.'

'I am doing no harm and that's hard for me … sometimes I think you want to stop my pain.'

'I don't want any trouble.'

'No! But you welcome me when you are suffering.'

'I am happy and I don't want to spoil it.'

'I am not interfering with your happiness … If! … You do not interfere with my sadness.'

'Is that a threat Lotus?'

'Yes Emerald.'

Ruby would often walk over when I was talking with daddy, and soon after she had sat down, daddy would make an excuse and leave us alone. Ruby would ask me what we talked about for such a long time. I would say, 'Oh! He tells me about his problems and his life … I think he simply likes to rub sun oil on me … there's no harm in that is there my love?'

'No I suppose not, taking into consideration he is paralysed from the waist down.'

'Well if he wasn't paralysed do you think it would make any difference?'

'No! Of course not.'

It was a hot day and I was lying by the pool. Ruby was out shopping and daddy was in the house. I rubbed sun cream onto my front and lay sunbathing. Soon I could hear the wheelchair approaching, so I turned onto my stomach as I knew daddy would put cream onto my back. 'Hello! My darling green eyes! How are you today?'

Lotus had not arrived yet. It was as if there was a switch which would call her, and daddy was now adept at summoning her appearance.

'I am fine thank you daddy.'

Daddy would not talk much until Lotus arrived. He would talk about trivial things such as the weather and the local news.

It was weird really ... like a secret we both shared that was a secret from ourselves. His hands were strong and comforting as they moved down my spine. Lotus would groan and push her bottom in the air while arching her back. She was like a wild cat. His hands would move over her tight, firm, round bottom and then it would happen. His hand would slide deeply between her legs and Lotus would instantly be there, *'You dirty bastard ... I will beat your fucking brains out.'*

They had this complex understanding that I could not fathom. Daddy would welcome her, 'Ah! You are there my love ... my Black Widow?'

'You will wish I fucking wasn't in a minute ... when you're blowing bubbles from the bottom of the pool.'

'I will tan your ass till it's raw if you speak to me like that.'

'OH! OH! Stop! Stop please! That hurts! That hurts! I hate you! You bastard,' Cried Lotus.

'You mean you love to hate me! You naughty girl.'

It was as if it turned daddy on ... or whatever? ... He loved the way Lotus talked to him. She would listen to his tales and stories of pain and suffering and that would turn her on even more. I let them have their fun ... no harm was being done and it made daddy happy, and I loved him. Their relationship also gave Lotus a contentment which drew her attention away from Ruby and me. I had become worried after the incident in the bedroom, when Lotus chased Ruby, because I knew she was jealous. When daddy was leaving, he would always give Lotus a light spanking on the bottom. He would say how he loved the way her bottom shimmered. Lotus seemed to have a way of controlling her rage. At one time she would have murdered anyone for spanking her. She didn't like it, but she seemed to like not liking it. As he spanked her she would growl at him, *'You dirty old bastard! I will murder you for this!'* Of course she never did. She would fling her head back and breathe in deeply, hissing like a snake. Luckily her eyes were closed, or I don't know what daddy would have thought.

It was embarrassing for me because I had to sit with daddy at meal times. He would keep winking at me as if we shared some secret. I suppose we did but it was nothing to do with me ... I was trapped between the two of them. I thanked the Lord for small mercies such as daddy being incapable of making love with Lotus, or God only knows what would have happened ... it was like some sort of sadomasochism practised between the two of them. It sent shivers down my spine ... but 'each to their own' I suppose. Everything was fine until one day I was lying face down by the pool and I felt daddy's hand on my back smearing sun cream. He began to feel my bottom but something was wrong. Lotus shouted at me and I knew she meant what she was saying, *'Get rid of that bastard who's fumbling on my arse or I will drown him like a rat.'*

I knew Lotus was serious and I turned around quickly. It was Thomas ... he had seen daddy with Lotus and decided to join in the fun. I was so annoyed, I shouted at Lotus, 'I told you 'no good' would come of this.'

She laughed, *'Well if I drown him it will look good, like an accident and that's good for me and good for you ... see! I am learning to be good.'*

I looked at Thomas, 'What do you think you are doing?'

'I'm feeling your arse like daddy does ... I have seen the two of you ... and I saw him spanking you.'

Lotus was almost coming out, *'I will tear the little swine's throat out ... Let me out! ... Let me out! ... He's dead!'*

I tried to get rid of Thomas as quickly as I could, 'Just piss off will you ... you zit-faced little prick.'

Thomas had been busy devising his devious plans, 'Alright then I will go ... I wonder what mummy will think when she hears about your fun with daddy?'

It was too late ... Lotus began to escape. She clawed at Thomas like a wild animal cutting his chest with her nails, *'Your dead you little maggot!'*

Thomas saw her black eyes and heard the growling voice of Lotus, *'I will tear your intestines out one inch at a time.'*

The hand of Lotus clawed at his stomach and her nail caught tightly into his skin. He rolled away screaming like a pig, 'No! No! Please! I will never say another word. Please let me go ... don't kill me.' Lotus didn't let him go ... he escaped, and he never spoke about the incident again.

I nearly died when Lotus told daddy the whole story of what had happened with Thomas. Daddy laughed until he cried, and for the first time ever I heard Lotus laugh ... or should I say attempt to laugh ... she sounded like a dog choking on a bone, and my throat was sore for days after.

At dinnertime 'things' became really peculiar. Thomas sat rigid like a man awaiting execution. Every now and then daddy would suddenly slap his son's leg hard; Thomas would jump out of his skin. Daddy would then burst into peels of laughter and make a remark such as, 'That's my boy!'

Mother would look her usual puzzled self and ask, 'What on earth is going on? Why do you keep holding your stomach Thomas?'

When we were alone Ruby commented on Thomas, 'I don't know what's wrong with that boy ... do you know why he's so quiet?'

I smiled and said, 'I don't know darling ... maybe he has had a near-death experience or something.'

TWO GIRLS IN LOVE

It was a Saturday evening and Ruby suggested we go to 'Mermaids' nightclub. I had noticed an advertisement in the newspaper for an 'Evening with Abba.' The group of singers had won a T.V. 'look-alike' competition and were to sing at a local disco. I showed Ruby the advert, and as we both liked the group Abba, decided to go to the club.

We showered and dressed. For a laugh we dressed like the two girl singers from Abba. I wore a blonde wig while Ruby left her hair colour auburn. I wore a bright red mini-skirt and Ruby was wearing a skin tight cat-suit. We laughed and I told her she would lose half a stone in weight from sweating by the end of the night. Lotus was excited; she told me, *'You're looking for trouble going out dressed like this.'*

We arrived at the club which was by the sea, around 9 p.m. Music was playing and when we squeezed inside the club, the two guys and gals from the group were singing and swinging. People were dancing and lights were flashing; we put our arms around each other as we pushed through people towards the bar and ordered drinks. We drank 'shorts' and drank them fast and furious. Soon we were 'Dancing Queens' and having the time of our lives. We danced slowly in each other arms when 'Fernando' a slow, song was being sung. Ruby whispered into my ear, 'I love you more than anything or anyone … I want to marry you now … I mean in a few weeks … will you marry me?'

'Well! I don't know Ruby … I mean I like your dad.'

We both burst into laughter and I shouted out at the top of my voice, '*Yes! Yes! Yes!* I will marry you.'

We continued drinking and dancing until we were dripping in sweat and the floor was slippery. We found an empty table and sat down panting. We drank until our heads were spinning and kissed and laughed; we didn't care about anything. All we needed was what we had ... an everlasting happiness and contentment from true love.

It must have been about 2 a.m. and we were thinking of calling for a taxi when two handsome guys came over to our table, 'Hi girls! ... Mind if we join you? ... Would you like a drink?'

I looked into Ruby's eyes and I knew what she was thinking. The lads were buying, so why not have one last drink before going home. One of the lads brought our drinks and placed them in front of us. I stared at the boys, 'I recognise you two ... you're the boys from the beach ... remember Ruby? ... The lads who offered to rub sun cream over us.'

We all started laughing and one of the lads said, 'That's us ... you really took us for a ride.'

Ruby rested her hand on one of the boys' shoulders, 'Well! No hard feelings lads.'

Everyone burst into laughter and the boys replied, 'No! No hard feelings.'

We had drunk far too much and I told Ruby I wanted to go home. I had never felt as bad as I did at that time. The room was turning and my eyes would not focus. I had lost touch with reality ... it was as if I was dreaming ... something like when Lotus took over. I looked at Ruby and her eyes seemed to be rolling around as if she could not control them. I could feel one of the boy's hands going up my skirt; he pulled me to him and kissed my lips. I had no control over my actions ... I was like some sort of puppet. The two boys lifted us from our seats and guided us out of the club. They had their arms around our waists, supporting us like rag dolls. I remember trying to scream 'help' to the door-man who was talking to somebody as we left the club ... but I could not speak. I remember seeing Ruby staggering in front of me, supported by the guy, holding her. They were big lads so they could carry us easily. I began to realise we had been drugged. I was screaming in panic inside, and I could hear Lotus growling and hissing like a wild trapped animal, but there was nothing I could do. The lads led us onto the sand and took us behind some bushes, 'So you think you're clever do you? ... Making fools of us! ... Well! You are not so clever now bitch?'

I blacked out which was probably for the best. I awoke in hospital and I was stinging like mad below. I was shaking ... shivering while at the same time soaking in sweat. A policewoman was sitting by my side and asked me what had happened. I remembered everything, but my only concern was for Ruby. I grabbed the policewoman's arm and cried out, 'Ruby! Ruby! Where is my Ruby?'

The woman looked at the floor and I knew what she was trying to say. I began to scream, '*NO! NO! NO!*'

A nurse gave me an injection and I fell into a deep sleep. Lotus shouted at me and would not stop, '*You stupid fool ... you were almost killed and those two animals used you while I just watched ... How could you be so stupid?*'

'I thought you liked pain?'

'*I like being a part of pain, not being humiliated and used. You stupid bitch! If I didn't need you I would tear your head off. And now your pretty Ruby and all your happiness has gone ... I told you love always leads to pain, and the more the love, the more the pain, leave things to me now ... do you hear me?*'

'Y ... Yes.'

'*What a fucking mess you've got me in Emerald! Two guys walking about and I don't know where they are ... how can I live without finding them. I can feel the happiness you had through the torture of the pain I now feel. What goes around*

comes around. You listen to me now and do as I say ...
understand?'

'Y ... Yes Lotus.'

'You don't remember anything! ... Understand?'

'But I .....'

'I said you don't remember anything!'

'Yes Lotus.'

'You have had your fun ... now it is my turn.'

The police returned to the hospital and asked me
what I remembered. 'I'm sorry ... everything is a blur and I
cannot remember anything.'

The police asked me lots of questions about what
had happened. They told me that we had been date-raped
and that an autopsy may reveal the drug, or drugs used.
For some unknown reason whatever the drugs were, they
appeared to have had an adverse affect upon Ruby.

I began to cry and I was left alone. Daddy visited
me and brought me bundles of flowers and boxes of
chocolates. I told him that money can't buy everything and
explained to him that my happiness was lost forever. We
both sat crying and daddy told me he would pay money to
see that the lads who did this were brought to trial. I told
daddy they would never end up in court. He stared at me
without blinking, and after a while he said, 'Your eyes went
black then ... it's Lotus isn't it? I can tell by your voice!'

'Go home daddy ... it's over!'

He left the room like a broken man with his head
held low and tears dripping from his eyes.

Two days later he died, and Lotus was mad ... I
mean really mad.

THREE BLACK WIDOWS

I returned to Ruby's home and attended the double funeral which was held for daddy and Ruby. Whilst attending the funeral I held Melissa in my arms and turned my ring of eternal love around on my finger ... it was as if I would wake up and all of the dream which had turned into a nightmare, would magically flip back into the illusion of reality which had vanished. I could not tell what was real or false anymore. It was as if I was watching myself from afar ... watching Lotus who was more able to cope with pain than I. I felt numb ... I was going through all the motions of life and yet I was simply existing. I wore black all the time and covered my body.

At the dinner table we ate mostly in silence. Mother would make general conversation giving reference to the weather or the news, but nothing much was said. Melissa would look at me occasionally but when I looked her way she would quickly turn away as if she was frightened. Thomas never spoke.

One day after dinner, mother came into Ruby's room where I was still staying. It was about one week after the funeral. Mother was shaking and lost her composure, 'Y ... You ... I want you out of this house ... you bring nothing but bad luck ... You are like that thing you always wear ... that 'Black Widow.' I knew about you and daddy ... you dirty whore ... I saw him fondling you and I told him to stop but he wouldn't listen to me ... And I know about you and Ruby ... I am not daft!'

Lotus replied, *'It's stupid!'*

Mother was shocked by the deep voice of Lotus, 'What is stupid?'

Lotus continued, *'You are not 'daft' the correct word is 'stupid' ... you are not stupid.'*

Mother raged, 'I want you out of my house as soon as possible.'

'It will be possible and it will be soon, and you killed your husband not me, he died of unhappiness ... happiness was the one thing he could not buy.'

Mother shook with rage as she screamed at Lotus, 'And you think that you made him happy ... letting him maul your body?'

'He made himself happy ... I did nothing ... I only felt his pain.'

When mother left, I asked Lotus why she had not killed her. She explained to me, *'Why should I free her from her pain? She will live a lie and hide from herself ... she will die a thousand times.'*

The next morning at breakfast I told Mrs Valair that I would leave as soon as I could. I explained I had something important to finish before I left.

Melissa cried out, *'No! No!* You're my friend, I won't let Lotus leave.'

I could see a look of puzzlement on Mrs Valair's face. I held Melissa's hand and told her, 'All good things must come to an end.'

I caught a taxi 'down-town' and wandered around the antique shops, led by Lotus. She had stopped speaking since daddy's death ... she just hissed and spat when agitated which was most of the time. As a result of the latter I had to carry a handkerchief, which was always ready in my hand, had I the need to cover my mouth. I had a credit card which I used sparingly as it had been arranged for me by Ruby; I had a feeling it could be cancelled at any time. We looked through many different antique shops and I dare not ask if we could stop and go home, or I would have been seen having a convulsive coughing fit as I attempted to cover a bout of hissing and spitting from Lotus. I was at my wits-ends and dying for a rest and some coffee when Lotus spoke to me for the first time in days, *'There! ... No! Over there stupid! ... Yes! ... Pick them up and hold them!'*

I found myself staring at two long stiletto knives. They had smooth black handles and long thin blades of about eight inches in length. The double-edged steel blades were shiny and looked sharp. The knife ends came to a point, and there was a small cross bar to prevent one's hand from slipping onto the blade. I was intrigued ... on each of the small cross-bars sat a spider which seemed to be staring down the blade. Lotus was excited and hissed, *'Pick them up! Pick them up!'*

I held the two knives and Lotus took over. She spun the knives in my hands ... first together and then alternately.

I felt like someone from a karate film. I looked around and people were staring. Lotus pricked my arms with the points and tiny drops of blood appeared, 'Watch it Lotus ... that fucking hurt!'

'Don't be soft ... I have to test them. They will do. Pay for them and go. Now you can drink your coffee ... if you can manage to drink it without burning your hand off.'

The shop assistant noticed my brooch and said, 'The two 'Black Widows' from the knives complement the one close to your heart madam.'

I replied, 'Yes! There are three Black Widows now.'

The assistant asked me what I was going to do with the knives. I paid for them and calmly replied, 'Oh! I am sure I will find someone to stick them into.'

Lotus wasn't happy about my remark to the shop assistant, *'You stupid bitch! You have to try to spoil things for me! ... Don't you?'*

SUN KISSED

I jogged down to the beach each day wearing a track-suit. I carried a large beach towel in one hand which was wrapped around the two knives. Lotus picked a spot on the beach which was fairly quiet and by the path that most people would use. Lotus sat watching like a hawk day after day. She called it hunting. Each day she would rise early and shout at me excitedly, *'Come on ... we're wasting time ... today could be the day! ... Remember! Happiness and Ruby ... Yesss! You feel it don't you ... well it's called revenge and it is sweet ... I can feel your lust ... hate can be as sweet as love and the kiss of death can be the same as the kiss of life, for passion will ride the black stallion and also the pure white mare ... yes we are the same you and I ... one burns with ice while the other burns with fire ... close your eyes ... we go hand in hand, we are love and hate.'*

I knew it would happen sooner or later ... Lotus caught sight of the two lads. I was frightened but I did as Lotus instructed; I thought of Ruby, and then I felt better as I was filled with hate. As the two boys approached, Lotus told me to act seductively. All I was wearing was a thong (nothing else; I was topless). As the boys walked over, Lotus told me to lie on my belly. She said, *'Whatever happens, do not let them see your face or all will be lost.'* She told me to bury the knives in the sand; one each side of my body where my hands would be. I was terrified and asked her to take over. Lotus explained that I might have to talk to the lads to get them to come over before she could make her 'appearance'; so she waited. The two boys were laughing and talking as they passed close-by on the path. I was struggling with the sun cream ... trying to reach my back.

156

The boys saw me and one shouted, 'Hey! You need some help babe?'

I mumbled, 'Yes please!'

The lads were over like bees to honey. They took my sun cream and squirted it down my back and began rubbing it in with their hands. Lotus shouted to me and she was so excited I could hardly understand what she was saying. I could hardly contain her. She said, *'Turn over onto your back or they may see the faint lines on your ass and recognise you.'*

I turned over and the lads' eyes almost popped out of their heads when they saw my naked breasts. Lotus shouted to me, *'You are doing fine ... cover your face with your arms so they don't recognise you ... all they will be looking at are your tits.'*

The lads could not believe their luck. Their fingers trembled as they massaged around my nipples while watching as they grew. Lotus hissed words to me, *'Now you will feel true ecstasy as I rape these two with death.'*

Lotus took over and I stood next to her watching. She lowered her arms from her face placing them by her sides. The lads didn't look up ... I could see her hands moving through the sand searching for the knives. She groaned at the lads, **'Suck me! Suck me!'** The lads' heads fell onto her nipples and I saw the glint from the knives blades reflecting in the sun as the sand fell away as fine as salt. Lotus said to the boys, *'I am going to fuck the two of you to death.'*

I think the boys were so aroused they lifted their heads in anticipation of what was to happen next. They both seemed to say *'Yes'* together and then it happened. One of them began to say, 'I know you....'

It wasn't quick ... Lotus crossed her arms as she did not have enough room to lift each arm upwards from the sand. I could see the two points from the knives slowly sinking in, between their ribs. Lotus arched her back as if there were thousands of vaults of electricity shooting through her body. She groaned deeply from her stomach and I knew it was a cry of death ... a sound which still haunts me now. Her body seemed contorted ... twisted ... I watched as the knives slowly sank deeper. She brought her face to meet the eyes of the two boys and the blackness they saw was death. The knives were in their bodies up to the hilt and blood was running over the spiders which seemed to be alive upon each knife. The faces of the boys were almost smiling as if they were somewhere else and not within the bodies where death was about to call. I thought to myself, *'Now you know how I felt.'*

Lotus kissed the life from each and it was over.

She removed the knives from their hearts and laid their bodies face down as if they were peacefully sunbathing.

She ran into the sea to wash the blood from her arms and took the two knives with her, to be left; her secret for ever with Neptune. As she walked back towards me, men turned their heads to admire her beauty. Her breasts bounced slightly, and she stretched her head backwards shaking the water from her hair.

Suddenly I was back in my body and I wondered what I should do next. I returned to the two boys who looked as if they were peacefully sleeping beneath the sun.

I put on my track-suit and I started to jog home. It had been a busy day.

When I arrived home ... I realised it wasn't my home; I had no home and nowhere to go. I had suffered so much pain from the loss of my love that nothing really seemed to matter much anymore. The only feeling that had mattered had now been fulfilled. I joined Ruby's family in the dining room where no-one spoke much. A T.V. was showing the news and could be seen clearly. I was glad the T.V. was on as I felt that it eased the tension at the dining table. I looked at Mrs Valair and spoke to her softly, 'I have finished what I had to do. I will leave tomorrow morning and I thank you for your hospitality.'

Mrs Valair glanced at me and nodded her head. Melissa pouted her lips, 'I don't want you to go … I will be left on my own with zit face.'

Our meal was interrupted, as our town was mentioned by the news reader, *'Today the bodies of two young men were found dead on 'Moordale' beach. The police are treating the boys' deaths as murder. They believe both boys to have been stabbed, and a murder hunt is underway. The police are appealing for anyone who saw the boys today, or if you have any information you should phone ………'*

Photographs of the two boys were shown on the T.V. screen.

Melissa shouted out, *'Look! Look!* It's Tom and Pete, two of daddy's drivers. They were here in the house a few weeks ago and I saw mummy give them some money … and when Tom was leaving he said ……..'

Mother interrupted Melissa, 'Eat your dinner and be quiet girl.' Mrs Valair spoke nervously and I noticed that her hand was trembling.

I asked Melissa, 'What did Tom say as he was leaving Melissa … honey?'

'He said he would want the rest of the money when she had gone.'

I looked at Mrs Valair and her face was red. She began to cough and excused herself from the table.

After dinner I returned to Ruby's room to pack a bag. Mrs Valair knocked softly and came into the room. She sat on the bed and tried to console me, 'You may take as many of Ruby's clothes or belongings as you wish. Do you know where you will be going?'

I continued packing my bag, 'Does it matter? … Do you care? … I came with nothing and I will leave with even less.'

She handed me an envelope, 'Here … this should help you to get started again.'

159

I was angry and spun to meet her eyes which were full of sadness, 'I don't want your money ... I have just had my heart torn from me and all you can do is offer me money.'

Mrs Valair lifted her hands to her face and began to cry, 'I ... I am sorry ... what have I done?'

I began to tremble ... I felt frightened. I asked her, 'What ... have you done?'

She lifted her head from her hands and her face was contorted with hate, 'Why did you have to turn up like a bad penny? I knew about you and my daughter ... planning to get married ... do you really believe I would have stood by and been humiliated by a cheap whore like you? ... Yes! You look shocked ... I saw you being familiar with my husband ... Who do you think you are, coming into my home and making everyone unhappy?'

I stared into her eyes, 'What have you done?'

She pointed to the brooch which Ruby had bought for me, 'You wear you brooch where your heart is ... Black Widow. I stopped you! ... That is what I have done ... I paid the two boys to get you to leave our town. Nobody was supposed to be hurt ... I just wanted Ruby to realise what a whore you are ... I wanted the boys to show her what you were really like.'

'Now I understand ... the two boys were meant to drug me ... and then Ruby was intended to catch me having sex with the two of them ... and of course I would have been sent away with my bags packed the next day. So your plan went wrong ... You should know that you cannot rely on youth and lust. The boys' could not resist two for the price of one. Ruby had an adverse reaction to the drug used and died. Game over.'

Mrs Valair sat crying on the bed with her head held in her hands, 'Why didn't you die instead of Ruby? ... Then everything would have been fine.'

Lotus was trying to come out, but I wanted to vent my anger without her help; I refused to let Lotus steal my rage. I was so angry I felt like killing her myself, 'You hypocritical 'two-faced', evil bitch. You dictate the right's and wrong's from your lists of petty rules as you sit on your throne of perfection ... And what are you really? ... You should be a politician! Dictating what is correct while offering the cup of friendship in one hand ... which must be held in accordance with etiquette. And as you smile over the rim of your delicate china cup, you drop your poison when no one is looking, from the hand which is always hidden behind shame ...'

She sat sobbing on the bed. I told her I was leaving immediately and threw the golden Black Widow brooch onto her lap, 'Here! Pin it on! The medal is yours ... four deaths in four weeks because your precious etiquette was threatened. Well done .... mother!'

ON YOUR MARKS! SET! ... GO!

I walked along a lonely road. It was dark and the stars were shining brightly. I sat down on a large boulder and stared into the dark night sky. There were millions of white dots ... each of the stars seemed alone like me. I could hear the wind humming its solitary tune of random notes stolen from the air, which is everywhere, while trying to find somewhere ... a simple energy of movement which will sail the mighty ships and will lift the metal of aeroplanes to meet with the gods of illusion who made the world round, so we may play our games and run as fast as we can ... to always return to the place from whence we started ......

~~~

Did you like that Wordcatcher?"
"What?"
"My poetic philosophy."
"Yes."
"And did you like my story?"
"Yes."
"Can I kiss you?"
"Yes."
"*Mmmmmmmmmmmmm!* Was that nice darling?"
"Y ... Yes."
"Would you like to meet Lotus?"
" ...."
"You didn't say yes darling.

~~~

I was given a lift by a long distance lorry driver. It's strange when you 'hitch-hike'. You may be given a ride and travel half a mile ... or hundreds of miles ... you never know until you ask where your journey will end. Lotus loved the mystery of travelling anywhere and everywhere. She didn't like routine or seeing the same people ... she didn't like people much anyway and yet she liked to help them, especially if they were suffering. As the lorry drove through the night I began to fall asleep while Lotus spoke to me as she often did, *'What is the use of going up ... you only have to come back down, and down is real because you know where you are and what you must do. I can't stand people who smile and stab you in the back ... if you're going to stab someone then just do it' why mess about doing it nicely. Pain is real and tells you where you are, and best of all it lets people know who you are ... or where I am. We are the most destructive species on the planet ... we kill everything, including ourselves and then when everything is destroyed we will start again ... if we get the chance. What you see is what you get with me ... Yes! I may kiss you ... and it may be the last thing you ever remember, but ....'*

I fell asleep in the lorry as Lotus whispered sweet nothings into my ear. I suppose even she had to speak to someone ... I didn't mind listening ... I was grateful to her for helping me to take revenge against Ruby's killers. It was as if we had worked together as a team. Sometimes I know that what she says is right. She has her little faults, but then we all do! Don't we?

The lorry moved from the night into the dawn. Country and Western music was playing as I opened my eyes. I felt like my back had seized-up. I stretched and moved about as much as I could. The driver, who was a bald man of about 35 years of age told me, 'We will be at the end of the drive soon. You can stretch your legs then; there will be a café if you want to grab something to eat and drink.'

The long articulated lorry stopped and I thanked the man for the ride. I was now on the other side of the country. I breathed deeply and stretched out my arms. Today was the first day of the rest of my life.

Feeling refreshed after washing in the 'Ladies Room', I ordered a big breakfast and lots of tea. I didn't know where I was, or where I was going to go, but I was happy and I knew something would happen; be it good or bad. I was wearing jeans and a cardigan under a short fawn coat with a sheep-skin collar. All my meagre belongings were held in a cloth bag. As I walked down the road I was experiencing an amazing feeling of freedom. I felt like skipping and singing and whistling ... it was as if life was nothing but a game. I told myself how lucky I was to be completely free. I watched as cars rushed by full of people living busy lives full of problems, commitments and debts; people chasing the fingers of the clock while not realising, that if they ever do succeed in their life-long ambition to dance the minuet's minute minute, and pass the finger of time ... it will soon revolve to greet with them within infinity. Several hours past by and the sun began to shine. I found myself beside a running track. There were athletics races taking place so I wandered in and sat on the grass to watch. There were lots of young girls, women, boys and men who were dressed in shorts and vests; waiting for the next race, and jogging around the outside of the track. I removed my jeans and took off my top. I felt free and I could feel the hot sun on my legs. I was wearing the training shoes that Ruby had bought me to go running in with her. We had done a lot of running and sprinting as we liked to keep fit, but I had never seen anything like this before. I watched as the different races took place. There were boys and men's races, and girls and women's races. There were short sprints and races which seemed to go on for half an hour. I was fascinated, and as I watched, my adrenalin began pumping. I felt like running. Lotus called to me, *'Go and do it ... it looks painful to me ... Go on do it!'*

I thought Lotus was joking, 'Of course it looks painful ... it would be wouldn't it ... dashing around in a circle to see who may win ... Ah! Win what?' I presumed there must be some nice prizes for the winners.

I walked around to where the table was with the runners' paper numbers. I asked a lady if I might have a race. She looked at me and replied, 'Hurry up, there is only the 1500 metres left for women and that starts in ten minutes.'

'Yes please! I will run in that.'

'What is your name?'

'Emerald.'

'Second name?'

'Lotus.'

'Woman?'

'What do you think?'

'Don't be cheeky! What club are you in?'

'Do I have to be in a club?'

'Yess! You ... have ... to ... be ... in ... a ... club!'

'Well! ... I am in the *'Black Widows"*

'Oh! That's not a local club!'

'No! It's a new club.'

'What is your age?'

'I am 21.'

'And what is your P.B.?'

'Err ..........P...B....?'

'Your 'Personal Best' time for the distance?'

'Oh! I can't remem............'

'Oh! Hurry! You will be late! ... Here is your number and four pins ... that will cost 50 pence please? You can get changed over there!' The lady pointed to a sports centre, and I thought it best not to tell her that I had ... already changed.

I copied the women who were warming up near the start line. I must have looked a bit strange as most of the women were wearing brief shorts; I was wearing black knickers and a black low-cut vest. The girls were stretching and doing short sprints on the track. I asked a tall girl with long dark hair how many laps the race was. She began laughing and ran away from me. I joined the girls on the track and tried a few sprints. I succeeded in gaining a fan club from the male section of runners who were sitting in the spectators stand. As I sprinted, my breasts were bouncing out of my shirt while my knickers decided to become a thong. The guys didn't seem to mind and began 'wolf-whistling' at me. Lotus was not amused, *'You always have to spoil things don't you?'*

'Well! It was you who wanted to do this Lotus ... shall we leave then?'

Lotus hissed, *'I never run away.'*

A marshal blew a whistle and I followed about twelve women around to the other side of the track. All the women put their toes against a white line ... so I did the same ... Lotus groaned ... *'Ahhhh! ... I can feel the pain already!'*

The race was underway. I could not believe how fast the start was ... it was like a sprint. I was trapped in the middle of the girls and being carried along with them. Elbows were digging into my ribs and the sharp spikes from their shoes stung my shins. Lotus 'came out', ***'Don't push me you fucking bitch."*** One girl was sent flying through the air and four others fell over her. I shouted to Lotus, 'Don't make my eyes black.'

Lotus hissed, *'Shut up!'*

Another girl fell over as Lotus clipped her heels from behind, ***'Ah! Sorry bitch.'***

A girl overtook and Lotus nudged her whilst discretely catching her foot with hers, ***'Woops! Sorry.'***

By the time we were on the third lap, girls were strewn around the track holding their legs and ankles. I knew we were starting the last lap because a bell had been rung. There was only one other girl left in the race with me. We ran side by side down the home straight as men whistled and cheered ... I felt as if my lungs were about to burst and I was going to die. We ran side by side towards the finish line ... Lotus looked across at the runner next to us and hissed ... the girl must have seen Lotus' eyes as her face turned completely white and her mouth dropped open. Lotus flew like the wind through the line and we had won. I lay flat on my back gasping for air. I felt like my chest had been filled with acid and every muscle in my body was about to explode. I shouted out, 'I never would have believed so much pain existed ... Lotus shouted to me, *'Yessss! Let's do it again!'*

A marshal walked over to me with a clip-board. I was still lying on my back in an attempt to resuscitate myself. He leaned over me and began to ask me questions. He was about sixty years of age and had one of those massive curly moustaches which twisted into a spiral at either side, 'Could you pull your vest from between your *'err emm!* Breasts please? I need to see your number! And well done ... you are the new Northern 1500 metre ladies champion ... subject to any complaints of interference ... This is supposed to be a non-contact sport you know?'

'Yes I know! ... I have never seen women being so unladylike before! ... Look at the cuts on my shins! How much have I won?'

'What did you say?'

'I asked ... How much is the prize for winning?'

'Don't be silly ... this is amateur athletics.'

Lotus laughed, *'Ha Harr all that for nothing for you! ... Well it was everything for me!'*

'Well make the best of it because you won't be doing it again.'

'*You really are a selfish bitch.*'

I was sweating after the race so decided to take a shower in the sports centre. The water was hot and I massaged my legs with shower gel. The showers were full of women runners and they talked together in groups. I was disappointed that I had no prize. My legs were aching … I was tired … I was hungry … and the last thing I wanted was trouble. The tall woman with dark hair whom I had spoken to before the race, shouted over to me. She was standing with a group of runners from our race, 'Do you know how many laps the race is now?'

The women burst into peels of laughter. I didn't want any trouble … I just wanted to leave and find somewhere to eat and sleep. I still had my 'visa card' which Ruby had given me. The card had been given to me by her and I believed I had every right to use it ... The tall girl continued speaking to me, 'Couldn't you afford proper running clothes … or are you punting for business?' Once more the shower room echoed from the sound of women's laughter.

Lotus was excited, '*Let's fight? … Come on! … Let's fight?*'

I spoke to her in my mind, 'We are going to leave here … you have had what you wanted so behave.'

I stepped from the shower and began to dry myself. I reached for a communal hair dryer lying on a shelf and the tall girl grabbed it from me. I turned away and began to dress myself. Lotus was finding it hard to contain herself, '*Let me smash her teeth … I promise not to hurt her too much … I wont kill her if that's what your worried about.*'

'Stop it Lotus.'

I slid into my jeans, finished dressing and moved to leave the showers. The women were standing in my way. The tall woman said, 'I think you owe me and the other girls an apology for acting like a wild animal.'

I really wanted to leave quietly, and I could feel a volcano bubbling from deep inside myself. 'I apologise to you and the other girls ... now can I go please?'

The tall woman grabbed my face with her hand and I could feel her nails cutting into my skin, 'You common tart ... I'm going to give you a slapping you will never forget.'

She moved her hand from my face and Lotus 'came out.' My foot flew into her groin and she began to double over ... as she bent forwards my knee lifted and met with her jaw which seemed to snap as it dislocated sideways. I screamed to Lotus '*Stop! ... Stop!* ... You will kill her!' Lotus continued. Before the woman hit the floor my foot kicked her in her nose which exploded, splattering blood all over the tiled walls. The woman lay groaning on the floor while all the other women stood like frozen statues. I picked up my bag and pushed through the women ... Lotus had to have the last word ... she cackled loudly in her deep groaning voice as we were leaving, '*She was right! That certainly was a slapping I will never forget.*'

CANDY

As I walked from the track I could feel Lotus inside me. I felt like my whole inside was bubbling ... boiling ... with excitement and energy. I tried to reason with Lotus, 'You have to control yourself.'

'*I saved you from that bitch.*'

'I know you did ... thank you!'

'*Don't mention it ... any time.*'

'That's the problem Lotus ... you are always looking and waiting for trouble.'

'*That's because it is always waiting to pounce ... you have to be prepared ... see what happened with those two lads when you didn't watch ... they took you and.....*'

'I remember what happened.'

'*And yet you still repress me.*'

'You frighten me.'

'*Why?*'

'Because if I wasn't there with you in the shower room, you would have killed that woman.'

'*You were there and you always will be ... how can you not be there, and if you were not there, then why worry anyway?*'

'Sometimes I am watching and you do things ... like with that girl who was bullying Melissa.'

'*But she was going to kill us.*'

'You don't know that! ... Do you?'

'*Well if I waited to find out neither of us would be here now discussing what happened ... would we?*'

'I suppose you could be right.'

'*I only do what is best for us. Remember one thing ... I am not self-destructive ... I touch pain and yet I know I must exist to experience, experience.*'

'We seem to be communicating a lot better now Lotus.'

'*Yes ... we do.*'

'We must try and work together.'

'*But it's not fair Emerald ... you make all the decisions.*'

'But you are too aggressive and violent to be in control.'

'*Yes! ... I understand ... but don't forget me ... will you?*'

'How could I ever forget you?'

I was walking into another city. It was 9 p.m. and the street lights created shadows where secrets whispered, hidden from whatever vision was reflected from a truth to be denied. I was standing on a street and it was still and silent. I was at a crossroads and as I stood beneath a street light I tried to decide which way to go. I was startled by a woman's voice shouting at me from a dark doorway, 'Fuck off bitch this is my patch.'

I realised I was in a 'bad' area so I crossed the road and continued walking ... a car pulled alongside me. The car's window was down and a man shouted to me, 'Are you working luv?'

'Yes I'm an undercover policewoman ... what's your name?'

The car drove away quickly and I walked faster down the street. I came to a nice looking public house. It looked quiet inside and there was a sign in the window saying that meals were being served. Starving, I went inside and sat at a table. I ordered a drink and a lasagne with boiled potatoes. The pub was warm and music played softly from a jukebox. I closed my eyes to bathe in the peace and tranquillity. A voice shouted in my head, '*It's too quiet in here.*' I whispered, 'Go to sleep Lotus.'

I ate my meal and ordered another glass of wine. I noticed an attractive woman with short blonde hair sitting at the bar. Her skin was fair and she was small and slim … petite and fragile looking. She was wearing a short grey coat and skirt, black stockings and black stiletto shoes. She was very attractive …… Lotus interrupted me, '*You're going after women again are you?*'

'Get lost Lotus.'

I noticed the woman at the bar was drinking double vodkas, and she had ordered at least four while I had been eating. She had a pretty face but looked sad … I began to imagine what her problems might be … maybe her husband was having an affair … maybe she had just lost her job.

I decided to leave the pub as it was 10.30 p.m. and I still had to find a bed and breakfast place to stay for the night. I walked to the bar as I had to pay at the till before leaving. I handed the barman my 'visa card' and looked at the blonde lady who appeared to be drunk and was smoking a cigarette. The barman shouted to me, 'Sorry! This card is showing invalid madam.'

'Oh! Are you sure?'

My heart began pounding … I half expected this to happen and I had no money. The man said, 'No! I am sorry madam … the card is invalid … I must ask you for cash please?'

I rummaged in my cloth bag wishing I could be, simply swallowed up inside it and vanish. My face must have been bright red, 'Oh! I seem to have left my purse at home!'

The man began to pick up the phone as he told me, 'I am sorry madam but you will have to wait while I call the police.'

It was all too much for me and I broke down crying. I was tired, homeless and had been through hell at the athletics track. The blonde woman who was sitting close by shouted, 'What the hell is going on over there?'

The barman seemed to know the woman and answered her, 'This lady has no money to pay for her meal.'

I shouted out through my sobs, 'I ... I have forgotten my purse.'

The woman began to laugh as she swayed drunkenly, 'How ... how much does she owe you ... 2000 pounds?'

'No ... her bill is for twelve pounds fifty.'

'Well! Will you stop yelling if I pay it for you?'

'Y ... Yes.'

The lady handed the barman a twenty-pound note, 'Here and give her a drink as well ... anyone would think there was an armed robbery going on or something. Now! Stop whinging and sit next to me.'

I sat next to the woman and I ordered a glass of wine ... Lotus told me she liked the woman and could sense her pain. The woman looked at me and I could tell by her eyes she was drunk. She was about 25 years of age and was very attractive. She gave me the impression of being very 'street-wise' and very strong if she had to be. She held out her hand to me, 'My name's Candy, what's yours? Ha! Let me guess ... Green eyes! ... Emerald!'

I couldn't believe she had guessed my name, 'WOW! How did you know that?'

'I'm a genius, and you're beautiful ... are you working around here?'

'No! I have just moved here.'

'Oh! Where are you staying?'

I was left staring into Candy's eyes ... I burst into tears.

'For God's sake! She's at it again ... so you've nowhere to stay ... stop making that row ... you can stay with me ... what the hell ... why not?'

The barman interrupted with a sly grin, 'She can stay with me if she wants to.'

Candy shouted, 'Piss off Pedro.'

It only took a few minutes before we arrived at Candy's apartment. She was staggering due to her drunkenness and mumbled, 'We're upstairs, *Shhhh!* An old 'nag bag' is living on the bottom floor.'

We climbed the stairs and found ourselves facing the door to Candy's flat. She fumbled in her handbag for the door key and we walked in. I was standing in a large lounge which had an archway in one wall. Through the archway was the kitchen and in the opposite wall of the lounge was a door. The room was clean and tidy and contained a two-seater settee a T.V. and a cabinet. The room was well cared for; it looked as if it had been recently decorated and had a new carpet. Candy opened the door which led from the lounge. She asked me to follow her and we entered her bedroom, which had one double bed, a wardrobe, a dressing table and two chairs, 'Leave your bag in here ... do you want a drink?'

'Yes please! I will have a cup of tea.'

Candy dropped her arms down by her side and pulled a silly expression with her face, 'For God's sake! Tea! Do you want some drinking chocolate of maybe a warm glass of milk and some biscuits?'

'*Ooo!* That sounds lovely! Thank you.'

Lotus shouted to me, '*Why do you always have to make me look like a fool?*'

I was surprised at Lotus, 'What do you mean?'

'*Emerald! .... Oh! ... Forget it*'

Candy came from the kitchen and handed me a glass of warm milk. She had a bottle of Vodka from which she filled a large glass for herself. She was sat next to me on the settee and brought her legs up over mine. She shouted to me, 'Bring your legs up so I can see you! ... That's right.'

We were sat facing each other and Candy pulled my shoes off. She nodded towards her feet which I presumed to mean she wanted me to remove her shoes. I removed her black high-heeled shoes and she groaned from the relief.

She slid forwards slightly as she made herself comfortable and her short grey skirt slid up above her stockings. Her thighs were white and I could see her black suspenders which gave an illusion of secret power against the feminine pureness of her silky fair skin. I began to rub her feet and she groaned from the relief, '*Oooo! I've never had that done before Oooo! That's wonderful.*' She took a drink from her glass and stared at me ... I looked back into her eyes, she said, 'I will tell you one thing! ... You're one of the most attractive women I have ever seen ... Your eyes are amazing ... a person could ... disappear for ever into your eyes ... you're beautiful.'

I wriggled my feet close to Candy in the hope that she might massage them as they were aching from the running I had done. She laughed while telling me, 'Drink your milk and I will tell you a bedtime story.'

I rubbed my hands together and chuckled, 'Oh! Goody!'

Lotus shouted in my head, '*Are you really stupid or did the girl at the gym bang your head?*'

Candy laughed, 'You can't be for real! ... Are you for real?'

I smiled and began to cry, 'I ... I am sorry ... it's been a long day and ... and ....'

Candy shouted to me, 'Don't start the water works again ... your face is too pretty for tears. Now if you're tired go to bed ... I'm not your mother.'

'I really am exhausted Candy ... I will go to bed if you don't mind.'

'No I don't mind babe ... Go to bed and we can talk tomorrow ... and go on the left side of the bed.'

I stood up and felt awkward ... I turned my head towards Candy's to kiss her and say 'Good-night.' She raised her hand to stop me, 'What are you doing?'

'I am saying 'Good-night.''

Candy shouted, 'There's nothing good about it. Go to bed.'

As I left the lounge Candy poured herself another drink. I jumped into her bed and made sure I was on the left side. I took all my clothes off and lay naked in the bed. I thought of Candy's naked thighs and her pretty little face, and the strength she seemed to have. I liked her and found her extremely sexy. I was disappointed when she did not let me kiss her ... She seemed very perceptive and I wondered if she knew what I was thinking ... I wanted to kiss her 'Good-Night' and I wanted to explore every inch of her body with my tongue. I wondered if she knew the pleasures I could bring to her. I was asleep ...

I was awoken by Candy getting undressed by the bed ... Through the darkness of the room a street light threw beams through a tiny gap in the curtains. I peeped from under the sheets as she undressed. She was swaying about as she dropped her skirt onto the floor. Her beauty took my breath away. She was standing with her back to me and was wearing tiny black knickers and the black suspender belt which I had seen earlier. Her bottom was round and firm looking; I wanted to reach out and feel her soft skin. She removed her stockings and fell onto the bed ... my heart was pounding as I pretended to be asleep. She removed her top and bra. The light from the window seemed to stroke her breasts which were small and firm-looking and appeared to merge into her large brown nipples which stood proud in the centre of wide-pooled circles of brown.

She climbed into bed and lay next to me on her back. I moved my hand onto her stomach and she groaned as if half asleep and dreaming. I slid my fingers between her thighs and she was dry. I slid down her body, running my wet tongue over her breasts. Sliding further down, I pushed my face between her legs and slid my tongue into her; wetting her with my mouth, and began to play with her ...

there was no movement from her body and no sound from her lips. I slid back up her body to look into her face ... her eyes were open and her face held a blank expression ... as if sleeping with her eyes wide open. I kissed her lips and her mouth opened slightly ... I pushed my tongue deep into her mouth and kissed her passionately. There was something wrong ... it was as if we were making love, and yet I was doing all the loving. I lifted my head and looked into her eyes. She stared at me and smiled and asked softly, 'Have you finished? ... I'm tired!'

I was astounded ... stunned, 'B ... But?'

'But what babe ... Let's go to sleep!'

'But didn't you like my loving you?'

'Did you like it?'

'Yes!'

'Have you finished?'

'Y ... Yes!'

'Then let's go to sleep ... I'm tired.'

'B ... But don't you want to make love with me?'

'Why would I want to make love with you?'

'You said I was beautiful!'

'I think thousands of things are beautiful ... I think my bottle of Vodka is beautiful but it doesn't mean I want to make love to it ... then again babe *Haa Haar* I suppose I have a deep loving relationship with my bottle every night. No offence intended babe ... don't let me stop you ... you have your needs ... I don't mind but hurry up I need some sleep ... Oh! Have you finished? Good! ... Sleep well and I hope you don't snore!'

I lay awake staring at the ceiling. I was absolutely amazed. I had just made love to a woman who had simply turned around and spoken to me as if I had been reading a story from a book to her.

I could hear laughter rising from deep inside myself. It was Lotus, "*Har Ha Ha Harr Har Ha Harr I like this woman ... it's about time you had things my way for once Har Ha Ha*

Harr Har Ha Harr Har Ha Ha Harr Har Ha Harr Har Ha Ha Har.'

I woke up and looked at the clock which was by Candy's side of the bed. It was 9 a.m. I remembered the night before and bit my lip. I thought to myself, *'You stupid fool.'* I wondered how I could face Candy after what had happened. I remembered my ...... I didn't even want to remember it ... I imagined her lay there after going to bed and ... and having someone you have helped, try to rape you. I could see her now lying there in fear and shock as another woman began to ... *Oh! No!*

I was so ashamed I slipped slowly from the bed and got dressed ... I just wanted to slip away and to never have to face her again. I would leave her a letter of thanks and apologise for my unspeakable behaviour. I had just pulled on my jeans, when I had the fright of my life. A hand slapped me on the bottom and Candy's voice shouted out, 'Morning babe! ... Stick the kettle on ... my mouth's like a cesspit ... and will you bring my cigarettes from the lounge?'

I was speechless, 'Y ... Yes ... sure.' I switched the kettle on and found the tea and coffee. I took Candy her cigarettes and asked her, 'How do you like it?'

She began to laugh and replied, 'Wet!'

I looked in the bedroom mirror and my face was bright red, 'No I ... I ... mean ... I mean ......'

She interrupted me, 'Don't worry I was tired last night ... if you want to do it again pick a better time ... I have my coffee white with two sugars please.'

I rushed off into the kitchen and made our drinks. I was at a loss for words and decided to simply carry on as if nothing had happened ... Candy didn't seem offended by my touching her ... she said she had been tired ... and she had, had a lot to drink ... maybe she did want a relationship with me after all. Candy drank her coffee and asked me where I had come from. I told her the truth about Ruby dying, except I said she had died in a car accident. Candy jumped from the bed and stretched ... I felt like throwing my arms around her and hugging her naked body ... I felt alone and needed love ... I couldn't help the way I felt. Candy opened a door that I hadn't noticed and there was a shower. She walked in and turned on the water. I sat on the bed drinking tea. Candy shouted to me, 'Come here babe.'

My mind began to fill with thoughts of love. The shower was all steamy, but I could see her shapely body clearly. She had her back to me and passed me a loofah and a bar of soap, 'Wash my back babe.'

I rubbed soap onto the louver and began to rub her between the shoulder blades. She sighed from the pleasure, '*Ahhh!* That's brilliant.'

I slid the loofah down her spine and she groaned, 'Harder! ... Press harder!'

She had placed her hands on the shower cubicle wall and was pushing her bottom out towards me ... her bottom was covered in soap ... I could not resist ... I slid my bare hand over her and let my fingers slip between her legs ... my hand was shaking from excitement ....

Candy laughed and threw her head back, 'Not again ... you're a horny little bitch aren't you?'

She turned around and said, 'Throw me that towel ... No! The large one ... thanks! Do you want a shower babe?' I shook my head. 'No! Well anytime you want a shower just have one. Hey! Stop puffing your lips out and looking all sad ... what are you crying for? ... You really are a sentimental softy aren't you? Come on let's have some breakfast.'

We walked into the kitchen and Candy told me to sit down. She was wearing jeans and a tiny pink top which left the middle of her body bare. I was wearing the same sort of clothes only my top was light blue. Candy offered me some cereal and toast and we sat at the table to eat. I leaned across the table to reach for some butter and Candy touched my stomach, 'What's that babe? ... That red mark on your stomach ... I've never seen anything like that before.'

'I've had it all my life ... it's a birth mark.'

'*Yeh!* Cool! It looks like an hourglass.'

We ate our breakfast and I still felt confused. Lotus whispered to me, '*Go on! ... Mess everything up! ... You always do! ... You can't keep your big mouth shut can you?*'

We finished our breakfast and Candy offered me a cigarette. 'No thanks honey, I don't smoke.'

I looked into her eyes as she blew smoke into the air and smiled. I found her beauty stunning ... she was so small and petite and yet she was like a 'tomboy'; strong and clever ... she gave me a great feeling of security ... I longed to be with her ... I mean .... Lotus shouted, '*I know what you mean ... you have to be in love and be all soppy ... you have to have things your own way and then when it all goes wrong, I'm left to pick up the pieces ... Why can't you leave things as they are for once? ... I like this woman.*'

Candy frowned, 'What are you crying for now?'

'I don't know where I stand with you!'

'I don't understand Emerald! What do you want?'

'I want to know if I mean anything to you?'

'What do you want to mean to me?'

'I ... I think I love you?'

Lotus shouted at me, '*Here we go ... I knew this would happen.*'

Candy smiled and stared at me, 'You have only known me for a few hours baby. Now! It's no good looking sad and frowning over those big green eyes ... If you want me to love you I will ... If you want to love me you can ... Are you happy now?'

'Yes!'

'Good! I will be anything you want ... just promise me to stop bloody crying.'

I jumped up and hugged Candy. She put her hand onto my shoulder and puffed her cigarette.

Suddenly through the silence, the *'William Tell'* overture sounded from a mobile phone like an instant panic to remind us that the world of reality is always waiting for the press of a button. Candy stared at the phone and read her text message. She looked at me and sighed deeply, 'Oh! Time to go to work.'

I was excited, 'Oh! Where do you work? Can I come with you and get a job?'

Candy smiled softly, 'Yes! I don't see why not.'

I cried out excitedly, *'Yesss! ... Yesss!* Where do you ... I mean we work?'

'I work for an 'Escort Agency' and I think we would be a great team ... guys will pay a fortune to watch two women like us having sex ... sorry ... making love.'

I burst into tears ...... Lotus burst into laughter, *'You never listen to me do you? ... Let me go with her? ... There will be lots of trouble! ... I know there will! ... Can I go? ... Please?'*

I was instantly submerged into reality. I understood everything now. While I was making love to Candy she was probably working out our prospective 'Job Opportunities.' I felt like I had been on a job interview ... there I was with my head between her legs tasting Candy, while she was planning our career together. I stopped crying and ran after her into the bedroom, 'How could you?'

'How could I what?'

'You let me be intimate with you and all you were thinking about was how much money we might make.'

'Intimate! ... You went down on me and gave me a 'blow job' ... Why call it some fancy word?'

'Because to me it was love.'

'O.K! It's love ... now let's go and make money.'

Candy had dressed up as a nurse and tied her short hair into pig-tails, 'That's me ready for work.'

I shouted at her, 'You look pathetic.'

'Pathetic enough to earn one hundred pounds in half an hour ... what will you earn today.'

'I will find a job ... a proper job ... how can you do it?'

'I don't do it ... they do it ... just the same as you did last night ... Oh! And don't worry that was free.'

'*Ooooooooow!*'

'I will be home soon ... here's a key in case you go out.'

'I won't be here when you get back ... '*WHORE!*''

'Of course you will ... you love me.'

'I hate you.'

'Do you hate to love me, or love to hate me? Either way you need me.'

'*Why didn't you go with her you selfish bitch?*'

'I hate you as well Lotus.'

I decided to go into the city and find a job. I had no money but I saw a twenty pound note on the kitchen worktop so I took it and swore to pay it back as soon as I got paid. I jumped on a bus and was in the city centre within minutes. I searched the city's shops asking if there were any vacancies. I was told '*Sorry*' a hundred times before I came across a sign in a window which read:-

Vacancy.
Switchboard operator required.
Apply within.

I was tired and this seemed like my last hope. I didn't want to return to Candy's without having found a job, but there was only one problem with the job opportunity facing me, and that was it was in the window of a police station.

I was experiencing a feeling of guilt ... my heart was pumping and I felt as if I had done something wrong. I remembered my last job on a switchboard and how I liked being alone. I was tempted; I might have my own little office again to work in. I decided that they could only say 'no', so in I walked. The police station was busy inside. I saw an elderly man standing behind one end of the reception desk. I told him I wished to apply for the job on the switchboard. He led me through a doorway and asked me to take a seat. A girl, who appeared to be about the same age as me, was sat facing me. She had her bare legs crossed and her arms folded. She was chewing gum as if it was the last piece on earth; frightened that someone might snatch it from her. She was wearing a short white skirt. She stared at me with wide, unblinking eyes. I felt uncomfortable. She asked me, 'What are you in for?'

I replied, 'I'm applying for a job.'

'What! To be a copper?'

'No! In an office.'

"Ave ye' got a ciggy?'

'No! I don't smoke.'

There was a short silence; I felt uncomfortable as the girl kept staring at me. Lotus whispered to me, *'Go on! Now's the time … say something stupid you always do.'*

'Are you here for a job?'

The girl began to laugh, *'Yeh!* A blow job … *Har Ha Ha Harr Har Ha Harr.'*

The door opened and a policeman shouted at the girl, 'Through here you!'

The girl walked away swaying her hips and pushed her bottom in the air towards the officer. She asked him seductively, 'Can I have a job sir?'

The officer replied, 'Yes of course you can … you can clean your cell.'

The door closed and I waited for Lotus to ridicule me but nothing was said. A lady popped her head around the door and asked me to follow her. She took me into an office and began to ask me questions. I told her that I had worked on a switchboard for several years and that I left my job because I had moved to a different area. She asked me the name of the firm I had worked for, and after filling in several forms she took me to a room where the switchboard was. I fell in love with the room straight away. It was small and bright with only one chair which meant I would be working alone. I was introduced to a lady who must have been in her late fifties, 'Emerald ... this is Ann.'

We shook hands and I was left alone with Ann while she explained what the job involved. The switchboard was familiar, and Ann said she could tell I would have no problem working it. I told her the one I had worked on previously was a lot bigger. She explained she was retiring at the end of the week and they needed a replacement operator quickly.

The lady who had interviewed me returned and told me she had contacted my previous employer. They had given me a good reference, but seemed concerned because I had left suddenly as my home had been burnt down. I began to cry and the lady put her arm around me, 'Don't worry my love you will be looked after here, we are one big team here and we all work together. Now! Here's a tissue to dry those pretty green eyes; wait here while I fetch you some tea.'

'Thank you ... you are so kind.'

'You should be nominated for an Oscar.'

'Get lost Lotus.'

I returned to Candy's to find she had not returned home. I looked in the cupboards and found some food and cooked a meal. I left some on a plate for Candy and turned on the T.V.

I must have fallen into a deep sleep because I was awoken by Candy returning home. She was wearing a fur coat over her nurse's uniform, and she was drunk. I looked at the clock and it was 11.30 p.m. I was lying on the settee when, suddenly, she fell on top of me as she took her coat off. She began kissing me in a silly way while laughing and telling me over and over, 'I love you ... I love you ... I love you.'

I stood up and I told her I had cooked her something to eat. Candy found the latter hilarious and spoke to me with a condescending attitude, 'Oh! You have been at home cooking all day ... What time do you call this to be coming home? ... I suppose you have been drinking with the guys at the pub *Har Ha Ha Harr Har Ha Harr!*'

'You're not funny Candy and I am going to bed ... and don't worry I wont touch you ... I might catch something.'

Candy fell onto the settee laughing, '*Har Ha Ha Harr Har Ha Harr Har Ha Ha Harr Har Ha Harr!*'

I marched into the bedroom and fell onto the bed laughing, '*Har Ha Ha Harr Har Ha Harr Har Ha Ha Harr Har Ha Harr!*'

I loved Candy ... she was wild.

When Candy came to bed I pretended to be asleep. As usual she was drunk, or possibly more drunk than usual. I watched as she undressed and wished she was mine. Lotus told me to keep my mouth shut for once and to go to sleep. I was almost asleep when Candy fell into bed. She seemed to always fall into bed ... she never lifted the sheets to gently lie down ... she was like a bloody horse. I peeped at her and began to breathe heavily as if I was asleep. She was lying on her back as she had the previous night; her eyes were open and she was staring at the ceiling. She suddenly shouted, 'I know you're awake.' She jumped on top of me laughing and pushed her crotch onto my mouth. I bit her and she screamed, 'You bitch.'

She jumped away and I bit one of her nipples. She put her hands in the air and shouted, 'I give in! ... I give in!'

Lotus shouted to me, '*Wow! This is fun! Shall I eat her?*'

Candy lay back on the bed panting, 'You're not as quiet as I thought. You're a wild bitch aren't you?'

'Yes! I suppose I am … deep down.'

We both laughed and I held Candy's hand. Her hand was limp but she didn't pull away. I suppose that was a beginning. We both fell into a deep sleep. Our heads were turned towards each other and our faces were only inches apart. Fortunately Candy did not open her eyes because facing her, were two black staring holes. Lotus liked Candy; wild and unpredictable. Lotus had never bitten anyone before and her mouth was wet as saliva dribbled down her face and onto the pillow. Her eyes moved down to look at Candy's pointed breasts. She could see the bruise from her bite and craved for more. The feeling she had was almost uncontrollable … it was an urge Lotus could not understand and did not want to give into; she liked Candy and wanted to save her … and yet part of her wanted to bite and bite and bite into her body. She sank back into her darkness … she had to.

In the morning we both showered (the shower was large enough for two). We washed each others back and played around like naughty girls. Candy shouted at me, 'You bitch … look at the teeth marks on my tits … I have to use these for work today.'

'Oh! Don't worry it will most likely turn your 'clients' on.'

There was no sex involved; we both realised it would be a waste of time; like trying to get blood from a stone.

I told Candy I had a job. She asked me where, and when I told her it was with the police she was shocked, 'Oh! Will you be arresting me and giving me a caution?'

'Yes …I must warn you that anything you take down, may cause things to be used against you.'

I picked up a large carrot and chased Candy around the room. She fell onto her back with her legs wide open in the air. She shouted, 'I admit it was me officer. I used all the carrots.'

I told Candy I would be working on a switchboard and she scowled at me, 'Are you sure you don't want to try working with me? We could make a film, or put a show on for several guys ... We could earn hundreds of pounds from one show lasting ten minutes and you can do all the things you wanted to do with me.'

'What I wanted to do with you, you have not the ability to understand.'

Candy cuddled up to me and started to 'baby talk', 'Come on, let's have some fun.' She put her hand up my t-shirt and began to feel my breasts. I felt all weak and ...

'Stop it! ... I will never sell myself for sex ... you use sex like a tool.'

Candy became angry, 'And you use sex as a tool for what you want.'

'What do you mean?'

'The first night you stayed ... you tried to seduce me sexually ... we had just met and you used sex for what you wanted.'

'No! I was trying to make love to you.'

'Oh! Love! ... You had known me for only a few hours and you decided you loved me?'

'Love is something that grows between two people, and is shared, and then they will do anything for each other.'

'Well I am asking you to do something for me.'

'But you don't know what love is!'

'I told you I loved you didn't I ... what do you want me to do 'put it in writing' or shout it to the world?'

'You are so cold and crude sometimes Candy.'

'Oh! How sorry I am 'little miss perfect' Emerald.'

'Candy! Have you ever loved anyone or anything besides money?'

'Emerald! Have you ever loved anyone or anything besides yourself?'

'I have never loved for money.'

'Well! Little miss perfect Emerald who never gets her sweet innocent self dirty ... where has the twenty pound note gone I left in the kitchen this morning?'

'I ... I ...'

'You! ... You! ... What?'

'I borrowed it and will pay you back next week from my wages.'

'Oh! But sweet Emerald ... that is dirty money. I was paid for doing dirty things ... but of course ... move the goal posts and justify stealing it.'

I was furious. I screamed, 'I didn't steal it ... I borrowed it.'

'You took it without permission and that's stealing ... tell them that at your new job.'

I was becoming really angry with Candy, '*Owww!* All right then! I will come with you to your sordid brothel and let men do whatever they want with me for a few pounds.' I was angry and expected Candy to tell me to forget it, but I should have been ready for the unexpected.

'Now you're talking! We can earn a fortune ... Good girl! ... Put those 'hot pants on' and those black boots.'

'Candy!'

'What?'

'Fuck off.'

I had been asked to start my new job the next day. It was a Thursday and Ann was to leave on Friday. I spent the day with Ann and she showed me the routine. On Friday I worked the switchboard while Ann helped me, until 5 p.m. when our shift finished. We walked from our office into a barrage of people. We were surrounded by officers carrying bunches of flowers and boxes of chocolates. Ann began to cry and I was worried in case she decided not to leave. We all went across the road to a public house for a drink and the chief inspector gave a speech telling how Ann had been loved, and would be missed by all the staff. After a few hours we all left the pub and a guy offered me a lift home in his car. He stopped outside the flat and remarked, 'Is this where you live? This is a bad area.'

'Oh! I know ... I am staying here temporarily with a friend until I find my own place.'

I bought some fish and chips from a takeaway shop and returned to the flat for a quiet evening's T.V. viewing. It was a waste of time preparing a meal for Candy. I emptied and washed her plate from the previous evening and made some tea. Candy came in about 11 p.m. - drunk as usual. She took off her coat; she was wearing her office suit. She grabbed a sandwich and sat down next to me and asked, 'Wha' 'av' ye' bin doin' today?'

'It's rude to talk with your mouth full and besides ... you're spitting half you sandwich over me.'

'Oh! Well! Forgive me ... I will go out and try to come in and act correctly ... or would you like me to leave?'

I thought for a moment, 'Well ... No! You may stay but behave yourself ... I don't like common people.'

We both burst into laughter as Candy dived on top of me. She threw me to the floor and held me down by my arms. She leaned over me and Lotus tried to bite her breast but luckily missed.

Candy was not amused, 'Stop that biting you vicious bitch.'

'Well! Don't mess that suit up I want to wear it on Monday.'

We sat down and Candy poured a Vodka for herself. 'Do you want a glass of milk and some biscuits ... and then I will read you a bedtime story?'

'*Oooo!* Yes please Candy.'

'You're one hell of a kinky bitch ... it's a shame ... a bloody sin ... you could earn a fortune on the street.'

'I will do my own milk and read a book in bed ... and where are the biscuits?'

'The biscuits are in the jar with the pink teddy bear on ... and you are unbelievable.'

'*Oooow!* Goody ... yum ... yum. I'm going to bed to read ... and do you mind not pouncing on the bed like a horse ... it does not become you.'

Candy sat with her mouth open, speechless. I reached the bedroom biting my lip and then burst into laughter when the door had closed. I ate my supper and read my book. Another day was over and I was happy, and in love.

It was Saturday morning and I awoke to the sweet smell of bacon cooking. I looked at the clock; it was 11.30 a.m. There was a cup of tea by the bed and ... and I was alone. Candy came into the bedroom carrying a tray with a plate on it, '*Oooo!* Candy that's lovely ... eggs and bacon ... What are you after?'

'That's lovely isn't it ... I cook you a breakfast and you think I am after something ... actually I was wondering if.........'

We both began laughing and I ate my breakfast. Candy sat staring at me with a smile on her face ... I stopped eating and asked her, 'Have you put something in this?'

She asked, 'Why, does it taste salty?'

'You bastard!' I threw a pillow at her and then finished my breakfast. I jumped into the shower and tried some of Candy's clothes on. They were tight and I had to sit down slowly in the jeans ... they would suffice until my first wage packet arrived. I walked into the lounge while looking down at a pair of Candy's shoes that I had squeezed my feet into, and that were trying to adapt to being a half size larger. 'These jeans are cutting my arse in two ... look!' I turned around so Candy could see my behind with a massive crevice up the middle where the jeans had decided to act like a cheese knife. I instantly knew something was wrong.

Candy whispered, 'This is John ... he said he gave you a lift home yesterday.'

I looked to my left and the guy whom I had met the previous day, was sat on the settee. He said, 'Oh! I think the pants are fine.'

I was flabbergasted, 'Wha … What? …'

'Don't panic, you left your coat in the pub last night … there you are.' John pointed to the coat.

'Oh! Right! Thanks.'

Candy stood up and grabbed the coat which was hers anyway, 'I am off out now … Watch out John she is looking for someone to love … and she's hot.'

I could not believe what Candy had just said. I shouted at her, 'You're dead when you come back.'

Candy couldn't contain herself, 'And be careful John she bites.' She walked out of the apartment singing the Queen classic………

'Need somebody to love bite
Need somebody to love bite
Can anybody find meee
Somebody to
Love'

I didn't offer John a drink of tea. I told him I had to go out soon. He asked me if I would like to go out with him one evening, but my heart was heavy and I didn't feel attracted to him. I told him we would see what happened, and he left looking sad. I was in love with Candy … it was a one-way trip but I hoped she would, or could have, or develop some feelings for me.

I stayed in the flat waiting for Candy to return. I read a newspaper which John had left and tried to complete a crossword. When Candy came home I told her John was in the bedroom getting dressed. She replied, '*OOOH!* You play for both sides then.'

I hit her with the newspaper and chased her around the flat shouting, 'I'll give you somebody to love bite.'

There was suddenly a loud banging on the door. Candy looked through the security 'spy-hole' … she suddenly went into a panic, 'Quickly ... Quickly, take your clothes off.'

I don't know why I complied but I was naked within seconds. Candy pushed me in front of the door and took the latch off. The door began to slowly open and I could hear an elderly woman's voice, 'You keep the bloody noise down you .... Oh! My God!'

The door had opened to reveal me and Candy, naked in each others arms, kissing passionately.

ROOM 103

Monday morning arrived and I was anxious and excited about starting my new job on the switchboard. I had to be at the police station for 9 a.m. to relieve the person who had been on the nightshift. I was told the nightshift was operated by an ex-police officer who had been crippled in a car chase accident. His name was Peter; a reclusive character who didn't speak much.

I squeezed into Candy's grey suit and put on some black tights. I caught a bus outside the flat and was in the city within minutes. I walked into the station and entered the switchboard office. Peter welcomed me, 'Hi! I wasn't told I would be working with an angel.'

I looked over my shoulder as if Peter was talking to somebody else, 'You're not! ... I'm a little devil really.'

'Well you can take me to hell anytime.'

Peter wheeled his chair away from the switchboard and took his coat from a hook on the door. I sat down and put on the headphones. I just wanted to be alone and get on with my work. Peter shouted, 'I will see you at five!'

I waved to him and the door closed. I rubbed my hands together and looked around my office. There was a coffee table against one of the walls with an electric kettle, tea and milk. I was not allowed to leave the switchboard except for visits to the toilet. At lunchtime a trolley came round with sandwiches and chocolate biscuits on it.

I was all ready to *'Rock and Roll'*. The switchboard was the heart of the police station. Almost all communications passed through my office. I enjoyed my day so much I could not believe it when Peter returned through the door. I looked at him and shouted, '*Oooooow!*'

Peter looked over his shoulder as I had done to him that same morning, 'I am not that ugly am I?'

'No Peter! ... I like it so much I want to stay.'

'Well don't let me stop you ... it's quiet through the night,' Peter smiled jokingly.

'Well! I would stay but I think I may distract you, and I was told you were quiet.'

'Quite a what?' asked Peter.

I returned home to the flat and Candy was cooking, 'I thought I would cook my princess her dinner after a hard day's work ... What's that on my suit?'

I looked and there was a chocolate stain on the skirt, '*Ohhh!* I'm sorry ... I will put some hot soapy water on it.'

Candy placed two plates onto the table. The meal was a kind of stew. I glanced over at the kitchen worktop and I could see several empty tins. There was a tin of beans, a tin of hot-dog sausages, a tin of boiled potatoes and a tin of Irish stew. As we began to eat I said, '*Mmmm!* This is lovely ... it must have taken you ages to cook!'

Candy smiled, '*Mmmm!* Wait till you taste the pudding.'

I tried not to smile as Candy filled two dishes with our desert. I glanced towards the left side of the worktop and saw another collection of empty tins. One was rice pudding, one was custard, and there was a sponge cake box sticking out of the rubbish bin. She placed a large slice of sponge into each dish before tipping the hot mixture over it. She placed my dish in front of me, 'There you are darling, made by my own hands for my hard working partner ... see I do love you after all.'

I was trying not to laugh as Candy was eating her sweet and staring at me whilst making little nods with her head, as if I was eating some rich gourmet dessert. I felt I had to comment on the food to stop her from nodding at me, as I was on the verge of bursting into hysterical laughter, 'This is marvellous darling *Mmmmm!* '

'*Oh!* I'm not just a pretty face you know … it takes years to perfect the art of making a perfect sponge cake … this one has the essence of lemon confined within it.'

I burst into peels of hysterical laughter. Candy froze, staring at me. Her eyes moved slowly sideways and she saw the sponge box popping out of the bin … she shouted angrily at me, 'You bitch! … Come here!'

She chased me around the flat with a large spoon which was covered in custard. When she caught me, she marched me back to the table, 'Now sit down and eat your sponge … bitch.'

I ate until I felt I was going to burst while Candy scowled at me, '*Emmm! Yum! Yum! This is lovely Candy.*'

After 'dinner' I showered and sat down to watch T.V., wearing my bath robe. Candy was messing with her mobile phone. She suddenly sat up straight while announcing, 'That's it … I'm off to work.'

She ran into the bedroom to get changed and left her phone on the settee. The screen was still lit-up with a text message so I picked it up. The message read:-

> ### Candy
> ### The Royal
> ### Room 103
> ### Maid

Candy emerged from the bedroom dressed in a maid's uniform and carrying a feather duster. She was wearing a tiny black skirt with fishnet stockings and pretended to dust a picture frame while sticking her bottom out in the air towards me, '*Oooo!* Master is their anything else sir would like me to do?'

I could imagine several things the master may like to do as Candy's white bottom could clearly be seen partially covered by tiny black knickers.

'For God's sake Candy whose fancy do you think you're going to tickle with that feather duster?'

'Oh! Shut your face … I will earn more in half an hour than you will earn in a week.'

'Well! You can never buy respect.'

'Oh! Emerald! Please don't go into one of your lectures.' She pulled on a long coat and all beneath was hidden.

I watched T.V. and had a glass of wine. I fell asleep to be awoken by Candy's return. I looked at the time and it was 9.30 p.m. 'Oh! You're home early babe!'

Candy didn't answer me and I knew something was wrong. She was limping slightly as she walked towards the shower. I peeped into the shower and watched as she pulled her clothes off. I was shocked at what I saw … blood was running down the back of her legs. She turned on the water and stepped into the shower. She began to sob as she washed her legs and bottom. She cried out in pain as she tried to wash herself behind and I could see more blood running down her legs. I shouted to her, 'Baby! What has he done to you?'

'Go away! Please! I'll be alright in a minute.'

'What has he done to you?'

'It wasn't a 'him' there were two of them. The bastards!'

'Well let's phone the police!'

'Don't be fucking stupid.'

'Candy! … You need a doctor!'

'I will be alright don't worry … on top of everything the two bastards never paid me … would you believe it. Go away Emerald and leave me alone. I'll have a rest and then I will feel better. I've had a lot worse done to me … pass me that ointment … leave me alone for a while babe … please.'

I waited for Candy to finish her shower. She pulled on her robe and limped into the bedroom. I looked around the door and she was lying on the bed sobbing. As I turned to leave Candy in the bedroom I caught sight of my face in the hallway mirror; my eyes were black, and for once I didn't care.

Lotus growled, *'Leave it to me!'*

'But?'

'There are no buts or questions anymore.'

'I know Lotus ... please be careful?'

'I always am.'

Lotus took a large knife from a drawer. It was long, slender and pointed. She knew the hotel name and the room number. She moved so fast it was amazing to watch. After phoning for a taxi-cab, she slipped into high-heeled shoes, put dark glasses on to hide her eyes and changed her bath robe for a long black evening coat with a fur collar. Before leaving the flat, Lotus checked herself in the mirror, then went down the stairs and walked outside to meet the taxi. Once inside the car, she stated her destination to the driver, 'The Royal Hotel please.' As I sat next to Lotus I felt as if the taxi driver (whom I'd never seen before), would shout out, 'That's not your voice ... that's the wrong voice.'

We pulled up outside the hotel and Lotus stepped out of the car. I was amazed as I watched her walking. She was so confident; she looked like a movie star. She nodded towards the doorman who stood aside and opened the door for her. She calmly walked into the elevator and pressed the button for the floor that room 103 was on. I was terrified as I watched her but I was also raging with anger at the thought of how these two men had treated the woman I loved. Lotus walked up to the door and knocked without hesitation. She undid the top buttons of her coat so that her firm white breasts could be seen. The door opened and a rough shaven man's face appeared. He was holding a glass in his hand, and by the smell of his breath I could tell it was whisky. He looked at Lotus and his eyes immediately fell onto her heaving breasts, 'Yes Luv … what can I do for you?'

Lotus tried to speak like an innocent lost girl which was difficult with her deep voice, *'I have been sent to make someone happy … I have been paid … is it you?'*

The man obviously thought he had a direct link with heaven, *'Yess! Yess!* It's me … come in.'

I followed Lotus into the room. Another man was lying on a double bed wearing only his underpants. The first man turned to his friend and said, 'It looks like we got two for one 'ere Jim.'

I noticed Candy's duster lying on the floor and I became really angry. It was weird because I was usually the calm one, while Lotus was always angry. Now I was raging with hate and anger, while Lotus seemed perfectly calm and in control. So calm in fact, she could have been the cleaner … simply cleaning the room … in a way I suppose she was. She opened the front of her coat and placed her hands on her hips. The knife was stuck through a piece of material inside the coat. The two men were shocked at her beauty … it was as if they could not believe their luck. Lotus spoke in her deep commanding voice as she addressed the man who had answered the door, *'You get undressed and lie on the bed … when I have finished with you, both of you will have gone from heaven into hell.'*

The man standing was so excited he ripped his shirt as he pulled it off. The two men were soon lying on their backs on the bed. Lotus stood over them dominantly, *'Get closer so I can have you together.'*

The two men huddled together tightly and Lotus sat on top of them with her legs wide open. One of the men tried to take off his underpants but Lotus stopped him, *'You will do nothing unless I say … you two are naughty boys and you have to be taught a lesson.'*

Lotus slipped her coat off; it fell onto the floor behind her at the bottom of the bed. Both of her hands were behind her back and in one hand she held the knife. The two men were shaking with pleasure. Their hands trembled as they tried to feel her body in order to release the pain from their sexual torment. Lotus threw her head backwards and her dark glasses fell off. She exhaled with a loud hissing and then looked down at the two men who seemed to freeze as the point of the knife swooped down like an angel of death. The knife stabbed into the eye socket of the first man and made a peculiar noise as it was withdrawn. Blood squirted into the air from his head while the second man began to beg for mercy, 'No! No! Please no!

Lotus spun the man onto his stomach and pushed the knife through his underpants at the rear while growling at him, *'How does it feel lover boy?'* The man screamed and she placed her hand over his mouth. She leaned over to the man who had been stabbed in the eye (he was almost dead) and kissed him while taking a deep breath. She then looked back at the other man; his head was turned sideways as she leaned forwards to kiss him. He was still alive and began to fight. Lotus bit his face ... she bit him again and again ... soon the man took his last gurgling breath through Lotus' mouth to meet death with a sigh of relief. Lotus flung her head back and hissed. I had never seen her like this before. Blood was running down her face and over her breasts. I shouted at her, *'Lotus! Lotus!* Let's leave.'

She hissed like a snake, *'Yesssss.'*

Lotus calmly walked into the shower in the hotel room and washed the blood from her body. She picked up her coat and glasses from the floor and put them back on. She left the knife stuck in the man and wiped the handle clean before placing the other man's fingers around it. As we were leaving the room she walked back over to a dresser where the two men's wallets had been lying. She opened them and removed a large wad of notes from each. She noticed their mobile phones were also lying on the dresser and dropped them into her pockets with the money. She left the room, closed the door and calmly entered the elevator, pressed the 'down' button and exited the hotel. She walked straight into a waiting taxi and told the driver to take her to the road where Candy lived. Upon arriving at the end of the road, she got out of the taxi and walked for about three minutes before reaching the apartment.

After entering Candy's flat, Lotus simply said to me, *'It's all yours.'*

I was back inside my body and in control of myself. I had been out of the flat for approximately forty minutes. I crept to the bedroom door and peeped inside. Candy appeared to be asleep. I took the two mobile phones from my coat pockets and stuck them into empty food tins which I then placed in the bottom of the bin, making sure more rubbish was covering them. I presumed Lotus had taken the phones as they may have been used by the men to call the Escort Agency, and may have provided a link to us. I took the two wads of money from my coat pockets ... there were two bundles of twenty pound notes. I began to count the notes. 'WOW!' One bundle held three hundred pounds ... 'WOW!' The other bundle contained seven hundred and seventy pounds. I stuck the larger roll of notes into the pocket of Candy's coat which she had worn to the hotel. I stuck the three hundred pounds into my purse as I thought I deserved something for helping Candy. I hung up my coat and put on my gown. The whole 'clean-up' had taken less than one hour. I drank a glass of milk and ate a cheese sandwich ... after all ... a girl had to look-after herself.

I must have dosed-off on the settee after I had eaten the sandwich because the next thing I knew was that it was 11 p.m. It had been a busy evening so I decided to go to bed and see how Candy was feeling.

I walked into the bedroom and turned on the table lamp. Candy was lying on her side and was awake. She asked me, 'What have you been doing?'

'I fell asleep on the settee.'

'You always seem to be sleeping ... you should be more aggressive and attack life ... take what you want from life and not be so 'laid back'.'

'I will try darling ... How are you feeling?'

'Sore ... and I mean sore about not being paid ... that hurts more than anything ... I should have been paid two hundred pounds from those two bastards.'

'Is it worth risking your life for money?'

'I would rather risk my life for money than work in a boring job all my life.'

'Turn over and let me look at you.'

'NO! Go away! Emerald! ... Please!'

I began to turn Candy onto her stomach ... she began to struggle so I shouted at her, 'You let me look or I will call for a doctor ... now stop being a pain in the arse.'

Candy shouted, 'You Bitch.' And we both burst into laughter.

I left the room and returned with a bowl of warm salty water. I bathed Candy and dried her with a soft towel. I smeared some ointment onto the swollen area. She asked me jokingly, 'How am I doctor?'

I replied, 'You had best leave the curries for a few days but I think you will live.'

I got into bed next to Candy and held her in my arms and told her I loved her. I kissed her gently on the brow and told her to go to sleep as everything was alright now.'

'Emerald?'

'Yes my love.'

'Thanks.'

The following morning I awoke for work. I rushed for the shower without noticing that Candy was not in bed.

I found her in the shower, '*Oooow!* Candy! Now you really are being a pain in the ass! ... I have to get ready for work.'

'Well jump in ... there's room for two.'

'How are you today Candy?'

'I won't be working that's for sure.'

Candy stepped from the shower and dried herself. She pulled on a bath robe and left the bathroom. After my shower I went into the bedroom to get dressed and got the surprise of my life. Lying on the bed was a new two-piece, black suit. Next to the suit lay a white shirt. I also found several pairs of black stockings a suspender belt and two pairs of high-heeled shoes.

I ran into the kitchen screaming with excitement and flung my arms around Candy, '*Ooooow! Oooooow!* I love you! I love you!'

'*Ahhhhhh!* Watch my arse!'

'Sorry! ... Sorry! I will try them on now *Ooooooooow!*'

I slipped into my new clothes and looked at myself in the mirror. The suite could have been tailor-made ... I even fancied my own reflection. I rushed out to Candy, '*Look! Look!*' I spun around in the middle of the kitchen.

'You look a million dollars babe ... now sit down and eat your breakfast.'

Candy had placed a dish of cereal on the table next to a bottle of milk. '*Oooow!* I'll have to rush or I'll be late.' As I sat down the muffled noise from a mobile phone could be heard. Candy looked around, 'What's that noise?'

I grabbed the black rubbish bag from the bin and rushed out of the kitchen saying, 'Oh! It's my mobile I bought yesterday ... I will have to go now babe or I will be late ... I will throw this rubbish in the bin on the way out ... *Byeee!*'

As I ran down the stairs in my new outfit Candy shouted after me, 'If any guys can't keep their hands off you tell them your girlfriend will sort them out ... and she's a man-eater.'

Lotus asked me nervously, *'How does she know about me?'*

I carried the bin bag down the side of the house and put it in the large 'wheelie bin'. I caught the bus for work and it was full of people. A man told me there was a seat upstairs and after climbing up the steps I was surprised to find the top seats were full. I shouldn't have been surprised ... I began to go back down the stairs and there were at least four men looking up my skirt. I realised I was wearing the black stockings and suspenders Candy had bought me. Lotus said, *'You will never learn will you? ... Well at least I'm here to keep an eye on you ... and if that's not enough I have to look after your friends as well now ... I don't know! ... I suppose I am becoming a big softy!'*

I was five minutes late for work and rushed into the office in a panic, *'Ooooh!* I am sorry Peter ... my phone wouldn't stop ringing this morning.'

'Don't worry ... there will be times I might be late.'

I pulled my chair over to the switchboard and sat down. I was still in a rush and panicking. As I reached up to the wall for my clipboard my skirt must have moved up my legs to reveal my suspenders which I kept forgetting I was wearing. I heard Peter taking a deep breath, 'What are you trying to do to me? ... I am an old man you know!'

'Oh! I am sorry Peter ... this morning has been hectic.'

'Well don't apologise ... I haven't seen or been as close to anything as sexy for years ... *Phew!* See you later.'

'Bye ... Peter.'

My day working on the switchboard passed quickly. Peter returned to take over and I gave him a kiss on the cheek as I left and asked him, 'Now do you think you can cope without me?'

He replied, 'Definitely not.'

I returned home where Candy had set the table. There was a new table cloth with pretty coloured flowers on it and a pink candle which expelled a perfumed aroma as its flame flickered with life. The table was set for two and Candy grabbed my coat, 'Sit down my darling.'

She was speaking in a soft romantic voice. I looked around the kitchen but I couldn't see any empty tins or boxes. I had to ask, 'Have you been torturing tins of food again?'

Candy seemed to instantly return to her normal self as she shouted, 'You bitch ... You always have to spoil everything ... don't you?'

'I am sorry ... *Ohhhh!* Don't start sulking ... wait till I tell you what happened on the bus to work this morning.'

I told Candy how the man had tricked me into going upstairs on the bus. She began to laugh, 'You're too soft with men Emerald ... if you were to go alone onto the streets you would be eaten alive.

There was a knock on the door and Candy ran to answer it quickly while shouting back to me in a posh voice, 'Dinner is served madam!' She opened the door and a young lad was standing holding a large bag in two hands. He stared at Candy who was still wearing her bath robe with the top partly open, 'Is ... Is your name C ... Candy?'

Candy laughed at the lad who must have been around 18 years of age and deliberately let one of her breasts slip out as she leaned forward to grab the bag. The delivery boy's eyes almost popped out of his head as her pointed nipple bounced inches from his face. She slammed the door and we both laughed. I asked, 'Have you no shame?'

She shouted, 'Don't be mean, the poor lad deserves a tip.'

I sat at the table while Candy took command of serving the meal, 'I hope you like Chinese ... nothing hot though ... not in my condition.'

'That looks lovely ... thank you ... how are you today?'

'Oh! I'm alright … I'm never down for long.' Candy licked her lips and we both burst out laughing.

'I wish you would stop being so crude Candy.'

'You are right! … I've stopped! … Would you mind awfully passing me the sauce please? .... Bitch!'

'You seem to be back to your normal self today babe!'

'Actually I am better than my normal self.'

'What do you mean?'

'I have an important announcement to make.'

'*Oooo* goody … you want to marry me!'

'Not quite babe … I looked in my coat pocket … the one I was wearing yesterday when I met the lover boys, and guess what?'

'Candy! … I could never guess.'

'Go on guess what I found?'

'Your feather duster.'

'You always have to spoil things don't you?'

'*Sorrrryyy.*'

'I found seven hundred and seventy pounds … Seven hundred and seventy pounds.'

'Oh! I wonder how that got there?'

'Well I thought about it for ages … and the two guys were drunk and one must have paid me … only, because he was drunk he has given me too much.'

'*Oh No!* Do you think you should return it Candy?'

'Are you serious? … You will have to get streetwise or you will end up getting hurt out there.'

While we were eating Candy said, 'Oh! You will have to give me your mobile number?'

'What mobile babe?'

'The one you had this morning that was ringing as you left.'

'Oh! That one …… I took it back; I'm getting another one on Monday … I didn't like the colour.'

We finished our meal and Candy poured us both a glass of red wine. She stared at me over the candle-flame and her lips looked full and moist. I asked her softly, 'Are you trying to seduce me?'

She shouted at me, 'You always spoil things … I am trying to say thank you.'

'What for?'

'For being there for me last night … nobody has ever been so kind to me before.'

'Welcome to love honey … there is a first time for everything.'

Candy held my hand and a tear ran down her face. I shouted at her, 'Don't go getting all soppy on me.'

We both laughed and lay on the settee to watch a film. Candy took my shoes off and massaged my feet.

I groaned with pleasure, '*Oooo!* That's the first time you have touched me like that!'

Candy whispered, 'Like you said. There is a first time for everything.'

When we went to bed later we held each other tightly. We fell into a deep sleep wrapped in each others arms. No words were spoken and nothing sexual was needed for we were in love.

It was a Sunday morning and Candy shouted at me, 'Get out of the shower bitch … I want one.'

I shouted back, 'Don't call me a bitch …… bitch.'

This was the usual morning banter which was bounced between the two of us. Anyone listening would have thought we hated each other … but we didn't.

Candy put a plate of eggs and bacon in front of me, '*Mmmmm!* That smells great … but there is too much … I don't want to end up with a fat arse …… like some people.' There was a silence; I peeped out of the corner of my eye at Candy. She picked up the Sunday paper which had been delivered, and began to run towards me. She chased me around the flat screaming, 'You bitch! How dare you say I have a fat arse.'

Candy twisted her head around while looking in the mirror and mumbling to herself, 'My arse isn't big ... honestly Emerald! Is my arse big?'

'No! Of course not! ... Can't you take a joke?'

'Well don't say it again Emerald .... Baggy tits.'

I screamed at Candy, 'You fat arsed bitch,' and proceeded to chase her with a glass of water until I had her trapped in a corner. I spoke to her in a deep voice, pretending to be Lotus, 'Say you're sorry you bitch.'

'I'm sorry! .... Baggy tits!'

I threw the water over her and we fell to the floor play-fighting. There was suddenly a banging on the floor. It was the elderly lady who lived below us. She didn't come to our door any more after our last meeting. Now she resorted to banging on the ceiling with a broomstick. We had agreed it was a broomstick because we had decided she must be a witch.

KNOCK ... KNOCK ... KNOCK

We both laughed and began singing the song:-
'Knock three times on the ceiling if you want me.'

THE SWITCHBOARD

Time flew by as only time may ... always being present whilst hiding in the shadows of doubt. "Did you like that Wordcatcher? *WORDCATCHER?*"

"Y ... Yes! ... What?"

"You are dopey at times Wordcatcher ... and you are always sleepy ... are you listening to me?"

"Yes! Of course I am."

"Well it's a good job I love you ... isn't it?"

"Yes! ... Emerald."

"Well pay attention and listen. Are you ready?"

"Yes."

~~~

"The relationship between Candy and me had grown as time passed by. It was as if she was learning to love ... learning how to love, and of course her love was my love because we became so close. We had discussed her work, and at the end of the month she was going to start a new job. Her new job was in a car showroom where she would ... what she called, 'Be a Model' to draw in the guys. She explained that it was an exclusive car showroom and they had told her they could not risk any adverse publicity. She had been instructed to wear sexy looking clothes and walk about the showroom posing and sitting on the cars ... on a soft piece of cloth of course. Candy chased me around the flat after I had asked her if there was a danger of dinting the cars' bodywork with her fat behind. My work on the switchboard had become more interesting. I began to listen to some calls. I found it amazing ... the things that were happening ... and some of the complaints and emergency calls were unbelievable.

A funny thing happened one day; a lady called complaining about two women who lived above her. I recognised her voice; it was the woman who lived below us. I couldn't resist - I had to know what she was going to say about us to the police. I pretended to put her through to the complaints department then asked her (in a more eloquent accent), 'Can I help you madam?'

'Yes you can. There are two women living above me and I think they are prostitutes.'

'And what makes you think this madam?'

'Well! ... They are always walking about half naked. I have seen them naked ... kissing and holding each other ... I mean two women ... kissing each other.'

'And where were they performing this indecent act madam?'

'I saw them in their apartment.'

'There is no law against two women kissing or being naked in the privacy of their own home madam.'

'But they are always making a noise; screaming.'

'I am sorry madam but from what you are saying, it could go against you if it were to go to court. In effect madam, you could be charged with intruding upon other people's privacy and held liable for court costs and wasting police time. Do you still wish to pursue this matter?'

'No, I don't want to get into trouble ... Can't we forget I called.'

'Yes, okay madam, but please be careful in the future – false allegations are a very serious matter. Good day to you.'

At that moment Peter walked into the room to start his shift, 'Any interesting calls today my angel?'

'No ... just the usual rubbish.'

Peter came over in his wheelchair and patted my bear thigh above my stockings with his hand. I didn't mind because I felt sorry for him and knew he was very lonely. He had asked me to go out with him once but I had found an easy way of letting him down gently ... I simply told him the truth ... I had a girlfriend who I was living with and loved more than anyone. He sighed as he felt my leg, 'What a waste ... if I could only turn back the clock.'

I liked Peter ... he was harmless and I could tell he craved for a relationship he could only dream of ... his dreams and fantasies were also limited by his disability.

When I returned home I told Candy about the woman downstairs calling to complain about us. We laughed and for days her curtains were closed and she was as quiet as a mouse.

Candy was finishing her last week of working with the Escort Agency. Our love had grown and we lived for each other. I showed Candy how to make love. She had to learn the difference between making love and lustful sex. She hated each day she worked for the Escort Agency and used to tell me about some of the awful things she had to do. She told me about some of the weird things men demanded and that she had one regular customer who would ask her to sit naked while he threw cream cakes at her. I said, 'That sounds like a tasty job.'

She replied, 'It's not funny ... bitch.'

She told me about things that happened that I found hard to believe ... like a guy who wanted her to urinate over his naked body. She scowled at me and said, 'If you say he was a pissing idiot I will murder you.'

She told me the worst thing was violence ... some guys would derive pleasure from making her suffer ... she used to pretend she was in pain and it would turn them on. It was very rare but sometimes she would get a real mad man ... she told me how a man had held a knife to her throat while he had sex with her. She said he never hurt her, and afterwards put on his suit ... politely paid her double the fee and returned to his job. She said she knew where he worked; he was a judge.

The Sting

I was working on the switchboard and was happy. It was Candy's last day working for the agency. I felt as if our life together would start the following day ... just me and her ... and the horrible life she seemed to live in secret would be no more ... It was in the afternoon when the call came.

'Officers required immediately at Hawthorn Avenue by the canal.
A woman has been found naked and unconscious.
Name of victim Candy Loach.'

I panicked and dived from my office. The officers in the police station stopped me and asked me what was wrong. I explained my girlfriend had been found unconscious. They told me to calm down, and that they would take me to her. Within minutes an officer shouted, 'She's been taken to the hospital.'

An officer drove me to the hospital where I was asked to wait. I must have been marching up and down for hours before a doctor came to see me, 'How is she doctor? Is she alright?'

'Might I ask who you are madam?'

'I'm her girlfriend and we live together ... I work at the police station.'

The doctor led me into his office, 'Miss Loach has overdosed on drugs.'

'But she doesn't take drugs ... what drugs?'

'The drug used was heroin.'

'But she has never used drugs doctor.'

'She does not seem to be a regular drug addict as there are no needle marks on her body. However, we are carrying out further tests in order that we may give her the proper medication to aid her recovery. I must also inform you that Miss Loach was found naked and that she has been severely sexually abused by several men.'

I broke down and cried. The doctor asked a nurse to bring me a hot drink while assuring me that Candy was in capable hands. I asked when I could see Candy and was told that I could sit by her bed, but that she was unconscious; in a critical condition in the intensive care unit. Worst thing of all though, I was also told that she might not recover.

I could not believe it when I saw her. She had tubes sticking out of her arms and was surrounded by machines. I stared at her ... she looked so helpless. I whispered to her, 'Only one more day my love ... and we would have been together for the rest of or lives. You will be alright, and then we can carry on forever ... tomorrow will be the first day of the rest of our lives.'

I sat by her bed for hours. A detective from the police station came and asked me questions. I told him Candy had never taken drugs before and that she must have been raped by a pack of animals. He told me to call him as soon as Candy could speak as the police had no idea what had happened ... he promised me they would catch these animals ... Lotus whispered, *'Not if I catch them first.'*

I had been so happy I had not needed to have any contact with Lotus. She asked me, *'Are you with me?'*

I knew what she meant and I told her, 'Yes!'

It was later that night when Candy began to speak. She startled me as I had fallen asleep,

'E ... Emer! .... E ... Emer!'

212

I woke up and she was holding my hand. I looked at her ... I was so happy to see her awake, 'My darling ... you will be alright now ... I will look after you.'

She spoke slowly ... she seemed so tired and weary, 'I am going to die ... I know I am.'

'Please ... don't speak like that ... you will be alright now... I will never leave you again.'

She spoke sadly and slowly, she told me, 'Heaven on earth was never meant to be for me babe ... I haven't got long so listen ... I want you to know it wasn't my fault ... you must tell the police what happened so they can be punished ... can you here me ... will you promise me you will make sure they are punished for this?'

'Yes my love ... I promise.'

THE LAST TIME

Candy spoke as if she was a million miles away. Her eyes were glazed and her heart was sad. 'After you had left for work the phone rang for the last time. I knew tomorrow I would throw my phone away and begin a new life with you. It was my last meeting and I knew who the lad's were. They were four local teenagers who were very inexperienced, sexually. Their fun was always over before they knew it had begun. They paid fifty pounds each and had seen me several times previously. I would call to where one of the boys lived which was in an apartment. The lads used to amuse me as they could not contain their excitement; I would tease them and usually a simple touch of my hand would fulfil their dreams. I had dressed myself in tiny red hot-pants and wore my small red top to match. I pulled on my overcoat and left our flat. I looked back and whispered to myself, 'When I return I will be free of this disgusting job.' I kept telling myself 'this is the last time.' I walked up the steps that led to a cobbled alleyway which was strewn with rubbish. This was the last day of my contract with the Escort Agency and it had to be fulfilled. If I left without giving the agency notice 'things' could have become nasty. The agreement wasn't legal and they had their own ways of handling problems. I knocked on the door and it was opened by Tim ... one of the four boys. I said hello and asked if he was ready to '*Rock 'n' Roll*' and he had said, 'You bet!' Once inside, I looked around, I was standing in the lounge and the other three boys, Les, Paul and Ray were sat around the room. I put my hand out and waggled my fingers. The boys knew the routine ... business first. They put the two hundred pounds into my hand. I let my coat drop to the floor and said, 'Let's party boys.'

I began dancing to music which was playing from a CD. I swayed my hips seductively and pushed my bottom towards them. The lads were drinking beer and had begun to undress. I took off my top and let my firm breasts point towards them. The boys were now busy playing with themselves. They talked to each other as if I was not in the room. I slowly slid down my pants and seductively opened my legs, 'Look at the tits on 'er!' one shouted.

'Look at the ass and the pussy!' shouted another.

I danced seductively over the boys, teasing them. I looked at my watch ... the way the lads were getting worked up they would most likely have relieved themselves shortly, and I was looking forward to leaving.

There was a knock on the door. I shouted to the boys, 'Don't open it ... they will go away.' I thought it might be the police but Tim told me that they had ordered something.

The door opened and a flash-looking man of about thirty years of age pushed his way in. The man was holding a 'Pit-Bull' dog on a metal chain. I was quick to understand the situation. The man pulled four packets out of his pocket and collected a wad of notes from the boys.

The boys shouted thanks to the man and told him it was Paul's birthday. They began to fumble with the packets. The man who was opening the door to leave turned around and looked at them ... he looked at me ... and I knew I had problems. He began to take control over the whole situation. I started to get dressed but he hit me across the face and shouted, 'You sit and wait slag.'

I took the money I had been paid from my coat and threw it to the boys, 'Here! Take your money back I'm leaving.'

The dealer grabbed the money and shouted, 'That's enough for a good trip babe.'

I shouted to the boys, 'I will tell the police!'

The boys began to panic and Tim shouted, 'I don't want the fucking police coming round ... let her go.'

The drug dealer shouted, 'She's a whore ... she won't go anywhere near the police.'

He prepared a syringe of drugs. I was fighting to escape, and the boys held me down whilst he injected it into my arm. I became weak and couldn't move but I could see what was happening. The dealer prepared the drugs the boys had bought and showed them how to inject them into their arms. The dealer turned to me and I heard him say to the boys, 'Now! ... Let's party ... I'll show you what she wants.'

I don't know how or where it came from but I had a sudden burst of energy and dived for the door. The dog grabbed my arm in its jaws. They all held me while I was injected with more drugs. I blacked out and that is all I can remember .... Will you ever forgive me babe?'

I spoke to Candy between my sobs, 'You have done nothing wrong babe ... just get well and we can carry on tomorrow like normal.'

Candy looked at me and smiled as she said, 'I am a silly bitch ... aren't I?'

In an instant all hell seemed to erupt. The machines were making loud noises and nurses and doctors ran into the room. I was screaming, '*Candy!* ... *Candy!*'

She never answered me again ... she was in heaven and I was alone in hell with Lotus.

THE SWEETEST KISS

I was asked by a detective if Candy had said anything before dying that may help with their enquires. I told him she hadn't spoken, and he promised me he would find her killers.

I was given time off from work which I needed. It was so different in the apartment. It was like a tomb. There was this silence; it was like I was falling into a well of solitude ... being swallowed up into a void. The night time was the worst ... I could hear Candy's footsteps, her voice. I might have been making a drink and I would reach for the milk and shout, 'Where's the milk bitch?' Then I would crumble up on the floor crying for hours ... because there was no reply and I knew there never would be.

The only thing that kept me alive and breathing was the address ... the address and phone number which was left on Candy's mobile phone from the day she had her last appointment.

Tim
Flat 6, Brookdale Terrace
Hot-Pants
Ph 8121203

Two weeks had passed by. I phoned my supervisor at work and said that I would be returning in a few days. Lotus was anxious and kept asking me to let her go. By 'let her go' I knew what she meant. It was time and we decided to work together. I would do the talking and Lotus would make them sorry.

I wanted to know from Candy's killers what had happened ... I wanted to know why they had left her to die like a dog ... naked and alone by the side of a stinking canal.

I had taken a large syringe from the First-Aid box in Candy's apartment. I thought how appropriate the needle would be to punish her attackers. I bought a cut-throat razor which I had seen in an antique shop; the blade was sharp and slid through paper with a magical hiss; a sound Lotus loved. Our work began. I found the address and name of Candy's last appointment from the text message on her mobile. I began to watch the property. I knew if this 'Tim' was working, he would most likely leave for work in the morning. There was a bus-stop close to his house so I would wait there and watch his house in the morning. He left for work at 8.30 a.m. I knocked on his door and there was no answer, which told me what I needed to know ... he lived alone. I waited until a Friday night and watched his flat. He had gone out for some 'take-away food' and a video at about 8 p.m.

I was trembling with fear. Lotus told me to remember Candy. I did, and I became angry and that made me strong. I walked up to his door and knocked. It was dark and I was wearing my long black coat with nothing on underneath. Tim opened the door cautiously saying, 'W ... Who is it?'

I stood with the top of my coat open so he could see most of my breasts, 'Hi honey! I was told there was a party here tonight ... Oh! Have I got the right place?' I spoke seductively and pushed my long white leg through my coat.

He began to stammer, 'Y ... Yes ... Y ... Yes ... C ... Come in.'

I walked in and Lotus grabbed him around the throat. He looked into her eyes and crumbled into the depths of fear. Lotus sat on top of him and hissed while the boy begged for mercy. She growled at the boy, *'And what mercy did you give to Candy?'*

'No! Please that wasn't me … honest it wasn't me.'

'Then who was it?'

'Everything was alright till he came.'

'Who came?'

'Max! … The drug dealer! We were just trying drugs for Paul's birthday party … I will never touch them again … honest.'

'I'm not bothered about your fucking drugs … you killed my friend Candy.'

'No! That's what I am trying to tell you … It was Max who injected her.'

'And you who held her down?'

'Please! … Please don't hurt me.'

'And who left her to die like a dog by the canal?'

'Max took her away … I didn't know anything was wrong with her till I saw it in the papers.'

'Where does Max live?'

'I only have his mobile phone number … I will give it you.'

Lotus let Tim stand up and he walked over with him to a phone book. He opened the book and ripped out a page, 'Here that's his number … it's all I have.'

'And what about Les, Ray and Paul?'

'Yes! I have their addresses and phone numbers here.'

'Do they live close by?'

'Yes … minutes away.'

Lotus told Tim to take her to his bedroom. She told him to take off his clothes. There was an excitement beginning to grow from somewhere deep inside him. Lotus stood facing him and the coat dropped down from her shoulder. They stood naked facing each other. Tim looked at the red mark on the stomach of Lotus and asked nervously, 'What's that?'

Lotus took him into her arms and whispered, *'Time.'*

The sting of the needle was hardly noticed by Tim as Lotus pushed her tongue deep into his mouth. He was trembling as he thrust his tongue into the open mouth of Lotus. The syringe was slowly squeezed and was full of nothing. Pure air filled the veins of the youth to stop at his lungs where all means of escape would be so close, yet ever so far. Lotus laid him on his double bed and he looked at peace. She hissed as if from ecstasy, *'That was the sweetest kiss.'*

She returned to the phone and called Les. She told me to speak sweetly so he would come to our web. 'Hello Les … were having a party here at Tim's I was told you're a big boy! … Come and show me.'

Soon there was a knock on the door. Lotus took hold of him as soon as he entered. He must have thought he was in heaven, until the squeeze of the needle when he dived into hell. His last words were, 'Why?' And the last words he ever heard were, *'Candy.'*

Lotus growled, *'Now phone Paul.'*

'Hi! Is that Paul … I am at Tim's pad and we are *dying* to see you … I am all wet and waiting for you.'

Lotus snapped at me, *'You always have to be clever don't you?'*

'Sorry.'

There was a knock on the door and Lotus pulled Paul inside. He took one look at the naked body of Lotus and took his last gasp through her lips. She laid his warm body on the bed with the other two and I didn't have to be told what to do next. I picked up the phone and punched-in Ray's number. When he answered, I said, 'Hello! Ray … There's a party going on at Tim's and Paul and Les are here. The problem is there are four girls here and only three boys.

I am all horny and haven't had sex for weeks. I'm disappointed so I will have to go home.'

Ray could hardly speak, 'W ... Wait ... I'll ... I'll be there in one minute.'

Ray was dead within seconds of the door opening. As the needle entered his neck Lotus covered his lips with hers and bit his tongue which he had thrust into her mouth. Blood squirted everywhere ... I shouted at Lotus, 'Why did you do that ... look at the mess you've made!'

Lotus whispered as her bloody lip's trembled, *'It's the sweetest kiss.'*

There was only one more call to be made. Lotus told me to be careful; she said she had a bad feeling about calling Max. I dialled Max's number.

'Yo! Max speaking.'

'Hi Max ... I was told you might be able to get me some sugar.'

'Who is it?'

'I'm a friend of Tim's from Brookdale Terrace.'

'Put Tim on the phone.'

'He's in the bedroom with a girl ... it doesn't matter it's just that ... well we're expecting about twenty people tonight who want to party ... I don't suppose you have enough stuff anyway ... bye .....'

'Fuckin' wait a minute ... I look after this area ... how many packets do you want?'

'Like I said, twenty.'

'That's five hundred quid ... c.a.s.h.'

'Fine ... no problem.'

'I don't like the sound of you ... bitch, and I don't know you. I will meet you under the bridge at Lostock Road by the canal in ten minutes ... Right?'

'Yes ... Fine.'

MAX

It was dark beneath the bridge. Cold misty spirals twisted over the canal like the ghosts of lost spirits in an earthbound confusion. As I waited, I whispered to Lotus, 'How ironic that death will once more visit the same spot again so soon. Candy I love you.'

Lotus told me to concentrate ... she said she had a bad feeling about this ... a feeling she had never felt before. I was worried ... Lotus was usually full of confidence.

I could hear footsteps approaching ... I opened my coat slightly and the light from the moon reflected softly on to my breasts. Through the darkness, a tall thin figure appeared. A dog began to bark that ended with a loud *'Yelp'* followed by an angry cuss, 'Fuckin' shut up.'

The man stopped and faced me while the pit-bull, at the end of the chain, snarled with dripping jowls. The man shouted, 'Stay where you are bitch. Money?' He held out his hand and his eyes were like steel ... cold and void of feeling. I didn't know what to do. 'Come on then bitch ... it's no good standing there flashing yer tits at me ... Money?' He waggled his hand at me ... waiting for me to comply.

Lotus whispered to me, *'Ask him for the stuff.'*

'Where's the stuff first?'

'You show me the money and I show you the stuff ... you give me the money and I give you the stuff ... it's not fuckin' rocket science ... silly bitch ... if you're lucky I might give you what you need as well ... and that's for free.'

I was raging with anger after what he had said, especially as this was where Candy had been found. I tried to ask Lotus what we should do next. She told me to, very slowly, hand him the money. Of course I didn't have five hundred pounds; I was holding about seventy pounds rolled up. As my hand moved towards him holding the money, Lotus took hold of the razor which was in my pocket. She whispered to me, *'As his hand is about to take the money, drop it.'*

He moved forward and his fingers began to close around the notes. I let them slip and he shouted, 'You useless cow.' As he bent forward to pick the money up, Lotus slashed across the back of his neck with the razor. He stood up holding the back of his neck while screaming, 'You bitch.'

The dog bolted free and jumped in the air towards Lotus' face. I was terrified … it was as if everything was happening in slow motion and I was now a spectator. I could see the dog's massive mouth of teeth moving into my face. Instantly, and yet slowly, I saw the razor cutting across the dog's exposed throat. Blood squirted everywhere and the dog dropped down dead to the floor.

Lotus looked at Max; he had pulled a gun from his coat. He took aim and shot at Lotus who seemed to swerve to one side and come up with her hand holding the razor. The last cut was across the front of his throat and as he stood gurgling and choking from his own blood he fell to his knees. There was a sudden **'BANG'** and I felt a tearing pain going through the left side of my body. I had been shot. I fell to the ground holding my side. I watched as Max rolled into the canal and lay still and silent, face down. I lay by the canal and could not move. I hoped someone would have heard the gunshot and called the police. I threw the razor and the syringe into the canal. I lay on my back gazing at the stars. Lotus mumbled, *'I told you I had a bad feeling about this.'*

Everything became black.

THE GOLDEN DAWN

I was running with Candy through fields of long green grass
The sun was shining and we were free
A rainbow arched across our path
We ran and ran towards the archway of colour
It kept moving away, as only rainbows can do
We were happy, and together and, Yesss!
The rainbow was coming closer and closer
We looked sideways into each others eyes as we ran
We were in love and free
The rainbow was almost above us
As we passed beneath it, there was, a golden dawn
And ....

There was a thumping on my body like and elephant bouncing on top of me ... again and again ....
I could hear somebody shouting ....

CLEAR   *CLEAR*
CLEAR   *CLEAR*

"She's Back ... She's Back"

I opened my eyes and a woman doctor was standing over me holding two large pads. She leaned toward me and whispered, 'Welcome back to life.'

~~~

Wordcatcher? Wordcatcher?"
"Yes! I am here!"
"Then hold me tightly."
"You are safe now Emerald."
"Sing to me Wordcatcher? ... Please?"
"But ... I can't sing!"
"You're a poet!"
"Yes."
"Then you shall write and read me a poem!"

In the dark of night
lying near the ground
with the stars above, so bright,
on a silken web
'tis a dead man's bed,
with a pillow of delight.

Beauty in the eye, of each one's nature?
or Past? or Control? or Abuse?
The hand that waves a Golden Wand
to stamp a print, a pretext.
To repeat the past,
in the 8-hourglass
the widow waits, so bold.
The secret is - the dye is cast
no secret - time unfold.

With an hourglass time entwine.
Patience, waiting, waiting,
Do you understand the riddle?
The secret of time and space?
Upon your belly, eternity, your figure 8,
your hourglass pointing to the stars
as you wait, and wait, and wait.

The sigh of joy, the cry of pain,
the sigh of life and death - to gain.
Within your grasp,
I stab and stab, with hate or love? Some say both the same.
Will you or I remain?
All I gave was love! Am I the felon?
Thank you Latrodectus
for your potent neurotoxin venom.

Am I just another arthropod,
A shell outside your web?
Another victim, a soulless male
who lay within your bed?

Why do you lie?
Why do you do the things you do?
From a spun thread web
in a place that's dead
'tis a lonely life for you.

Sitting on a spider's web,
on a sticky death trap wait,
waiting for your sacrifice
for a time to consummate.

Lying on a spider's web
playing with a knot
to tie or die, or live a lie
to play a game, with cost
and you will sigh, 'tis a mind game ply
soon to cry when all is lost.

A lifetime spent.
Is revenge so sweet?
Hate outside or love within.
Love within or hate outside.
Do you love to mate, to desecrate?

Do you hate to love, so hide the blood?
Beneath your web,
is a well to hell,
a spiral, one way trip,
To take the bait, at Satan's gate,
'tis just one more soul, to slip.

I am the male, I am half your size,
so, in my mind I have to grow.
I may turn up late and hesitate
I have the power, 'tis here to bestow.

Little spider, watch and wait
What's in your eyes? What see?
She lies on her back, is this a trap?
She's so big, but her scent is free.
Stay or go, one's nature to unfold.
What I see is a golden tree
with a fleece and a pot of Gold.

Dancing in the twilight zone,
all that glitters is not gold,
for the jewels are black
in a poison sack
but of course! You will not be told.

I rest upon your golden breast,
I stab to my delight,
It feels so good, that Mother Nature could,
endow with such delight.
I dig so deep, and stab you,
Full of life.

'Tis my time now, yet you seem to wait,
Yes! I wonder what my fate.
Stabbing in the deep dark night,
is this hate or love surreal?
Or is it just stolen lust,
Purely nature's way to feel?

Such a bond, created life,
you two are one, the seed to grow.
Can neither of you stand the pain,
one to stay, and one to go?

Wincey spider run now quick,
now your task is surely done,
or will you stay, in a death grip pay,
to be part of an endless sum.

"Well that wasn't very romantic was it Wordcatcher?"

"That depends upon your perspective of romance. I think to risk death for one moment of passionate love could be the height of romance."

"And would you Wordcatcher?"

"Would I what?"

"Risk your life ... your soul for one moment of loving?"

"But Emerald! My darling! I am!"

Our lips meet to steal surreal so sweet the taste
Natures golden dew
Tongues searching caves
Moist warm juices mix as one

"That's lovely Wordcatcher ... kiss me again."

And yet ...?
Through love, your bite surrounds the tongue
White talons rows from death sublime
For in the end through love or hate
Bloods kiss taste sweet
The eyes lids tightly close
Life and death as one will meet
Propose, Suppose, Black Rose.

"*Oooo!* That sounded nice Wordcatcher. Hold me tight and kiss me again ... and I promise not to bite, if you don't bite."

We kissed and stared into each others eyes. Her eyes reminded me of some trick pictures I was once shown. I remember one was a vase ... and then instantly the vase become a face; and then 'flick' back to being a vase. Emerald's eyes were like the pictures I had seen. I was staring into her beautiful green eyes ... so soft, calm and peaceful ... and then I would catch a sudden brief glimpse from the dark depths of her pupils, and a shiver would travel down my spine. I kissed her lips and closed my eyes for ignorance is bliss, and the taste of honey is so sweet when the queen is out of sight.

"Wordcatcher! Are you there! ... You're kissing me and your eyes have gone all dreamy. Sometimes I don't understand you. I suppose it is true what they say. 'Love moves in mysterious ways.' Do you love me?"

"Yes."

"Good! ... All we need is love. Now! Where was I?

~~~

I was told by the doctor that I was very lucky to be alive. The bullet had just missed my heart by inches and I had lost so much blood I had actually died and had been brought back to life.

A detective came to the hospital to ask me questions. I had remembered what had happened and, lying in a hospital bed, had given me a lot of time to think.

'Could you tell me exactly what happened prior to your being shot?' asked the detective.

'Yes! ... Of course! It's all a bit vague but I will tell you what I can. I was visiting the place where my partner had been killed. I often go down to the canal to speak to her and have a cry. I could hear several voices approaching and I was frightened. I hid in some bushes and four boys came walking past. They were met by a man with a dog and they began to talk. It looked as if they were selling something ... the next thing ... all hell broke loose. The people began to fight and I jumped up from the bushes to run away. The next thing I was aware of was waking up in hospital.'

'Have you ever taken drugs?'

'Never ... Look at my arms.'

'There was a roll of money ...£70 ... found with your fingerprints on it ... do you know anything about this money?'

'Yes ... I had a roll of money in my pocket ... can I have it back?'

'Have you ever *and I have to ask you this.*' Have you ever been involved in prostitution?'

'Oh! How dare you? No! Definitely not.'

'Could you tell me why you had no clothes on beneath the overcoat you were wearing on the night of this incident?'

'Was I breaking the law?'

'No ... it just seems a bit unusual to be standing by a canal in the dark naked ... except for a coat!'

'I've been told many times that I am unusual, but I assure you I am not a prostitute, a drug user or a murderer. Yes! I suppose I am guilty of being unusual. Do you know!

... I remember once, standing under the moon naked and I
............'

'I think that will be all for now madam.'

'Oh! Goodbye officer.'

After my recovery I returned to Candy's flat and continued
with my work at the police station. Life seemed one long
boring routine. I was worried about the deaths of Max and
the boys as some forensic clue or evidence may have been
found to lead the police to me. I was relieved when I read
an article in the newspaper:–

MAX

Drug barren and four youths murdered
In drug land wars.

*Max, a known drug dealer was found dead by Lostock
canal. His death seems to have been the result of a
gangland war. Four other youths were also found dead
under suspicious circumstances, and their deaths are
thought to be from the inadequate use of syringes.*

HOLLY

Lotus seemed to have disappeared since our evening by the canal. I think it had disturbed her in some way ... as I suppose a near death experience may do.

I felt my life held no purpose or reason. I seemed to be going through the motions of living with the only satisfaction in my life being that I had battled through another day. I didn't bother about wearing sexy clothes anymore. People seemed to give me a 'wide berth.' Even Peter seemed to be on ice when he was around me ... I felt guilty as I had shouted at Peter when I had returned to work after Candy's death. He had put his hand on my leg as he usually did and I had shouted at him, 'Is that all you can think about? ... Sticking your hand up my skirt?'

Peter had rolled out of the office with a bright red face and his wheelchair tyres burning rubber. I held his hand the next day and apologised. He said it was alright, but he wouldn't touch my leg again and I wished he would; it was one of the things which I had told Candy about, and she thought it was really cute.

My life seemed to have become founded upon routine. The only place I went to out of doors was the police station and shopping for food. I was given the opportunity of learning to drive and received free lessons through the police service. I had bought a small car and I was pleased that I did not have to rely on public transport anymore.

Within my nights of solitude, began to grow an unusual experience; my dreams became more and more vivid ... almost real. I began to see things ... flashes ... some sort of premonitions. I remember one that frightened me. I was looking out of a window and in the distance I could see clouds of black locusts. Somehow I knew they represented death in some macabre way. The next day on the T.V. news a catastrophe had happened in India; thousands of people had been killed in a major earthquake and land slide.

I would have the occasional vivid dream and would usually find the dream gave reference to some situation from life. One night I was asleep and I could see Candy in my dream. Seeing her in my dreams was not an unusual occurrence as I believed she was always with me. In this particular dream I was standing facing her and we were in a dark, cold street. I could see buildings and there was a misty glow with a yellow hue as if from a street light. Candy was staring at me, and she looked sad. I asked her, 'What is the matter my love?'

My eyes seemed to float down to Candy's feet and there, lying on the floor was a young girl. The girl looked as if she was dead. I could see her face and she looked like she was only about thirteen or fourteen years of age. The girl was thin and frail and was wearing a short skirt and a cardigan. I looked back into Candy's eyes; I knew she was showing me the girl for some reason but I could not understand.

In the morning I contemplated on the dream. I never knew the answer to the riddles I was shown and could only surmise as to how they may materialise in everyday life. I thought that Candy may have a daughter she had not told me about, and that she maybe in some trouble. I had no way of finding out if she had a daughter, as Candy had told me that her parents were both dead and she had no brothers or sisters. I was troubled by my dream but had no choice but to continue with my mundane life.

The cold, dark nights crept in like a blanket of misty raw ice. It was a wintry Saturday and I was off work. It was around 7 p.m. when I was driving home from the supermarket. Close to my apartment was an area which was frequented by prostitutes. Candy used to tell me, 'They won't bother you if you don't bother them, and our rent is half the price because of the area we live in.'

It was so misty I could hardly see. I was leaning forwards to see out of the car window. Suddenly my heart jumped into my mouth. I could see a street light and standing under it was the young girl from my dream. She had a short skirt on and was wearing a short thick coat. She was shivering and I could see her mouth trembling from the cold. I stopped the car and stared at her. Lotus spoke to me for the first time in months, '*Keep going … I have a bad feeling about this.*'

I thought of my dream and Candy. I looked at this poor child … I couldn't just drive away and leave her like this. I thought … I would at least ask her if she needed help. As I waved to the girl a man appeared at my window. I wound the window down and the frosty air swooped in as if to eat the warmth from inside my car. The man was about 35 years of age, he was rough shaven and his teeth were yellow, 'Looking for business luv?'

'How much is the girl?'

'What girl?'

'Are you blind? The child over there! Standing beneath the street light?'

'Ah! That girl! She's special … a virgin she is … guaranteed.'

'Well! How much?'

'Depends what ye' want to do? If you want full sex with 'er it's £500 but you're not taking her virginity are ye'? … Ye'd 'ave a job, *Ha Har Ha Ha.*'

The man's breath stank like a sewer and I was beginning to feel cold. I opened my purse and took out twenty pounds, 'Here's twenty quid ... put her in the car and I will bring her back in fifteen minutes.'

'Oh! *Ha Har Har Har* sorry luv she ain't goin' anywhere. You come wi' me, I 'ave a place round the back 'ere. Lotus whispered, *'Let's go now while we can?'*

I handed the man the twenty pounds which he grabbed, 'Thanks luv ... Hey, it's fifty not twenty ... what do ye' take me for?'

I was tempted to tell him but I was busy thinking how to get the girl out of this mess. Lotus said, *'If you are taking us down some back ally with this guy we had better 'tool up' there could be more of them down there in the dark.'*

I was frightened; I was pleased that Lotus was with me again in case there was any trouble. I handed the man another thirty pounds and he told me to follow him. Lotus reached under the car seat where there was a long handled screwdriver in a tool bag. She slipped the long shiny shaft under my coat sleeve and held the handle tightly. The man shouted, 'Come on then ... this is her first time and I wanna make some money tonight. Hey! Yer a good looking chick! Why don't ye' work fo' me?"

'I don't think so.'

We walked down a dark ally-way and I looked at the girl. She was a broken spirit. Her eyes were blank and she was shivering. I decided I had to take her away from this ... Lotus asked me, *'What if she doesn't want to go with you?'*

I didn't have an answer for Lotus. I couldn't imagine her wanting to stay with this man ... but if she did then there was not a lot I could do to help her.

We came to an area at the back of the ally where I could see a large white van. The man opened the back door and the girl reluctantly climbed into the back. I looked inside and it was lit by a small interior light. The floor of the van had a double mattress laid on it. The man looked nervous and began whispering, 'You've got ten minutes ... I don't know what people like you do, but hurry up.'

The man closed the back door of the van and the girl began to cry, 'What are you going to do?'

'*Shhhh!* I'm not going to hurt you ... I'm here to take you away from this.'

The girl sniffled and stopped crying, 'He has a big knife ... he poked me with it and said he would cut me into pieces if I didn't do as he said.'

'No one will hurt you, but we have to get away from here ... do you want to leave with me?'

'Yes! ... Please don't leave me with him.'

I peeped through a crack in the door and jumped in fear; there was an eye ... it was the man looking in. He shouted, 'I'm watchin' ye' ... I don't like this ... yer a bleedin' weirdo ... you've got one more minute.'

I looked at the girl ... she was nothing more than a child. She was shivering as tears began to run down her face again. I spoke to Lotus, 'Can you help me Lotus, I'm frightened?'

Lotus whispered, '*If I must ... anyway ... I don't like him either.*'

The girl whispered, 'Who are you speaking to lady?'

I told her, 'Just a friend ... Listen to me carefully. When the door opens and I lift you down, run to my car and I will take you home. If I don't come, run to a phone box, call '999' and ask for the police ... they will help you ... understand?'

'Yes ... don't leave me will you?'

'No!'

'Don't let him hurt me will you?'

'No I promise.'

The van door opened and I jumped down. The man shouted, 'That's fifty pounds!'

'I just gave you the money.'

'No ye' didn't ... anyway it's extra 'cause yer a weirdo. I run a respectable business.'

I stood in front of the man and lifted the girl from the back. As soon as her feet touched the ground I shouted, 'Run.' The man's hand went inside his coat but Lotus had taken over. The screwdriver shaft slid through the inside top of his open mouth and sank into his brain as he began to shout, whatever word was to remain upon his lips forever in a mask of death. His arms dropped to his sides and a large serrated knife fell with a clatter onto the black, cold, stone cobbles.

Lotus asked me, *'Can I go now?'*

I said, 'Yes and thanks.'

She said, *'What are you doing now?'*

'I'm taking my money back.'

Lotus laughed, *'You really are unbelievable.'*

I ran around to my car and the girl was waiting for me. When she saw me she began to jump up and down excitedly, 'Oh! I knew you would save me ... has he gone?'

'Yes! You will never see him again.'

The girl jumped into my car and I turned the heater on full. I told her my name was Emerald and she replied, "I thought your name was Lotus."

I asked her why she thought that, and she told me that when I had spoken to myself, I had used the name Lotus. I told her Lotus was my guardian angel. She asked if Lotus was also her guardian angel and I said, 'Yes.'

Lotus whispered to me sarcastically, *'Oh! I'm here to save the world now! ... I'm some sort of evangelistic vigilante now am I?'*

The girl thanked me for saving her and told me that her name was Holly.

Upon arriving back at my apartment I covered Holly with a blanket and turned the heating up. I asked her if she would like something hot to eat and drink and she nodded her head. I felt as if she was suspicious of me, but I would not have expected anything else after what she had been through. As I prepared our food she asked me, 'What are you going to do to me?'

'I'm doing nothing to you that you don't want me to do. I work at the police station and I know a nice lady who will help you ... Where do you live Holly and where are your parents?'

'My father is dead and the man who lives with my mother used to touch me when I was alone with him. I was sick of it all so I ran away. Don't send me back will you?'

'No ... I won't send you back.'

'That man I was with when you saved me; he told me if I did what he said I would have lots of money and my own place to live ......'

'Holly! That man is ... was ... an evil man and he is back in hell where he belongs.'

I set the table and gave Holly a dish of hot soup while I mashed some potatoes to go with two hot pies which were heating in the oven, 'Do you like chicken pie?'

'Yes! ... I usually get chips from the 'chip shop'.'

I placed a plate full of mashed potato with pie and peas in front of Holly and she began to eat as if she was starving, 'Take your time Holly ... there is more food if you want it.'

I sat at the table facing Holly, "That's a nice name Holly!"

She answered me without pausing from eating her meal, 'I was born on Christmas day.'

I decided to heat up some rice-pudding for Holly and then looked to see if I had some cake, 'You are going to cost me a fortune to feed young lady!'

Holly suddenly stopped eating and looked sad ... she put her hand into the pocket of her cardigan and pulled out a five pound note, 'I have some money ... I'm sorry.' I was shocked at her reaction. I flung my arms around her and told her not to worry, that I was only joking, and to eat as much as she could.

Holly must have been starving - or had a tape worm in her stomach! She sat at the table and held her belly, 'Oh! I'm ready to pop!' ... She stood up and lifted her cardigan, 'Look! I look like I'm pregnant.'

Holly had a pot belly because of all the food she had eaten. She let out one massive long burp and then looked at me with her big round eyes, 'Excuse me.'

I looked at the clock; it was 10.30 p.m. I asked Holly what she wanted to do. She looked at me and asked, 'Can I stay here live with you?'

'You can stay here for now; I will make sure you don't go anywhere you don't want to.'

'Why can't I stay with you for ever?'

'I won't lie to you Holly ... it's not my decision, you are still a child and I have to tell social services that you are with me.'

'Oh! Can't you just hide me here?'

'It's not that simple honey ... I have to work each day and you need to be looked-after.'

'I can look after myself! ... Honest!'

'I noticed that when I found you Holly.'

'Oooow! ... That wasn't my fault ... he lied to me.'

'I can see your tired Holly ... have a good-night's sleep and we will see what happens on Monday... I promise you everything will be alright.'

I showed Holly the bedroom and I noticed there was a slightly unpleasant aroma coming from her. 'When was the last time you had a shower honey?'

She looked at me with her big round eyes and whispered, 'No! ... My name's Holly, not Honey.'

'I called you honey, because you are sweet.'

'Oh! Well I suppose that's alright then ... Lotus.'

'Why did you call me Lotus?'

'Because she is inside you and she helped me.'

I turned the shower on for Holly and left her a dressing gown. I put her dirty washing into the machine and gave her some of my underwear, saying, 'I've put your clothes in the washer and your underwear made a run for freedom.'

She looked at me and said, 'Sorry.'

After Holly had showered, I said, 'You look nice and clean now ... come on let's tuck you into bed.'

She took off her gown and she had a pair of my panties on. She looked so young and vulnerable ... I was proud of myself for stealing her away from the evil that was on the streets ... the evil that had stolen my Candy. Holly closed her eyes and I think she was asleep before I closed the door. I watched some T.V. and then decided to go to bed and squeezed in next to Holly. Soon I was in a deep sleep and I had the most unexpected dream. I could see Candy again ... she was standing alone and still staring at me with the same expression of despair as in my previous dream. She began to shake her head and I knew something was wrong. My glance floated downwards once more to fall upon Holly. She was kneeling at Candy's feet and was covered in what looked like bruises. I raised my eyes to see Candy and she was shaking her head from side to side as if something was wrong.

I woke up in the morning and opened the curtains. I couldn't understand my dream and I thought it to be a warning that someone was after Holly, or going to hurt her. Holly was lying in bed and staring at me. I shouted to her, 'Come on Holly honey ... out of bed and let's have a gigantic breakfast.' Holly was quiet and lifted the covers back to climb out of bed. Suddenly I was shocked, 'What's that?' On Holly's shoulder was what looked like teeth marks from a bite.

She said slowly, 'Oh! It doesn't matter.'

'I didn't see that on your shoulder last night!'

She stared at the floor, 'It wasn't there last night.'

'Then how did it happen?'

'Oh! I don't mind.'

'Mind what? .... What?'

'I ... I don't mind. If ... If you want to bite me.'

I was totally shocked and devastated. I told Holly to put her gown on and to come to the dining table. I prepared breakfast while my heart pounded ... I asked Holly softly and slowly, 'How did you get bitten honey?'

She replied, 'Don't you remember? You kissed me in the night ... it's a 'love bite!' ... is that why you call me honey ... *Ha Ha Ha* ... do I taste sweet ... I don't mind, it didn't hurt much.'

She began to eat her breakfast while I went into the bedroom to get dressed. I fell onto the bed crying, *'what have I done?'* I felt guilty ... I had abused an innocent child. I thought of my dream. I suddenly realised what had happened ... I shouted, 'Lotus? ... Lotus? I know you are in there ... come out!'

There was nothing but silence. I decided it was important to move Holly away from Lotus as soon as possible. It was Sunday and I had to wait until the next day to speak with the social worker at the police station.

I was sitting on the bed crying when Holly walked into the bedroom. She sat next to me on the bed and reached her arm around my shoulder, 'Don't worry Lotus ... I won't tell anyone ... I have lots of secrets I never tell.'

THE LOTUS BUD

I couldn't risk going out of the flat with Holly. I didn't know how many people may be involved with the awful man who Lotus had killed. Holly watched video's while I prepared dinner. I was glad to get through the day, but I was worried about the night. Holly was watching a film about a were-wolf in the city of London. I thought to myself … *'Is that what I have become? … Was I some kind of weird creature that only comes out at night, to bite people?'*

At 'bedtime' I tucked Holly in, and closed the door. I decided I was going to try and stay awake all night, so I lay on the settee reading a book about tales from the Isle of Lewis in Scotland. It was past midnight and I was really tired. I got up and turned on a small table lamp, they lay back down on the settee. I tried to speak to Lotus, 'Why are you doing this to me?' There was no answer, so I told Lotus she wouldn't be able to touch Holly after tonight.

I must have been half asleep when the door opened and Holly walked over to me. I asked her, 'What are you doing out of bed honey?'

She whispered, 'You can come to bed if you want … I don't mind if you want to give me a love bite.'

'No! I don't want to give you a love bite … it is wrong … now go back to bed and sleep.'

Holly went back into the bedroom. I felt sorry for her as she did not understand what was happening. I began to cry and Lotus came … she was angry and asked me, *'Who do you think you are?'*

'No! Who do you think you are?'

'She said she didn't mind my kiss!'

'That so-called kiss was a bite.'

'What has it got to do with you, it was me who saved her.'

'You saved her from abuse, to abuse her?'

'I got carried away … that's all … I won't hurt her.'

'Leave her alone … you evil bitch.'

'Oh! I'm an evil bitch am I … that's not what you said when I saved your ass, I don't remember how many times.'

'You don't bite children!'

'She said she didn't mind … are you deaf as well as stupid?'

'Well I mind, so go back where you came from.'

'She is my mine … my Lotus bud. I won't forget this you bitch … I will pay you back.'

When I awoke in the morning I was warm and in my bed. I felt something on my shoulder and looked … it was Holly's head. I began to regain my senses. I looked at the clock; it was 8 a.m. I had to be at work for nine so jumped out of bed to have a quick shower. As I stood up, everything hit me at once. I looked in the mirror and my chest, breasts and stomach were covered in blue marks tinged with red. I realised I should have been sleeping on the settee. I looked down at Holly and she had about twenty bite marks similar to mine. I swore at Lotus, 'You fucking bitch.'

Holly woke up and looked terrified, 'Please don't hit me … please don't be annoyed … I promise not to tell anyone about it.'

'I'm not shouting at you Holly!'

I went into the shower and looked at my body. I looked like I had been playing in a rugby match with a bunch of vampires. Lotus shouted to me, *'Next time you will get worse.'*

I showered and then returned to the bedroom. I dropped my bath towel to the floor and stood naked in front of Holly and asked her, 'What are all these marks on my body?'

Holly looked frightened and told me, 'Lotus bit me again … it hurt and I thought she was going to eat me. She told me to bite her … she kept shouting, *'Bite the bitch … harder … harder.'* I didn't know what was happening and I was frightened. Have I done something wrong? Am I in trouble?'

'You must never bite anyone again Holly … it is wrong.'

'I'm sorry … I wont do it again.'

I told Holly that I was going to work and she must not answer the door. I left her some food and video movies. I kissed her as I was leaving and she gave me a kiss and nibbled my face. I was shocked and jumped away. She laughed. As I closed the door I could hear Lotus in convulsions of laughter.

I arrived at work early and asked Peter if he could stand in for me a while longer as I had to see someone. He said, 'Sure … what's with the polo-neck sweater; got love bites or something.' I didn't answer him … I was worried.

I met with Kay the social worker and explained that I had found Holly walking the streets. I told her the story relating to her abusive step-father and her running away from home. Kay told me that Holly would have to be taken into care and that she would be placed with suitable foster parents. I arranged to call for Holly with Kay in the afternoon, and I was happy that she would be cared for and most of all … safe from Lotus. Lotus was angry and hissed at me all afternoon, *'You have no right to nip my bud … She is mine! … Do you hear me? … I will get you back for this.'*

Kay called for me in the afternoon and a temporary replacement was allocated to the switchboard. We drove to my flat in Kay's car; I was terrified. I was crying in the car and Kay thought it was because I was sad to see Holly go. Really I was crying because I felt frightened and guilty.

Frightened in case Holly showed her bite marks to anyone and ruined my life. Guilty, because I blamed myself ... even though it was Lotus.

We entered the flat and I shouted for Holly. There was no answer so I looked in the bedroom where Holly was asleep on the bed. I gently woke her saying, 'Wake up Holly! A nice lady is here to meet you.'

Kay introduced herself to Holly, 'Hello Holly I'm Kay ... You are a big girl for thirteen years of age ... and haven't you got lovely big round eyes?'

Kay told Holly that she would be taking her to a nice house, and people would be there all the time to look after her. Holly asked, 'Can't I stay here with Lotus?'

My heart was in my mouth and I had to swallow before answering and praying Kay did not ask who Lotus was, 'No I am sorry honey.'

'*Ooooow!* Alright then.'

Holly handed Kay her coat. As she lifted her arms while Kay held it out for her, her blouse button came undone and opened revealing the bruises across her chest. Kay recoiled in horror, 'What in God's name are all those marks?'

I was so frightened I felt faint. Kay opened Holly's blouse with her finger, 'I have never seen anything like this in my life ... those look like ... teeth marks. Who has been biting you girl?'

I bit my tongue as my whole life flashed before my eyes. Holly pouted her lips and looked at the floor and then she answered, 'The same person who did it to Emerald.'

Kay gasped, and her mouth was wide open as she whispered, 'What in God's name is going on here?'

Lotus shouted to me, '*I told you I would pay you back.*'

Kay rushed out of my flat with Holly ... I didn't blame her. I was left sitting alone and crying. I had no idea how to talk my way out of this problem. I thought to myself ... 'how ironic that I had saved Holly from a fate worse than death and as a result … I was wishing I was dead.'

Lotus said, '*I told you I would pay you back!*'

I was too depressed to argue, 'Well done Lotus!'

'*You shouldn't mess with me.*'

'You are going to destroy us both Lotus.'

'*No! You are … Why should I remain repressed?*'

'You are hardly repressed … you're a living fucking nightmare.'

'*Don't swear, I don't like it. You want everything your own way Emerald … you are a selfish bitch.*'

'You are there to help me if I ask.'

'*And you are there to help me. We said we were working together when we killed Max and his cronies … remember?*'

'Because we worked together does not mean you can take over my life.'

'*Your life is my life … you cannot use me to kill people and then pretend I don't exist.*'

'Oh! Leave me alone Lotus, don't you see I have a problem and I need time to think?'

'*Yes! Of course I see. I am that problem. I want my bud back!*'

I decided the best thing I could do was to return to work as soon as possible. I had to phone for a taxi to take me to the police station as my car was still in the car park at work. I went into my office and took over on the switchboard. My stomach was turning over with fear, how was I going to talk my way out of this situation.

As I was preparing to go home I was asked to call to the superintendent's office. Upon entering I found Kay was also sat waiting to see me. The superintendent directed me to sit down; he asked me how I was feeling. I told him I was fine … I felt like shouting, 'Oh! Get on with it.'

'Kay has reported an incident regarding a young girl who you were caring for.'

'She was homeless sir. I only took her into my home on Saturday night ... I couldn't leave her out on the street.'

Kay was sitting with her nose in the air and her bottom lip was trembling.

The chief continued, 'How did you manage to have all the bite marks on your body?'

'We were hungry at dinnertime last night and had no food, so we tried to eat each other ... unfortunately she was too skinny so I was going to fatten her up an.........'

The superintendent interrupted me, 'Please! I have to make these enquires!'

'I'm sorry sir ... I find it hard to accept that I helped this child and Kay ran away and left me at my home with no transport.'

The chief looked at Kay, 'Is this correct?'

Kay stuttered, 'I ... I......'

I interrupted Kay, 'My concern was for the child's safety and personal welfare.' I looked at Kay and asked, 'What did you think I was going to do, 'eat the two of you?'

Kay continued, 'Well! I have never seen anything like this in my seven years of working in social care; what about the marks on your body?'

'Excuse me! What I do in my relationships is private and personal.'

The superintendent interrupted us, 'Now ... Now ladies we must not let this situation get out of control. I will have to seek further advice regarding this matter. Please carry on as normal with your work and I will be in contact with you both soon.'

As we were leaving the superintendent's office Kay looked down her nose at me and smirked. I drew my lips back and showed her my teeth while sucking in air; doing an interpretation of Hannibal Lector. She looked terrified and ran down the corridor screaming as if her knickers were on fire. I returned home and sat to drink a bottle of wine and drown my sorrows. I could find no peace. Lotus would not leave me alone, *'Drinking to hide away from your mistakes?'*

'I haven't made any damn mistakes ... it was you who bit Holly.'

'Oooo! ... Nasty temper! ... Drunken bitch!'

'I have only had one small glass of wine.'

'Well what will you be like when you have drunk the bottle ... No wonder you're ruining your life ... Alcoholic!'

I threw the bottle across the room and screamed, 'Leave me alone ... go away.'

'You always were a loser ... Emerald.'

'I will lose you if I ever have any luck.'

'You can be really hurtful sometimes Emerald.'

I retired to my bedroom and pulled the blankets over my head to hear a whisper upon the wind, *'I'm still here! ... Don't worry!'*

THE WEB AND THE BLACK WIDOW

I awoke early the next morning for work and had a shower. I felt depressed; it was as if my whole life was like a jigsaw falling to pieces.

When I went into the office Peter moved away from the desk and began to tut, 'I have been told you are now eating children.'

'Only little roasted ones. Peter ... Your looking tasty today ... can I have a bite?'

'You can eat me anytime my darling.'

I worked nervously all day waiting for, and imagining the inevitable quick call from a head popping around my office door, 'Emerald ... the super. needs to see you immediately,' and then, those omnipotent words, spoken by the super. *'Oh! Sorry your career and life have gone down the drain ... and you are to be charged with child abuse. Will you close the door on the way out please Emerald ... thank you.'*

Thankfully, I completed my shift without any problems and returned home to meet with a bottle of wine and my worst nightmare, *'Drinking again are we?'*

'Piss off Lotus ... I will probably be out of a job, out of a home, and possibly staying in prison because of you tomorrow ... well done! We're finished!'

'You always were a pessimistic loser.'

'Well I don't care anymore! ... You fucking psycho!'

'Take that back ... you bitch. You can be really cruel and hurtful sometimes.'

'Don't you understand ... it doesn't matter anymore ... We are finished ... This time tomorrow we will both be looking at the sky through the bars of a prison cell.'

I finished my bottle of wine and opened another one before going to bed around midnight. I decided; my life was in the hands of fate.

I awoke and my eyes were closed. I could hear the birds singing so I knew it was morning. I didn't want my night to end; at least I felt safe, tucked into my nice warm bed. I was almost letting myself fall back into sleep to escape from the day. I thought, 'how simple it would be to stay in bed and ... and maybe the world would leave me alone and carry on turning without my help.'

I was suddenly startled as I felt something move in the bed next to me. I opened my eyes and almost jumped out of the bed from fright. Holly was in the bed next to me fast asleep. Lotus was with me and said, '*Go to work.*'

I looked at the clock and it was 7.30 a.m. 'What the hell is going on Lotus?'

'*It's none of your business ... just go to work.*'

'What's Holly doing here?'

'*It's none of your business ... go to work.*'

'Of course it's my business ... she's in my fucking bed.'

'*There is no need to swear in front of the child.*'

'Now you have really finished us!'

'*How many times can you be finished? You said everything was finished last night, and nothing matters anymore. Don't you understand Emerald? ... You are the web and I am the 'Black Widow.'*'

'If anything ever happens to that child you will be answerable to me Lotus.'

'*Nothing can ever happen to the child.*'

Holly began to wake up. She yawned and stretched out her arms. She flung her arms around me and shouted, 'I knew you wouldn't leave me with that horrible woman *Hoooray!* I'm home again!'

I was shocked and disorientated. I walked from the bedroom and into the shower. It was as if I was in a trance ... simply acting out my daily routine. When I looked in the mirror; I noticed scratches down my legs. I traced my steps, back through my mind over the previous day's activities and I could not recall any time when I may have scratched myself. The scratches were deep and stung when I showered. I put some ointment on them and wore some baggy pants for work.

In my mind I had accepted that I was going to be arrested and put into prison. I had also accepted that my next night would most likely be spent in a prison cell, and yet there remained one flicker of hope ... as if I was trapped in a deep hole and yet still hoped for a way to climb to freedom. I assumed Holly had escaped from Kay's and therefore expected a knock on my door at any moment.

I decided that on arrival at work, I would tell Kay that Holly was back in my home. I would ask Kay to stop being an official pain, and to let Holly stay with me. I knew the latter would be a waste of time, but at least I had a straw to clutch onto.

When I arrived at work I noticed the whole police station was in a state of chaos. Officers were running around like headless chickens. I walked into my office and asked Peter what was going on. He looked at me sadly and spoke slowly, 'It's ... It's Kay. You're not going to believe this. Some maniac has killed her ... she was strangled in the night.'

I caught hold of the table as I felt faint, 'Oh my God! No!'

'Yes ... I'm afraid so. I don't know what the world is coming to. You are not safe in your own home these days.'

'Well you go home and have a sleep Peter, you must be exhausted.'

"Yes! … The switchboard has been alive with calls. I feel like a bloody octopus, or should I say I wish I was. The calls seem to have eased off now. I will see you at five, darling … Bye for now.'

'Bye Peter!'

I made some tea and sat down like a frightened mouse. I didn't have to be a genius to work out what had happened. Lotus must have been busy in the night. She would have known where Kay lived from the time she had driven to my home to collect Holly as she had stopped at her own house on the way to collect some files. I also remember her remarking how she was happy living alone without a man in her life. I thought about telling the police that Holly had turned up at my home but … there were a lot of 'but's. If Holly was found at my flat, she would be questioned until the police found out what had happened. This was a murder investigation now, and not some query as to how a few bite marks occurred.

I suppose I was like an ostrich and buried my head in the sand. I kept clinging onto what tiny fragments of hope I could imagine. I had a day full of reassuring 'maybe's'. Maybe nobody new Holly was staying with Kay; maybe no one noticed that Holly was missing; maybe if they knew Holly was missing they would not suspect me … why should they?

I returned home and found Holly watching T.V. As soon as I walked into the room she shouted, 'Kay's picture has been on the news. She was murdered and they are asking for information. Don't worry … I can keep secrets.'

The only answer I had to my predicament was to do what Lotus had advised … to carry on as normal with my mundane life, which I prayed would remain that way.

As Holly ate her dinner she asked me questions which I had no answers for. 'Am I a fugitive Emerald? Am I on the run from the police?'

I told Holly she must ask Lotus her questions as she had brought her here and was making all the decisions for her. She asked me if I was still her friend and I told her that I would always be her friend. I realised how confusing everything must be for her, because it was confusing for me. I washed the dishes and then I washed some clothes. I had to keep busy for I knew the dark would come soon.

It was a freezing winter's night. The woman was standing under a street light; she shivered while her naked legs trembled. Her skirt was short and she wore black stockings which left a seductive white area of skin leading into the unknown, where most men search endlessly. She chewed on gum and held a cigarette in one hand. She looked at her watch; it was 12.30 a.m. She would finish working in one hour then return home and carry on with her life. A car passed by slowly with the window down and a man shouted, 'How mush is oral?'

She shouted back, 'Twenty-five pounds.'

'Is that without a condom darling?'

'No! Fuck off!'

'You Fuck off you slag.'

The car sped away to leave the woman grumbling and swearing. She could hear footsteps approaching and thought it might be her pimp. He would not be happy tonight as she had seen only two clients.

Through the mist a young girl slowly appeared ... she looked about thirteen years of age. She wondered what such a young girl was doing out so late, 'Hi! What are you doing?'

'Nothing.'

'What's your name?'

'Holly.'

'Well you stand there Holly and when a car stops, move behind me. If I pull a trick I will give ye' ten pounds.'

'Alright ... can I have the money first?'

'I 'ave to get it from them first ye' silly cow. Stand there ... that's right ... quickly there's a car coming.'

The car slowed down and a man shouted to Holly, 'How much darling?

Holly shouted, 'Ten pounds.'

The man shouted anxiously, 'G ... Get in! ... Get in!'

The prostitute jumped forwards and shouted at Holly, 'You stupid fucking bitch ... you don't tell 'em ten pounds. I said I'll give you the ten pounds.'

The driver panicked and sped away. The prostitute was raging with anger and grabbed Holly by the hair throwing her into the road, 'You stupid bitch, fuck off away from my patch or I'll rip your fucking head off.'

There was a slight clicking noise as her neck broke. Her body was limp and still being supported by Lotus. A car drove up and the man looked at Lotus who was wearing dark glasses and dressed in black fishnet stockings which seemed to stretch upwards for ever from her high-heeled shoes, eventually to disappear up to her short black leather skirt.

The man shouted to Lotus, 'How much?'

Lotus replied in her deep voice, *'I'm not for sale.'*

The man looked at the prostitute whom Lotus was holding and said, 'She looks drugged up ... how much is she?'

'Ten pounds.'

'Right! Put her on the back seat.'

When the girl had been placed in the car, the man shouted, 'I can do anything I want with her! Right?'

Lotus shouted back, *'Do whatever you want ... she won't mind I promise.'*

The man sped away to a heaven where hell was waiting.

Lotus asked Holly if she was alright. Holly said to Lotus, 'I don't know what she was so upset about ... I had got her the ten pounds she wanted.'

Lotus said, *'Sometimes people are never happy … people are greedy … she got her ten pounds in the end anyway. Let's go home now … it's sad when you can't have a walk without people causing trouble. I'm sorry you had to listen to that woman's swearing.'*

As they began to walk home a man drove up to them in an expensive looking car. He shouted out of the open car window, 'Where my bitch? … Where my bitch? Watcha' man …'

The pimp never finished his sentence as Lotus rammed his head down onto the edge of the glass window which was partly up. Blood ran down the white paintwork of the car from the man's torn throat.

Lotus walked home with Holly and they both held hands. Lotus explained to Holly how dangerous the world was and told her how important it was to be strong and defend yourself. She told Holly how I was soft and would let people do anything with me, until she arrived to protect her.

The two returned home and went to bed. They kissed each other and said goodnight. Lotus told Holly to say her prayers. Holly was happy; she had never been cared for by anyone as much as Lotus had done. She felt safe with Lotus and trusted her. She knew Lotus would look after her. Lotus wrapped herself around Holly in the bed and held her tightly, for she knew she would not be with her again until I slept once more.

In the morning I was sweating. I pushed Holly from my body, 'Holly I'm soaking in sweat … why do you cling so close?'

'It was Lotus she wrapped herself around me like a spider.'

There was a sudden banging at the entrance door of the flat. I jumped out of bed in a panic not realising I was only wearing a t-shirt. I opened the door and a policeman and woman walked in as they showed me a search warrant.

The policewoman explained to me, 'We are investigating the death of Kay Brooks and have a warrant to search your premises.'

I didn't know what to say. Several police officers then came into the flat and started searching in cupboards; they kept looking towards my legs. I realised I was wearing a shirt halfway up my bottom and dived for the bedroom. The policewoman followed me and I told her, 'I am putting some clothes on ... is this the way you usually treat a respectable woman.'

She replied, 'We have our work to do madam.'

I looked around the bedroom and could not believe that Holly had gone. The policewoman asked me when I had last seen Holly and I told her that it was when she had left with Kay. They finished the search and left the flat telling me to call them immediately if I found out any information which may help them with their enquires. I got ready for work and arrived at my office on time.

'Hi Peter my darling! ... How are you today?'

'I'm shattered ... it's been another mad night. There were two murders last night. One was a prostitute and the other was a 'pimp' ... cars and ambulances everywhere. It's so annoying when I have to phone people in the night and they are half asleep ... all you get from them is, 'What? ... What? ... What?''

'You sound like you need some sleep Peter.'

'Yes! ... Maybe tonight will be a bit more peaceful. Bye my darling.'

'Bye Peter.'

I began working on the switchboard, but I was anxious to return home and find out what was going on. Because of the way I was feeling the day seemed to go on for ever. Eventually Peter returned and wheeled his chair over to the desk. I removed my chair and as I leaned over him I caught the smell of his aftershave lotion, '*Mmmm!* That smells good.'

I jokingly gave him a kiss on the cheek and pretended to nibble him. I felt an unusual urge to bite his face and I had to use all my will-power to stop myself. As a result I gave him a 'gentle bite' on the neck, 'Oh! You tease … Oh! Go on bite me again … or even better let me bite you.'

I had to make a quick exit from the office with a red face whilst wondering how I was ever going to face Peter again. I shouted at Lotus, 'Why did you do that?'

She laughed, *'Can't you take a joke?'*

'I have to work with him.'

'He liked it, and I like him, and you like him. Why do have to make everything so complicated?'

'And when he says something to upset you, and you murder him … that's not complicated for you! But I have to pick up all the pieces from the web.'

'You always have to exaggerate and be a 'drama queen.' Sometimes I think you have a really twisted nature.'

I walked into my flat and Holly greeted me, *'Hooray!* You're both home at last. I asked her, 'Where did you vanish to this morning?'

'I ran down the fire-escape and into the flat below through the window.'

'But the flat below belongs to the old lady.'

'No it doesn't … Lotus has given it me now … the old lady has died.'

I was shocked, 'What? When did the old lady die?'

'Last night.'

I shouted at Lotus, 'How did she die … you murdering bastard?'

'Please don't swear in front of Holly.'

'Tell me how she died? …………...'

'Quickly.'

THE COUNSELLOR

I was experiencing a kind of denial. I had questions I wanted to ask but simply did not want to face the answers. I decided to let Lotus carry on with her life while I carried on with mine. What choice did I have? ... What could I do? ... Who could I talk to? I think that was one of the most difficult parts of my relationship with Lotus. She made herself a secret. I decided to see a private counsellor; I would be able to talk to someone secure in the knowledge that everything would be confidential. Lotus wasn't happy, *'What do you want to see a counsellor for ... I know you worry about things too much but there's nothing wrong with you. You can talk to me ... I have always looked after you ... I will counsel you ...Lie down ... are you relaxed? Why are you always looking for problems?....... Come on tell me!'*

'I don't know ... all I want to do is live a peaceful, normal life.'

'And why do you swear in front of children?'

'Because I am annoyed.'

'Well you must not become angry anymore.'

'I will try ... I know you are right.'

'And why are you always looking for problems and causing trouble which other people have to help you with? And then why do you blame the people who have helped you for the problems you had?'

'Oh! This isn't going to work ... You're not a counsellor.'

'See! The truth hurts ... All you will do is waste your money.'

'It's my bloody money ... at least I work.'

'Stop shouting ... Stop!'
'You would make the devil shout ... I ... I hate you.'
'You really can be cold and ... and hurtful sometimes.'

I sat in the chair facing Mrs Bates. She lived in a different area which was over an hour's drive away. She was a kind calm lady of around forty years of age. She explained that our first meeting would be informal and would be intended to see how we worked together, and to determine if we both wished to enter into a journey of enlightenment.

Mrs Bates told me that I could call her by her first name, Jenny. We sat facing each other in an ordinary sitting room in her house. The meeting was very informal and I felt comfortable and relaxed. We sat facing each other upon soft chairs. Jenny made tea and offered me cake and biscuits. We sat staring at each other whilst munching digestive biscuits and discussing the world news and weather. Jenny was a very attractive lady with short blonde hair. She wore a long black dress which hugged her shapely figure. I asked her if she had a partner and she told me that her mother had died last year and she lived alone and was not involved in a relationship.

Eventually she asked me, 'Was there something in particular you wanted to talk about?' There was a long silence. I felt a slight panic. It was as if I didn't know why I had come to see Jenny. Was I a fool, who looked for problems which didn't exist as Lotus had repeatedly told me? I stared at Jenny ... her lips looked soft and wet and a strand of blonde hair was hanging down her forehead near her eyes. She had kind-looking blue eyes. I leaned towards her and brushed the hair from her brow with my finger. She seemed slightly startled, 'Oh! Thank you Emerald.'

'You have beautiful blue eyes Jenny.'

'Thank you and your eyes are beautiful as well.'

'I don't really know what to say ... maybe I should go ... I think this may be a mistake.'

'You may leave whenever you want to Emerald.'

'Emer!'

'Pardon!'

'You can call me Emer ... if you want to.'

We sat staring at each other for several minutes then I asked, 'Is everything I say just between us?'

'Of course it is ... I give you my word that what is said in this room will go no further.'

'Sometimes I hear voices.' There was another long silence. 'And sometimes I talk to myself.'

'A lot of people talk to themselves Emer.'

'Sometimes I think I change into somebody else.'

'What makes you think that you can be somebody else?'

I sat looking at the carpet and I felt very agitated. 'My father would whip my bare bottom ... when I was a child ... then he would wipe ointment over the marks.'

'That must have been dreadful for you.'

'No! That's the problem I have ... It haunts me.'

'What haunts you?'

'I was excited ... I enjoyed it.'

'Emotions are often mixed up when we are young. Sigmund Freud once said – *'Analyse any human emotion, no matter how far it may be removed from the sphere of sex, and you are sure to discover somewhere the primal impulse, to which life owes its perpetuation.'*

'But why would my emotions still be mixed up now?'

'It's like a jigsaw which we make as we develop and grow through life ... we all have our own jigsaw to make and sometimes the pieces may be put in the wrong place.'

'I watched as my father killed himself.'

'How did he kill himself Emer.?'

'He took an overdose of tablets.'

I began to cry and Jenny gave me a tissue and put her arm around me, 'I think that is enough for today Emer.'

I stood up and Jenny was close to me. I could feel the heat from her body as she held me comfortingly. I placed my hand on her hip. Lotus shouted at me, *'Here we go ... go on mess things up and cause problems like you always do.'*

I pulled Jenny toward me slightly ... I wanted her to put her arms around me and hold me tight. I began to cry more, 'Hold me Jenny ... please?'

She put her arms around me. My body was pressing against hers and it felt wonderful. It seemed so long since I had experienced love, or making love. I lifted my eyes to meet Jenny's and pulled her body against me tightly. We were staring into each others eyes; I moved my lips to meet with hers. Her lips were wet and I felt her body go limp, but it was only for an instant. She gently pushed me away, 'No! Emerald! Please! You must not feel this way about me ... your emotions are mixed up at the moment ... you are emotional.'

'Of course I am emotional. Don't you love me?'

'Emerald ... your eyes are going black.'

Lotus threw Jenny onto the floor. She sat on top of her and ripped her dress open so her breasts could be seen. She hissed and bit her breasts until the floor was red with blood and Jenny's crying became no more than a whimper. Jenny watched as Lotus's dark eyes changed to become big and round. Lotus whispered, *'Kill her Holly ... it's time for you to learn.'*

Holly put her hands around Jenny's neck and began to squeeze. It was a long time before Jenny stopped breathing and was still. I stood up and began to cry, 'All I wanted was to love you Jenny ... we could have been so happy, and I could have lived here with you.'

Holly shouted excitedly, 'I did it Lotus ... is she dead?'

As Lotus left the room she looked back at Jenny and whispered, '*You were right my love – Analyse any human emotion, no matter how far it may be removed from the sphere of sex, and you are sure to discover somewhere the primal impulse.*'

I had a shower when I arrived back at my flat. There was blood on my mouth and clothes. I tried to think where I had been but could not remember. I asked Holly if she knew where the blood had come from and she whispered to me, 'Maybe it's a secret.'

I cooked dinner and then settled down to read a book while having a bottle of wine. It was not long before I was asleep; all in all, it had been a busy day.

DOMESTIC VIOLENCE

The man was drunk as he walked home from the football match. His team had lost ... again, and he was angry. His wife was waiting at home and had made sure the children were in bed. She knew he would beat her, but hoped it would be quick and easy. She had learned a lot of tricks over the past years, such as falling to the floor holding her stomach, or arm, or where ever the last blow had been. She had to call the police several times as she was frightened for her life and the safety of her children.

On this particular occasion I had been working a little later on the switchboard when the woman called. She explained to me what her husband was like. I asked her address promising to send someone who would be able to help, round to her house. I told the woman my name was Emerald and that one of my colleagues would call. I also promised that once my colleague paid her a visit, she would never have any more trouble from her husband.

Lotus was dressed in black and Holly was close by. They peeped in the back window, through a tiny crack where the curtains met. It was a bungalow and they watched as the man came home and walked into the lounge from the front door. The man threw his coat onto the floor and began looking around for an excuse to punish his wife, 'Where's my fucking dinner you lazy cow?'

'It's here my love.' She placed his dinner on the table and began to walk away.

'Wait a minute … what's the fucking rush … been up to something have you?' The man looked at his dinner, 'What the fuck's that?'

The woman looked at the dinner she had made and knew this was going to be a bad beating. The dinner was perfect; with roast potatoes, chicken and peas covered with rich onion gravy. The man grabbed her by her hair and flung her across the room. She tried not to scream as she didn't want the children to wake up. He dived on top of her and began to twist her arms and pinch her skin. He took hold of her hand and began to bend and twist her wrist. He could hurt her like this for several hours knowing that, later, nothing would be seen even though she would cover her body because she felt shame and embarrassment.

Lotus asked Holly if she wanted to stop this badness. Holly asked Lotus if she would be with her, and Lotus told her she would always be with her. She gave Holly some thin gloves and told her to put them on.

Holly tried the back door which was open. She walked in and found herself standing in the kitchen. Lotus guided her, *'You need something which will be easy to use, and you must decide if you want him to go quickly or to suffer.'*

'I hate him Lotus!'

'Use a long thin knife that is strong … not springy or it will snap.'

Holly felt the different knives and chose one. Lotus continued to guide her, *'Good choice … I couldn't have chosen better myself.'*

Holly slowly opened the door to the lounge and the man was sitting on top of his wife twisting her arm. His wife was trembling whilst crying in pain, and had her eyes closed tightly.

Lotus whispered to Holly, *'Don't hesitate … stab hard into his back … remember … hard and deep as if your hand is to pass through him.'*

Holly crept up behind the man and lifted her hand high into the air. Her big round eyes looked even larger and her mouth was wide open as she concentrated on her task. Her hand trembled slightly and she hesitated ... Lotus shouted, *'NOW!'* The man turned his head and his mouth dropped open. Holly cried out like an angry child as the knife swooped down. Because the man had turned his body sideways, the blade travelled downwards into his chest. He began to screech like a baby in pain. Lotus praised Holly, *'Well done! ... He will die slowly now, unless you want to finish him quickly?'*

Holly looked at the woman who was shaking and staring as if she was in a dream. Holly asked the woman, 'Do you mind if I eat the lovely dinner you have made ... and ... and have you any cake please?'

The woman nodded her head and walked into the kitchen in a state of shock. The man was bleeding profusely while whimpering and struggling for breath.

Holly ate the dinner while speaking to the man, *'Mmmmm!* You should have eaten your dinner mister ... it's lovely ... you're a bad man hurting people ... it's not nice to hurt people ... *Ooooo!* Cake ... I love cake.'

Holly finished her dinner and asked the man, 'What's it like dying mister?' There was no reply. 'Time to go home ... Goodbye and thank you very much for the dinner and cake lady.'

As the two walked home Lotus said to Holly, *'I'm very pleased with you Holly. You are very well mannered, that's something which has been lost in the world today. The way you said 'thank you' to the nice lady really made me happy. I feel really proud of you.'*

'That's what is important in life ... being happy, isn't it Lotus?'

'Yes it certainly is Holly.'

THE PSYCHOLOGIST

I walked into work as usual and was asked to go to the superintendent's office. I felt nervous; I was aware that a visit to see the superintendent must warrant a matter of great importance, not that I had anything to worry about of course.

'Come in Emerald. How are you today?'

'I am well thank you sir. How are you?'

'I would like to introduce you to Graham.'

I turned my head to see a young man of around 35 years of age sitting in a chair to my right. The superintendent continued, 'Graham is here to talk with you about Holly.'

Graham extended his hand which I shook, 'Hello Graham, I am pleased to meet you.'

Graham told me that he had an office which was more comfortable and private where we could talk. He walked with me to a quiet office and asked me if I would like something to drink. I asked for a tea and Graham soon returned holding two plastic cups. I remarked to Graham, 'Everything seems to be plastic these days ... don't you think?'

Graham was busy wiping his scalded hand on a tissue, 'Yes, especially cups.'

I grabbed Graham's hand and began to wipe it with a handkerchief, 'There! ... Now you are dry and back to normal. I kissed his hand and crossed my legs so he could see the top of my stockings. I saw his eyes wander down and hoped that I may be able to interfere, or influence what ever he was going to talk to me about. He cleared his throat, '*Err Ermm!* I would like to ask you about Holly?'

'Are you a policeman?'

'No … I am a police psychologist.'

'Does that mean you are a policeman who rides a peddle bike?'

'*Haa Haa Ha!* I suppose in some cases it might.'

I crossed my legs again and my black skirt moved up several inches revealing my naked white thighs.

'You … You certainly are a very attractive woman Holly.'

'My name's Emerald.'

'Oh! Sorry … Emerald.'

'Do you like my legs?'

'You have lovely legs … but I would like to talk about your emotions. Would you like to talk about your emotions Emerald?'

'Yes.'

There was a silence while Graham stared at me. He waited for me to continue …… 'Yes! … Emerald!'

'Yes … Graham?'

'You said you would like to talk about your emotions.'

'Analyse any human emotion, no matter how far it may be removed from the sphere of sex, and you are sure to discover somewhere the primal impulse.'

'"Amazing … where did you learn that Holly?'

'My name is Emerald.'

'Sorry … Emerald.'

'Why do you keep calling me Holly?'

'I'm sorry Emerald. What do you think the statement you have just made means?'

'What statement?'

'The one you made regarding human emotions?'

'It means that one way or another you are trying to fuck me … either physically or mentally.'

'And would you like that?'

'Would you?'

'I am not trying to hurt you Holly.'

'**E.M.E.R.A.L.D.** My fucking name is Emerald.'

'Then who is Holly?'

'This is silly, we are going round in circles. Tell me what you want to know and stop talking through a maze. Is that what they teach you to do at your cycling school ... play 'mind games?' What do you want to know? ... Graham?'

'Alright Emerald we will play it your way.'

'I'm not very good at playing games Graham ... I like to get straight to the point.'

'Emerald ... do you realise you walked into your bedroom when Kay, the social worker was visiting you, and transformed yourself into another person called Holly.'

'Who told you that rubbish?'

'Kay.'

'Well that is easy to answer. Kay didn't like me for some reason ... she thought I ate children ... maybe if you had seen Kay, she may have still been alive.'

'And that brings me to another question ... Where were you on the night that Kay was murdered?'

'I was out at the roasted children's buffet.' There was a tense silence .... 'I was where I am every damned night ... sat in my apartment.'

'You had a girlfriend ...... Candy.'

'Yes! ... Disappointed Graham? Well don't be, I like men as well as women ... the problem is that most men are like you.'

'What do you mean?'

'They're all out to fuck you one way or another.'

'And how does that make you feel Emerald?'

'It doesn't make me feel anything because I am with a woman.'

'What woman?'

'What?'

'You said you are with a woman … What woman?'

'I was thinking of Candy.'

'And now Candy is dead.'

'She was murdered by M.E.N…….. MEN! Now do you understand?'

'That was tragic … I'm sorry.'

'Why are you sorry? … Because you are a man?'

'Do you hate men?'

'No! I don't hate anyone … there is no one alive who I hate.'

'Did you ever see Holly again?'

'Holly was with Kay.'

'Holly left Kay's before she was strangled. Do you know where Holly is Emerald?'

'If I did, why would I tell you?'

'I am only trying to help.'

'So if I tell you she is at my home now … what would you say?'

'I would ask you to come with me to see her so we may be able to help her.'

'You're one big fucking bundle of help aren't you Graham?'

'I try my best! … Can I help you?'

'Oh! Very clever … You're asking me, how you can help me?'

'I only want to find out what is happening.'

'Come with me now then, and I will show you Holly.'

'Oh! ………………'

'You seem surprised?'

'No! … Alright then! … You mean now?'

'Yes, now!'

We walked from the office and I whispered to Graham, 'We must keep this a secret; I don't want her taken into care.'

'I understand Emerald ... Anything you say.'

'Follow me down the back stairs and we will go in my car.'

It was around 5 p.m. when we arrived at my flat. I showed Graham into the lounge and told him I would call Holly. I went into the bedroom and Holly was asleep, 'Wake up honey ... there is a man here to see you.'

'Who is he Emerald?'

'He just wants to see that you are alright.'

'But didn't you tell him I am happy.'

'Yes but he didn't believe me. Put on your pretty floral dress and your pink head band. Now! You look like a princess ... Go and see him, his name is Graham. I will tidy up in here.'

Holly walked into the lounge and Graham gasped. Holly was pretty; she looked beautiful in her clothes. He said, 'Hello Holly ... How do you feel today?'

Holly jumped onto the settee next to Graham and shouted excitedly, 'Are you going to ask me, lot's and lot's of questions?'

'I have come to see if you are well.'

'Do I look well?'

'Yes ... Where is Emerald?'

'Oh! She is tidying the bedroom.'

'Shall we go and see her?'

'*Yess! ... Yess!* ... Shall we shout *BOOO!* And open the door quickly?'

'Is that what you want to do Holly?'

'*Yess! Yess!* Follow me ... Let's creep quietly.'

Holly held tightly onto Graham's hand as they approached the bedroom. They both stood together and Holly put her hand onto the door handle. She whispered to Graham, '*Shhhh!* Are you ready? .... *BOOOOOOO!*' .... *Oooooow!* There's nobody in here Graham ... That is peculiar isn't it Graham? I wonder where she could be hiding. Where do you think she is Graham?'

'I think you're the only one who has the answer to that question Holly.'

'Well! I think she may be in the shower. *'Tip-toe ... Tip-toe don't let any beasties know'* ... that's right Graham hold onto my hand tightly. Listen I can hear the water running, can you?'

'Yes ... maybe this isn't such a good idea after all.'

'Oh! Don't be frightened Graham ... after all it's only a game and you like games ... don't you?'

'I will wait by the door Holly.'

'Alright! ... You wait here and I will go in and scare her ... and ... and then she will come out to see you.'

Holly crept into the shower room and Graham could hear her shout, **'BOOOOOOO!'**

Graham could hear the sound as if two people were laughing. Holly pushed her head around the door and shouted to Graham, 'Guess what Graham?'

Graham was smiling, 'What Holly?'

'It wasn't Emerald Graham .... it was Lotus.'

Graham's expression became serious, 'Who's Lotus?'

Lotus walked out of the shower room naked and wrapped herself around Graham. He struggled but she clung to him and he could not escape. He was limp and weak from shock and fear. Lotus stabbed her tongue into his mouth and bit through his lip. He fell to the floor and Lotus lay on top of him. She bit his face and he began to gurgle and choke on his own blood. The last thing he saw was the endless darkness from deep within the eyes of Lotus, and the last words he ever heard were hissed from her bloody dripping lips.

'Game over.'

I grumbled as I rolled up the short hall carpet. I passed it to Lotus who carried it down to the flat below.

I mopped the blood stains from the floorboards in the hall, 'You two are really difficult to live with. You make more mess than ten children ... sometimes I don't know what I am going to do with the two of you. I will have to buy more carpet now ... do you think I am made of money?'

Lotus hissed, *'You brought him here ... what did you bring him here for?'*

'He knew about Holly so I ....'

Lotus interrupted me, *'Holly is my girl ... if anyone goes near her I will bite them.'*

I continued with the cleaning saying, 'One day you two will be the death of me.'

Lotus sneered, *'Ha! You would have been long gone if it were not for me ... but of course ... I get no thanks for my efforts. At least Holly listens to me ... she's a good girl and is following in my footsteps.'*

Holly interrupted, 'I wish you two would stop arguing all the time ... don't you know that a child who is brought up within a disruptive environment may be emotionally disturbed?'

THE WEB

I walked into the office and joked with Peter who was sitting at the switchboard, 'How is the only man in my life?'

I pulled my chair close to Peter who looked into my eyes and replied, 'Happy now you are here my only true love.'

I crossed my legs to reveal my white thighs to Peter. Lotus hissed to me, *'You are a common flirt ... a hussy.'*

Peter looked at my legs and placed his hand on my thigh. I was pleased to feel his touch; this was the first time he had touched me since I had shouted at him after Candy's death. I could feel the heat from his hand on my cool skin and I felt aroused. It had been so long since I had made love or been touched. I opened my legs slightly whilst looking at the switchboard and talking to Peter. His hand moved further up my thigh and it sent shivers down my spine. Peter suddenly pulled away and moved from the desk to leave the office. He looked at me and smiled. He had a tear in his eye as he wheeled through the door, 'You should find yourself a proper man my love ... I'm no good to a woman.'

I was left frustrated and sad at the way Peter felt about himself. I cared for him and felt that I could easily love him. He was so kind and caring; I felt so comfortable when we were together. I didn't want some *'big superman'* all I wanted was love and to be loved. I thought to myself, 'It's typical of men ... they always have to spoil things ... I felt like shouting out in anger at Peter, 'You have hands and lips ... love me with your hands and mouth.'

I decided to let Peter know how I felt when he returned in the evening.

It was 2 p.m. and I was asked to go to the superintendent's office. I felt annoyed. Why did he keep pestering me?

'Hello Emerald! ... Sit down ... please.'

'Hello sir, how may I help you?'

'Have you seen Peter since your meeting yesterday?'

'No sir.'

'I ask because his car was left in the car park last night and his wife has said he did not return home.'

'I left him at the office at about 5 o'clock and went home sir.'

'Most peculiar ... have you any idea where he could be?'

'No sir.'

'That's all then ... bye for now ... and Emerald?'

'Yes sir.'

'Could you ... *errrm!* ... Wear something less revealing?'

'Yes sir.'

Lotus had to say something, '*You shouldn't be looking up people's skirts ... dirty old pervert.*'

The superintendent was startled by the different tone of voice, 'What ... What did you say?'

'I said ... I will be a bit more covert sir.'

'Good! ... Goodbye.'

Peter arrived back for his shift at 5 p.m. and sat next to me. I looked at him and held his hands, 'How's my man?'

'I'm fine my darling.'

'I hope I didn't upset you this morning Peter, only I am very fond of you.'

'And I am very fond of you. Sometimes I feel too fond of you.'

'How can you be too fond of me?'

'I'm old enough to be your granddad Emerald.'

'And you are wise enough, and kind enough to make us both happy. Where love grows all boundaries can have no resistance.'

'Emerald … It wouldn't work, the age gap between us is too great, and I could never give you children or even satisfy you sexually.'

I kissed Peter on the lips and pushed his hand between my thighs. He began to tremble. The office door suddenly opened and the superintendent walked in shouting, 'Emerald Carter I am arresting you ……..'

I was cautioned and read my legal rights, then two policewomen placed handcuffs onto my wrists.

I shouted out in panic, 'I was only kissing him!'

They took me by the arms and led me out of the office to an awaiting police van outside. I sat in the back of the van for what seemed like hours. A large woman sat facing me. She stared at me without blinking. I asked her, 'Where are we going?'

She continued to stare without speaking. I decided to try again, 'What have I done?'

The woman was big and ugly and sneered at me, 'Your pretty looks won't help you where you're going.'

'And where might that be?' I asked as Lotus became restless.

'You will know when you get there … be patient … you will have all the time in the world to think about your past mistakes.'

Lotus was out in an instant and kicked my foot towards the guard while twisting my body sideways. I was still wearing my high-heeled shoes, and the long pointed heel stuck into the woman's throat. Lotus hissed as the woman stared for one last time into the black void of her killer's eyes, *'Now you have all the time in the world to think about your last mistake.'*

The van stopped and the back door opened. Lotus kicked out and her heel passed through the eye socket and into the brain of the other woman who was escorting her. She looked out at her surroundings. The van was parked in a large empty courtyard. Towering walls hid the light from the day amongst shadows that crept to find the elusive light of escape.

An elderly lady walked over and Lotus was ready to kill her. As Lotus was about to strike the old lady began to talk to her, 'Are you my friend? … Are you Mary, mother of Jesus?'

Lotus stared at the woman, *'No! I am Lotus, and I don't have friends.'*

The woman continued, 'Well you're dressed in black so I will call you the Black Widow. I think you have killed those two women. Let's go and pray for forgiveness before the nurses come and jab you.'

'Nobody will jab me.'

'Here let me take the rings from your wrists that you may pray with Jesus in your heart.' The old lady reached for a key from the belt of the guard and removed the handcuffs from Lotus, 'There you are, free from sin … now follow me.'

Lotus began to follow the old lady who led her by the arm, *'Don't pull me! … I don't like to be pulled.'*

MARY

The lady led Lotus to her room through a back door. Her room was small and bare. The walls were covered in religious pictures. Lotus felt uneasy as hundreds of pairs of eyes stared at her from the walls. The lady seemed to be in a rush, 'Quickly ... you must change from the clothes of a harlot or you will be punished.'

The lady was small and in her seventies; she threw clothes onto her bed. Lotus felt uncomfortable and decided to leave, 'Hello! My name is Holly ... Are we playing a game?'

The lady turned around to meet the gaze of Holly, 'Oh! Where has the sinner gone? Oh! A little girl with big round eyes ... you must put these clothes on and dress respectably. You look shamefull dressed like that ... You dirty girl.'

Holly looked sad, 'They are not my clothes ... They belong to Lotus.'

Holly rummaged through the clothes which had been thrown onto the bed, '*Ooooow!* Look what I have found ... some nice baggy jeans and a T-Shirt with a man's face on the front ... Oh dear! The man is crying and he has blood on his head ... he looks sad.'

The old lady became angry, 'That is Jesus ... don't you know who the Lord is?'

'I thought Lotus was the Lord ... She told me she was the Lord of justice.'

'There is only one Lord my child ... Are you a catholic, a protestant or ... one of the others?'

'I think I am lost.........'

'Oh! Now don't cry my dear, take that shirt off ... it is only to be worn by a catholic.'

Holly was handed a shirt which had flowers embroidered on the front, '*Oooow!* That's beautiful ... Thank you ... What's your name?'

'My name is Mary.'

Suddenly the sound of sirens could be heard screaming. Mary looked frightened, 'Oh! We have to stay in our rooms now. You sit on the bed and I will sing to you.'

Holly lay on the bed and rested her head on Mary's lap. Mary began to rock while singing a lullaby,

> *'Angels singing, go to sleep*
> *Little children should not peep,*
> *When the night begins to creep*
> *Close your eyes now*
> *Sleep, Sleep, Sleep.'*

Holly was fast asleep when the door was opened. There were too many nurses to enter the room all at once and they were panicking. 'Heads would roll.' Two guards had been killed and the staff had made mistakes. There should have been at least two nurses outside at the gates for the van's arrival. The front gates had been opened for the vehicle and then closed again in accordance with procedure. The inner gates had then been opened and closed, and the van was parked in a secure position. The guard operating the gates had then left his desk to go to the toilet, leaving the security cameras unmanned. He had admitted the van and presumed the nurses would be in the yard, as he had given notification that a van with patients had entered the 'Mental Institution.'

Holly was sleeping deeply ... she had found the day tiring and just wanted to rest. It was ironic that the nurses were standing watching Holly sleeping, as they panted and gasped for breath after their running and panicking; it was ironic because they were holding syringes which contained a sedative to put their patient to sleep. One of the male nurses whispered with a tremble in his voice, 'Shall we leave her she looks peaceful?'

Another nurse replied, 'Oh! She's peaceful alright ... she's just killed two guards.'

Another nurse noticed Lotus's high-heeled shoes, 'Look at the blood on her shoes!'

Mary was affected by all the excitement and began to shout hysterically, 'Tis the blood of Christ redeemed.'

Holly awoke and spoke softly, 'What are all you people dressed in white for?' She was calm and half asleep as the nurses grabbed her. Three of the nurses had syringes but only one made contact before Lotus came out. Lotus was fast and hissed a warning, *'Leave my girl alone.'*

Lotus was fast and strong. She grabbed her stiletto shoes (one in each hand) and began to strike with the accuracy of a martial artist.

The first male nurse died instantly as the long sharp heel sank through his eye and pierced his brain. The other hand from Lotus flew upwards passing through the bottom jaw of the next nurse to enter her skull. Lotus moved with the grace of a cat ... to her it was as if everything was in slow motion. Each move made by her enemies was clearly seen and calculated. She would not hurt anyone who was not attacking Holly, Mary or herself ... that would have been wrong and she had principles.

Soon there was silence. The room was covered in blood which was splattered all over the walls and the pictures of Jesus to resemble a scene from hell. Six nurses lay still and at rest; their white coats splattered in blood.

Mary was sitting in the corner rocking while sucking her thumb and humming a tune. She looked into the dark eyeless sockets of Lotus and said, 'I knew you would come my Lord Jesus.'

Lotus did not consider Mary as a threat. She hissed at her with her deep groaning voice, *'I am not Jesus.'*

Holly returned and was shocked, 'Oh! Look at this mess ... I must have a talk with Lotus. Emerald will go berserk if she sees this mess.'

Holly yawned and was tired. She fell asleep again as the sedative began to take affect. The battle between the nurses and Lotus had only lasted for seconds.

Mary held the head of a female nurse on her lap and began to sing. The nurse stared back at her from wide unblinking eyes.

'Angels singing, go to sleep
Little children should not peep,
When the night begins to creep
Close your eyes now
Sleep, Sleep, Sleep.'

THE NATIONAL GUARD

The military arrived and helicopters circled above. Marksmen, armed with rifles which contained sedatives, crept down the corridors of the asylum. A thousand faces stared from behind doors through panes of glass, which could not hide the pain within the eyes of forever.

When the soldiers came to the prayer room they began to heave at the sight which faced them. The worst war they could imagine could not begin to resemble the holocaust which lay before them. Pools of blood seemed to flow, one into another as if trying to find a way of escape. The soldiers looked into the room and saw a woman covered in blood rocking and singing. They shot her with the sedative and she collapsed. They lowered there weapons as they had completed their assignment. That was their first mistake. Lotus was there in a flash. She threw her shoe at the soldier's face. His second mistake was having his face visor raised. The stiletto heel from the shoe had a sharp metal tip which stabbed into his skull killing him instantly. Several soldiers immediately shot at Lotus who dropped to the floor. The soldiers radioed for medical assistance to help their injured colleague, for whom help would be too late, as the dead ask for nothing in return for their mistakes.

When I woke up I was wearing a 'straight -jacket' and could not move. I lay on my back staring at the ceiling and mumbled to myself as I stared at the strange surroundings, 'I should have known you could not be left alone Lotus.'

Lotus shouted angrily, '*It was Mary's fault ... she said she had a friend called Jesus who would forgive us and set us free.*'

Holly cried, 'It is true Emerald ... she gave me some clothes and said she would lead us to happiness.'

'Mary spoke softly, 'You must have faith and all will come to those who believe.'

I began to cry as I looked around my padded cell and everything was green. Psychologists watched me from a hidden camera in another room but I could hear them saying, 'Look! Her eyes are bright green. She has multiple personalities. I have never seen anything like this before.'

Eventually the restrictive clothing was removed and I was given a chair and allowed to enter through a door leading to another room to sleep. The psychologists watched and recorded my every move, 'Look! It is as if she is talking to somebody ... as if there is someone sitting in the chair ... listen ....'

~~~

"It seemed so frightening Wordcatcher ... one minute I was working and living a normal life ... and then the next minute ... I am here locked up with my arms tied. People can be so cruel ... can't they Wordcatcher?"

"Yes Emerald ... I suppose they can."

"Wordcatcher! Are you going now?"

"Yes ... I have no choice."

"Will you kiss me one last time?"

"Yes."

"Do you love me?"

"Yes."

I suppose I never was the one
The one whom you could be
When you became the one I was
Another was set free.

Farewell for now my friend ... take care
For within the mind infinity rules
Where ghosts forever hover
Trying the keys
Ah! For one will always turn
To grant your dream?
Or nightmare?

Be careful of who you wish to be.

The Wordcatcher
Colin Demét

Wordcatcher

Wordcatcher Publications

Books and Verses

Unique verses for all occasions.

© *Wordcatcher Publications*

www.wordcatcherpublications.com

Books and Cards handmade and printed
on the Isle of Lewis, Outer Hebrides